W9-AVX-137

The Significant Seven

Books by John McEvoy

Blind Switch
Riders Down
Close Call
The Significant Seven

The Significant Seven

John McEvoy

Poisoned Pen Press

Copyright © 2010 by John McEvoy

First Edition 2010

10 9 8 7 6 5 4 3 2 1

Library of Congress Catalog Card Number: 2009931417

ISBN: 9781590587058   Hardcover
       9781590587157   Trade Paperback

Poisoned Pen Press
6962 E. First Ave., Ste. 103
Scottsdale, AZ 85251
www.poisonedpenpress.com
info@poisonedpenpress.com

Printed in the United States of America

*For my family and
its newest member,
Noah McEvoy*

I hear the Shadowy Horses, their manes a-shake,
Their hoofs heavy with tumult, their eyes glittering white...
—W. B. Yeats

Truth is never pure,
And rarely simple.
—Oscar Wilde

Chapter One

Six tremendously excited friends, middle-aged white men who had known each other since college, chattered and laughed and occasionally shouted in triumph.

Their faces were flushed, and not just because of the Saratoga Springs heat layer that hovered over the old upstate New York racetrack like a giant steam-bath towel. The late afternoon sun boiled down upon the departing crowd where many looked with curiosity at the half-dozen obviously revved up men still seated at their picnic table near the paddock, one occasionally slamming the table with his palm to emphasize a point, another passing around the iced beer cans he'd pulled from their cooler. The men grew even more animated when big Arnie Rison approached. Rison was sweating, grinning, doing a lumbering dance of celebration, and shouting loud enough to shake the leaves off the old elm trees, "We got the money, boys. We *got* the money!"

Walking just behind the jubilant Rison was a stockily built, thirtyish man with a bemused smile stamped on his broad face. Rison stopped at the table and gripped the young man's arm and raised it like a referee with a winning boxer. "This is Ira Kaplan," Rison announced. "He's a reporter for *Racing Daily*. He wants to write us up in the paper. What do you think of that?" They hooted and clapped as Kaplan sat down at the picnic table bench.

"Ira," said Rison, "let me tell you whose happy faces you're looking at. That little guy at the end with the big brain is Chris Carson, a CPA from Milwaukee. Next to him, with an old fullback's beer belly, is attorney Mike Barnhill, lives in Chicago, defending society's dregs for hefty fees. To his left is Joey Zabrauskis, 'Mr. Z', the Peoria area's biggest beer distributor."

Rison paused for a swig of beer. He nodded approvingly as Kaplan thrust his tape recorder farther into the middle of the table. "This side of the table," Rison said, "at the end, sits the honorable Henry Toomey, circuit judge of Dane County, which includes Madison, where we all met years ago as young, degenerate horse players." The others cheered that description. Rison continued, "Next to him is Steve Charous, one of the Chicago area's top insurance adjusters. We love him anyway. To your immediate left is Marty Higgins of beautiful Evanston, IL, Realtor supreme. Me, I'm from Skokie, IL. I run a car dealership."

"Or two, or three," interjected Carson, the little guy at the end. "He's no small potatoes, Kaplan, don't let him yank your chain."

Rison reached for the red cooler beneath the table and offered a beer to the reporter, who politely refused, saying, "Not while I'm working, thanks." Kaplan glanced at his notebook. "I've got a few questions to ask you."

To Kaplan's first query, Rison said, "We've been friends and horse players since we met back in Madison over thirty years ago, at the U. I don't remember exactly how we came together in the first place, probably in Doherty's Den, our favorite saloon, watching the Kentucky Derby the first Saturday of every May. The owner, Tim Doherty, came from Ireland. Great guy. Loved horses and betting. Doherty did a little bookmaking on the side. That's where we got to know each other, found out we liked horse racing, and each other, for that matter. For years now we've been going to the races together at Heartland Downs outside Chicago at least twice a month in the summer. And, for the last fifteen years, we've been leaving our wives and families and meeting here at Saratoga for a week of betting at this grand old place.

"And," Rison continued, "I guarantee you that we never, *ever* had a day at the races like we had today." He reached into his pocket for his wallet. He extracted a check. After glancing over his shoulder, he hunched forward and displayed the front of the check to his friends, then to Kaplan. Judge Toomey put on his glasses to see it clearly. Little Chris Carson had to stand up and lean forward.

"Holy shit," Carson said. "I didn't calculate it to be *that* big."

"Neither did I," Rison said. "Until the pari-mutuel manager told me I was bringing him today's *only* winning ticket in the carryover Pick Six."

Kaplan said, "What was the payoff? They wouldn't give me the figure earlier. Said they had to wait until they'd paid off the winner."

Rison slid the piece of paper toward the reporter. Kaplan saw $999,976. "Wow," Kaplan said. "That's a million, rounded off."

"Round it off, my new friend," Rison said, "and that's after taxes. I had to sign the IRS form having the track deduct 25 percent. I paid that tax in my name. When we split this up, I'll write checks to each of my guys here, deducting their portion of the tax from their shares. We're each going to get nearly one-hundred fifty grand."

Mike Barnhill let out a whoop. He shouted, "I'm ahead for life betting horses!" Barnhill's laughter was interrupted by Rison's coughing jag. Zabrauskis pounded his friend on the back, then reached over to snuff out Rison's Marlboro. "Arnie, you got to give up those damn cancer sticks," he said. "I know, I know," Rison managed to gasp before he'd completely recovered.

Kaplan said, "What did your ticket cost you guys? Do you mind telling me?"

Steve Charous laughed. "We had tickets, not a ticket. One main ticket, then some backup tickets. It was the main ticket that hit. This was the biggest shot we ever took. We knew the Pick Six pool was going to be huge. So last night, after several enlightening hours of drinking and handicapping at the bed and breakfast where we're staying, we decided to put in two hundred bucks each. That gave us $1,400 to invest. Far and away the biggest bet we'd ever made."

Judge Toomey, his long face stolid but eyes alight with excitement, said, "We're getting to that point in life where chance is more appealing. We're pretty much past midlife crises, if we ever had any, and still the near side of the grave with some juice left in the tank." He took a sip of beer. "We took a fucking shot," declared the normally austere jurist, making his buddies roar with laughter.

Kaplan looked around the table, memorizing some details for his story of these faces, old friends on a late afternoon at Saratoga Race Course, enjoying what was undoubtedly the pinnacle of their horse-playing careers.

"I want to ask you about your handicapping, how you put together your ticket," Kaplan said. "Would you talk about that?"

Rison said, "Why not?" He looked around the table. "I think we'd all agree it was a combination of smarts and luck. The first race of the Pick Six, we used five horses. We had the winner, she pays $18.80. Five again in the second leg. A real bomber, this time, pays $42.20. Third leg, we singled a grass sprinter trained by Hinda Rice, she's dynamite with those kind of horses. He wins for fun as the fourth choice in the race. For fun! Hey, we're starting to get kind of excited now. There are people all around the racetrack crumpling up their dead Pick Six tickets and tossing them into the trash."

"Tell Ira about the next one," Charous said.

Rison said, "We bowed to the expertise of Mr. Carson. We had all kinds of different opinions, some fierce arguments. Then Chris said, 'I don't care what other horse you use, but you've got to throw in Sean's Dream. Sean's the name of my first grandson, born two weeks ago.' Well, we couldn't argue with that. We tack Sean's Dream on as our fourth horse in that race. The son of a gun wins at 33 to 1! We're leaping around now. Mike Barnhill is starting to pace up and down, wearing a path in the grass. Like he's depending on a place kicker he doesn't trust to hit the winning field goal. The Judge? The Judge appeared to be in silent prayer.

"We had three horses in the fifth leg. One of them, CC's Camp, wins in a photo finish and pays $27.20. This is unfucking-believable for all of us. We're not just excited, we're starting to sweat. Scrotums are tightening. We've never been in a position like this before. Chris tries to calm us down, says 'At least we'll have five out of six for the consolation payment.' I thought Mr. Z was going to strangle him."

Zabrauskis, like Barnhill another ex-footballer but a lineman, laid his large right hand gently on little Carson's arm. "What I was thinking," he said softly, "was that we're going to goddam *win* this thing. Honest to God, I knew it was going to happen. I could feel it in my Polish bones."

Kaplan said, "Okay, going into the final leg of the Pick Six, you're alive to how many horses?"

The men at the table answered in chorus, "Two," then laughed uproariously at this sign of unanimity. Higgins stood up hoisting his beer can. "Two for the fucking money. That's what we had." Cheers from his table mates ascended.

Kaplan looked down at his notes. "The favorite didn't win," the reporter said. "I see who did. That old hard knocker trained by Cecil Granitz." Kaplan looked inquiringly around the picnic table. He said, "How the heck did you come up with him?"

Rison said, "Ask the insurance guy." Charous sat back, spreading his arms expansively. Track custodians were working their way around the picnic area that was now deserted except for this table. Rison waved them off. Their foreman, a young Latino, signaled okay, and the green-suited crew moved their brooms and rakes to a different area.

"What can I tell you? It was an act of pure genius," Charous said, eliciting some derisive comments from Carson and Higgins. "Seriously, we all thought we'd single the big favorite in the final leg of the Pick Six. He looked like the cinch of cinches, the lock of locks. But I had a feeling, and inkling…"

Rison said, "For Chrissakes, Steve, get to it."

"All right," Charous replied, "I insisted—I'm saying *insisted*—that what turned out to be the winner be used on that ticket in the last leg."

Kaplan examined his racing program. He shook his head, chuckling, as he looked up at the insurance man.

"Horse named Actuarial Tables," Kaplan said. "Nips the favorite and pays twenty-three to one. He closed the million-dollar deal for you guys. I'll be a son of a gun." He was chuckling as he closed the cover of his notebook and put it in his sport-coat pocket.

Kaplan looked at his watch. "One last question. What are you going to do with this bonanza?"

Rison got to his feet. The others followed. "Gentlemen, I say that we all go next door and spend some money before we address that question." He patted Kaplan on the shoulder. "You, too, scribe."

Almost all of the track crowd had cleared out by now. Maintenance men were spearing discarded papers and cups from the grassy patches between the numerous picnic tables. The sun was momentarily obscured by a procession of clouds. Kaplan and those he would call "The Significant Seven" in his story—a title soon to become famous in racing circles—trekked out of the track grounds into the nearby patio bar of one of this expensive little city's most expensive restaurants. Zabrauskis carried the ice-filled beer cooler in one big hand until he reached the patio entrance, where he handed it to a waiter who staggered slightly on receipt.

"All yours, buddy," Zabrauskis told the young man, patting him on the shoulder.

This restaurant/bar had been derisively described for years by one racetrack wag as the "Home of the $17.50 Cocktail."

For that reason, the long-time friends had never ventured into this always crowded spot. But when they entered the patio area, many people there seemed to know who they were. They were getting smiles and nods and waves from strangers. Money news travels through racing people as fast as champion sprinters run. Chris Carson said to Zabrauskis, "Joey, I'm glad you dumped our cooler. This doesn't look like a cooler crowd. Or place." Rison led his pals to the bar. "My man, haul out a few magnums of Verve Clicquot, if you will." He laid two $500 bills on the bar.

"Right away, sir," said the bartender. He signaled a couple of waitresses. They quickly produced plates of hors d'oeuvres, offered with winning smiles. An hour later, the party of eight was led to a choice table inside the restaurant. There was no stemming the tide of expensive French champagne. Kaplan, his tape recorder now stored away, remained in tow. Hours later, when the steak and lobster dinner plates had been cleared away and Courvosier orders taken, Kaplan said to his newest best friends, "Fellas, I got to ask again. What are you going to do with this money? I don't mean for publication," he hurriedly added, "just for me."

"Ira," said Arnie Rison, "for both you and for publication, I think I can speak for the bunch of us. Some of us who have kids to educate will lay away money for college tuitions. We'll probably each take our wives on expensive vacations—believe it or not, we're all still married to our originals after all these years of horse playing.

"But," Rison continued, "we'll still have a good chunk left, every one of us. And I would venture to say that with that part of the winnings, we're going to do what we've talked and dreamed of since our days back in college, in Madison."

Rison looked around the table. "Am I right, men?"

The reaction from this emotionally transported group was made obvious by their huge smiles and upraised thumbs. At the far end of this table, just as he had been in the Saratoga paddock, little Chris Carson got to his feet and answered for the seven. "Ira, we're going to buy some racehorses!"

Their waitress came to announce dessert choices. Judge Toomey said, "I'm so full, I'm recusing myself." Orders for coffee, ice cream, and a slab of peanut butter cake, a house specialty, were put in. The waitress waited, pen poised.

Rison said, "Steve, you want something else?"

Charous, cursed with a lifelong and once before nearly fatal allergic reaction to peanuts, said, "I'd like the lemon tart sitting over there in the booth with a codger, showing off her beautiful yellow dress and hair, but I think I'll settle for the lemon torte."

"Wise choice," said Rison.

Next morning The Significant Seven assembled for breakfast, slightly hung over but with traces of the previous day's jubilation still coursing through them. Chris Carson said, "I thought I dreamed what happened yesterday. But I didn't." Their talk soon turned to possible horse ownership. Judge Toomey brought out a notebook and began writing down names of trainers they would consider hiring once they got in the business.

It was agreed each one of the seven would interview at least one possible trainer choice face-to-face, then report back to the group. A hiring decision would evolve from this process.

"We've got to go about this in a business-like manner," Carson cautioned. There were nods of agreement all around the deck breakfast table of the Mansion Inn, where the seven men had stayed each August for so many years.

It was agreed that each syndicate member would put up $50,000. With a $350,000 bankroll, they calculated they could purchase three or four horses in the mid-forties/fifties range and pay for their training costs for one year. If one of them did very well, they theorized, and a "couple do decently," as Carson put it, "we might beat the odds. We sure as hell did yesterday," he laughed. Judge Toomey said, "We all know, of course, that 95 percent of horse owners lose money. Year after year. The fallout rate in horse ownership is as bad as the restaurant business."

"Ah, Henry," Arnie Rison said, "let us put that depressing statistic behind us." He beamed at his old friends around the table. "We defied the odds yesterday. Let's ride the goddam waves, that's what I say. All these years, we've been playing the horses. Up one year, down the next, on and on. Some of us were looking at it like what many an old horse player has said, 'Please, Lord, let me break even. I need the money.'"

Joe Zabrauskis picked up the orange juice pitcher and filled his glass. He said, "Remember that story about one of the horse-playing movie actors—Jack Klugman, maybe Mickey Rooney, Walter Matthau. I'm not sure. One of those guys."

"No," Charous said. "I don't." Neither had the others.

Zabrauskis said, "He's at Del Mar one day when this regular, a guy he's known at the track for years, comes rushing up to him. Guy called Harry the Hopeless Horse Player. Says he's got a huge problem. Harry's wife needs major surgery the next day. Yeah, they have health insurance, but with a big deductible. Could the actor loan him $2,500 for the operation that's set for the morning?

"The actor, a good-hearted fella, thinks it over and says, 'Well, okay. I'll have to cash a check. I'll meet you back here in twenty minutes.' When he comes back and hands over the cash, Harry is extremely grateful. He says thanks about a dozen times. Then they hear the bugle for the first race. The actor, he's in kind of a generous mood now, says, 'I know that money I loaned you is going for the operation, right? But, Harry, you need a few bucks to bet the double?'

"Harry the Horseplayer looks at him, shocked, his eyebrows raised, like he's almost insulted. Harry pulls out his wallet, which is thick with cash. He says to the actor, 'I don't need a few bucks for the daily double. I've *got* betting money!'"

The other six broke up, laughing. Joey Z stood up and took a bow. "I only tell you that story," he said, because I *know* we're going to do better than Harry the Hopeless Horse Player. We did all right, and had a helluva lot of fun, over the years. We did *terrific* yesterday. We made the biggest score we could ever imagine ourselves making. We are definitely going to keep this going. Why shouldn't *we* be in the 5 percent that makes money?" He sat down to a round of applause that caused the other veranda breakfast guests to look up from their omelettes.

Steve Charous signaled the waitress to refill their coffee cups. The men discussed what flight times they had that afternoon. Six were destined for Chicago's O'Hare Airport. Chris Carson was headed for Washington, D.C., to plead the case of one of his clients before an IRS official. "And I'm going to tell that son-of-a-bitch," Carson vowed, "how insane our U.S. tax system is regarding gambling earnings. Do you know we're the only major country in the world that taxes them? You win a lottery in Britain, or Ireland, France, or Italy, wherever, the damn government takes nothing in taxes." His little face had turned red. Joe Z patted him on the back. "Chris, Chris, you've said it before, and I'm sure you're right. And I'm sure you'll tell us again. We love you anyway."

"I've got to say," Rison interjected, "on this wonderful August morning in Saratoga Springs, I never in my craziest dreams thought the seven of us would be sitting here on a day like this, planning what we are."

"Graduates of the Doherty's Den Unofficial School of Horse Playing," said Mike Barnhill.

"Here's to a great University of Wisconsin education. In horse playing and friendship," Marty Higgins added.

Joey Z raised his glass of orange juice. "Here's to horse ownership," he said. "I think we're going to do this right. Honest to God, I really think it's going to happen."

The next day, the following story appeared at the bottom of page one of *Racing Daily* under Ira Kaplan's byline:

SARATOGA SPRINGS, NY—Saturday's huge Pick Six payout here at Saratoga Race Course went to a group of Midwesterners who have decided to parlay their pari-mutuel bonanza into horse ownership.

Fans of American Western movies are familiar with "The Magnificent Seven." Horse racing fans are certain to be interested in the prospects of an entity hereby dubbed "The Significant Seven."

This fortunate group combined talents, money, and, as they admit, luck, in purchasing the only winning ticket on Saturday's Pick Six here. It paid nearly $1 million after taxes. The men, who each put up $200 toward their $1,400 ticket, are Arnie Rison, Chris Carson, Judge Henry Toomey, Joe Zabrauskis, Mike Barnhill, Marty Higgins, and Steve Charous. They became friends some thirty years ago while students at the University of Wisconsin-Madison, bonding through their shared passion for thoroughbred horse racing. They have been playing the horses and attending races together on a regular basis ever since. This was their fifteenth straight year of coming together at old Saratoga. It was their first monumental betting score.

"We've cashed a couple of small Pick Six tickets over the years, and a few five-out-of-six. But never anything like this," said Rison, a Chicago area automobile dealer. Five of the others are also businessmen. Toomey is a Dane County, Wisconsin, circuit judge.

After taxes, each member of The Significant Seven enjoyed a return of some $150,000 for his initial $200. They decided to devote a portion of their winnings to realizing another "life-long horseplayer's dream," as Zabrauskis put it: "Owning some race horses."

Whether they create what they say will be their "small stable" via the sales ring or private purchases "has yet to be determined," according to Judge Toomey. "We'll iron that out in the next couple of weeks," he said. "We'd love to have a horse good enough that we could bring him here to run at Saratoga in a year or two."

Considering their experience here last Saturday, who can discount the chances of The Significant Seven?

Chapter Two

April 14, 2009

Jack Doyle loped around the south east corner of his north side Chicago block, then finished his morning run with as good a fifty-yard sprint as he could muster at age forty-three. It wasn't enough to shake the leaves off the nearby trees, but it wasn't bad. He was blowing just slightly as he pulled up at the front entrance to his condominium building. Blowing like he used to do after many minutes jumping rope or hitting the heavy bag, back in his amateur boxing days. He bent over, collecting his breath, feeling the kind of pleasure produced by righteous pain. Then he looked up to see two familiar figures emerging from a car so nondescript that it had to belong to an arm of law enforcement. It did. "Oh, Christ," Doyle said, "You two again?"

"Morning, Jack," said FBI agent Karen Engel. She offered her hand. Doyle accepted, smiling at the tall, attractive woman.

"What about you, Damon?" Doyle said to Engle's dour looking companion. Like his partner, agent Tirabassi was in his early forties. "No friendly greetings for the man who made you a Bureau legend?"

The short, stockily built Tirabassi grimaced. "Doyle, I suspect you're just as much a pain in the ass now as you were when we first met." Tirabassi managed a brief smile as the men shook hands. Doyle said, "Ah, Damon, you can't help it. You've still got that same cheery aura about you. Like somebody about to have their second colonoscopy of the morning."

"You continue to have that effect on me, Jack."

Doyle's thoughts flashed back to that pivotal first meeting. It had come after he had been fired, unfairly in his view, from his advertising account executive job with a major Chicago ad firm. An acquaintance, Moe Kellman, reputed to be Chicago's "furrier to the Mob," had convinced Doyle to help fix a horse race at a local track and earn $25,000 in doing so. The plan worked, but Doyle's illegal proceeds had been stolen from him. Worse than that, the FBI had linked him to the crime, then coerced him into helping break a ring of criminals who were killing thoroughbred horses for their insurance values. It was an unsettling period, even for a life like Doyle's that was generously dotted with stratospheric highs and ocean-bottom lows. He looked back upon that period with lingering angst.

"We've been following your career, Jack," Engel said. "From aide to us, for which we are truly grateful, to racetrack publicist, to your current period of between opportunities. As you might put it on one of your résumés," she said smiling, amusement lighting her eyes.

Engel hadn't seen Doyle in three years. He hadn't changed, she thought, same fit looking ex-boxer, sandy hair, same lively and knowing expression. She said, "You look good, Jack. Really, it's nice to see you again."

"I'll be the judge of that," Doyle said before asking, "Karen, are you still happily divorced?"

"Yes, Jack. You too?"

"Yeah, I had some rewarding times with a couple of very nice women, but nothing permanent came out of it. Story of my life. So far."

Leaning against one the few remaining trees on his block, he stretched his legs, saying over his shoulder to the agents, "Let's go into my place. I don't want my law-abiding neighbors to see me talking to the likes of you two." He went ahead of them and opened the building's front door.

He ushered the agents into his third-floor condo. Tirabassi gave an appreciative whistle. "This is several steps up from that dump you used to rent where we first met you."

Doyle said, "I've made some decent money in the past few years, Damon. Honest gelt. Betting horses, even a paying job as a racetrack publicist. And I had some luck in the market before it went in the dumper, which my broker saw coming, God love him. I bought this place from a grain trader who'd coked himself out of his fortune and was desperate for cash. I had some."

"How'd you find the condo seller, Jack?" Karen said.

"He found me, as a matter of fact. My friend Moe Kellman pointed him my way. And don't give me that look of yours about Kellman. You think he's mobbed up, maybe he is, but neither of us can prove it. I've got no need to, and obviously you and your people can't. Moe's a friend of mine, Damon." He peeled off his old, gray, sweat-soaked shirt. "I've got to shower, then we'll talk. There's coffee made in the kitchen."

Fifteen minutes later Doyle, his hair damp from the shower, dressed comfortably in khakis and a short-sleeved shirt, sat down across from the agents. "Karen," he said, "somehow you've managed to get even better looking since we last saw each other. You still playing volleyball as well as nailing criminals?"

She said, "Yes, as a matter of fact. I play beach volleyball on Sunday mornings. I still love the game." Engel, Doyle knew, had gone through the University of Wisconsin on a volleyball scholarship. "You're obviously in great shape," Doyle said, adding, "women's beach volleyball is my favorite outdoor specta-tor sport. Love the uniforms. As for you," Doyle said, turning to Tirabassi, "you still genuflecting each morning before your photo of J. Edgar?"

"Doyle," Tirabassi said, "let's get down to business. We're not here to have you assess us."

"So, what do you want?"

Karen said, "We need your help again, Jack."

Doyle looked at the two of them incredulously, just staring. Then he started laughing. "Are you two fucking kidding me? The last time we did business, you had me by the proverbial, factual, realistic balls. I knew you could ruin me if I didn't cooperate, and to tell you the truth I wanted to. I hated what those insurance thieves were doing to those horses." Doyle took a breath. "But now, friends, things have changed. You've got nothing on me. And I've got no interest in again becoming an arm, no matter how unofficial, of federal law enforcement."

Engel leaned forward in her chair. "Jack, at least listen to why we're here." Tirabassi barked, "You're not exactly number one on our list of people to deal with, believe me."

Engel signaled her partner to let her proceed. "Jack, have you heard of the sponging of horses?"

"Sponging? Of course. What the hell, that's what I did when I was working as a groom for that little dictator Angelo Cilio. Horse comes back from working out, you cool him out, then wash him and sponge him off till he's dry. So what?"

"There's another sponging," Engel said. "It's rare, it's cruel, and it's criminal. And it's going on at Heartland Downs right here outside Chicago."

Doyle said, "Damon, what the hell is she talking about?"

Tirabassi said, "This is the deal, Doyle. Say somebody wants to bet not on, but against, a big favorite, wants to insure that the horse runs poorly. One way to be certain to accomplish that is to insert a small, egg-shaped piece of sponge in the horse's nasal cavity. That cuts off between forty and fifty percent of its normal oxygen supply. Horses breathe only through their noses. With a sponge in them, it's like, well, like a car's not getting enough gas when it's being driven. The horse doesn't *look* in distress. And it sure can't tell anybody about what happened."

"How many cases have there been? And, how do they determine the horse has had this done to it?"

"At least three races at the current Heartland Downs meeting have been involved," Engel said. "In each case, the horse that looked like the favorite on paper, but didn't get as much money bet on it as you would expect. Then it ran terribly. With the favorite guaranteed to run poorly, the crooks could structure their bets leaving him off their tickets. As a result, the exacta and trifecta payoffs were huge. Winning tickets were cashed both on-track and at area off-track betting parlors, but not many of them. There were only a few people involved in the cashing. Each one was an old guy, what they call a ten percenter at the track, a person who pays almost no income tax because he's retired. He signs the IRS forms. Then, from what we can figure out, he gives the cash proceeds to whoever asked him to carry out this chore, and is paid with a tenth of the winnings. Ten percenters.

"*All* of the names used to fill out the IRS forms were completely fictitious, backed up by phony Social Security numbers. This tells us this is a pretty sophisticated and widespread ring. If we hadn't kind of stumbled upon one of these cashers, as I guess you could call them, and scared the crap out of him, we wouldn't even know this much. What we don't know is who is running this ring. Who is doing the sponging to the horses."

She said, "I need another cup of coffee." Doyle and Tirabassi waited in silence until she returned.

"The spongings were discovered," Engel said, "after the horses' trainers noticed unusual nasal discharge, sometimes accompanied by a strong, foul odor. They'd call in a veterinarian. Using an endoscope, he'd find the sponge. There were a rash of these sponging cases at the New York tracks back in the 1930s, then nothing for many years until the mid-nineties in Kentucky. They convicted a former horse trainer down there of carrying out these more recent ones. Then he disappeared before he was imprisoned."

Doyle said, "Well, that's some nasty business. But what have I got to do with it? What's your point?"

"Our point," Tirabassi said, "is this. We want you to help us catch whoever is doing the sponging."

Doyle's laugh was long and loud. "Aw, Jesus, Damon, you've developed a real sense of humor over the past couple of years." He paused to look directly at the now red-faced agent. "How would I do something like that, Damon? More importantly, *why* would I do something like that?"

There was a momentary silence before Doyle said, "I'm Irish, and I was raised Catholic, and we don't have any statute of limitations on guilt. But don't think you're going to hold that race-fixing caper over my head again. You gave me your word I was signed off after we broke the insurance ring. Right, Karen?"

"Yes, Jack," Engel said. "And we'll keep our word. We're not threatening you with anything. We're pleading with you to help us. We've arranged for you to begin working as a groom for a trainer named Ralph Tenuta. His barn is centrally situated on the Heartland Downs backstretch. It'll make a good spot for you to base yourself."

Doyle stood up and walked the few feet into his condominium kitchen. "I'm making more coffee," he said. Karen sat back in her chair, crossed her long legs, and gave Tirabassi a discreet thumbs up sign.

As he waited for the coffee to perk, Doyle thought over what he'd just heard. For some reason that he couldn't understand, he felt a sense of excitement. He hadn't done anything but travel and laze about for almost a year now, after his work as publicity director at old Monee Park. He'd made a good deal of money during that venture. He didn't really need money. What he needed was something to do.

Following his amateur boxing days, Doyle had held a succession of advertising jobs, moving up the corporate ladder until he'd been abruptly dismissed for brandishing his wise ass persona too broadly in a business world that he'd never really enjoyed or cared about. Next came his first association with the FBI, then the Monee Park publicity job, a bittersweet experience at best because of his dealings with, and feelings for, the track's very attractive co-owner Celia McCann.

His thoughts went back to the first horse he had groomed, City Sarah, the one he'd stiffed and which later won the race that the Mob guys had bet on. He'd developed a real sense of respect and liking for that little black filly. He'd come to not only admire but like City Sarah and her backstretch colleagues, fey, one-thousand pound animals that, for the most part, tried to do their best. The thought of some asshole purposefully stopping that quest aroused a deep anger in Doyle.

He brought the coffee cups into the living room. "Tell me this," he said, "how in the hell can somebody manage to stuff a piece of sponge down the nose of a horse."

Tirabassi sipped his coffee, giving Doyle a nod of approval. "Good coffee. As to your question, what Karen and I have been able to establish is that it would probably take two people to manage it. One has to hold the horse's head, the other handles the insertion. These would have to be people who know horses. These spongings are an inside job. If you can call 'inside' anything that happens in a racetrack barn area, hundreds of acres, a couple thousand stalls at Heartland Downs."

"Damon," Doyle said, "you're talking needle in a haystack shit here. Say I went to work for this Tenuta. Say I wander around, doing my usual nosy business, eight, ten hours a day. What are the chances of me finding the person or persons who are doing the sponging?"

Karen said, "You were a huge long shot to bring the insurance creeps to justice. But you did it. We've got no one in the Bureau who can carry off working as a plant on a racetrack backstretch. A reward has been offered, a good one, $50,000 by the racetrack and the horsemen. But nothing's come of it. Jack, you're our best bet."

Doyle walked over to the living room window. He looked down at traffic-heavy Halsted Street, considering. He laughed again before turning back to the agents. "Tell me about Tenuta."

Tirabassi said, "Man's been training for years and doing well. He's got more than forty horses in his barn. He could use a stable agent to keep track of business, workouts, scheduling of owner visits, generalized stuff that Tenuta the horseman doesn't want to deal with. He had a guy like that, but he retired. Now he needs another. That, Jack, would be you. It would give you perfect cover on the Heartland Downs backstretch."

"How did you talk Tenuta into this?"

Karen said, "It was easy. Ralph is a super straight shooter. He's appalled at this sponging stuff. And his brother-in-law, Bud Dorsey, is a good guy in our Chicago bureau. Tenuta called him, asking for help. Then the track's security people chimed in. That's how FBI involvement in this investigation started."

"Well, hell," Doyle said, "why don't you rope the brother-in-law, Dorsey, into this and not me."

"Bud Dorsey knows *nada* about horses or horse racing. But he told us Tenuta would be agreeable to a set-up like this. He swears Tenuta is a good guy, honest, loves racing, doesn't want to see it tarnished."

"Why can't the horses be tested before their race?" Doyle said. "You know, use the endoscope on them before they run?"

"Can't be done," Tirabassi answered. "A horse undergoing an exam like that wouldn't be able to run that day. That kind of pre-race testing is impossible. For one thing, it's too expensive. Also, most horses do not take kindly to such an invasive examination. It can throw them off for a day or two."

Doyle sighed. "Our government must be in dire straits for its representatives to tab me as a best bet." He looked out the window, shaking his head. "You gotta laugh at this situation," he said. "Count me in."

Chapter Three

August 29, 2002

A week after their triumphant return from Saratoga, the newly christened Significant Seven met for an afternoon of racing, and business, at Heartland Downs northwest of Chicago. They sat in Arnie Rison's seven-person box, situated under the cantilevered roof and in the shade, enjoying its comfortable chairs and small television that enabled them to watch the racing action not only down on the track in front of them, but around the country. Hovering nearby was a friendly young woman armed with a portable bet recorder. Thus, they didn't have to leave their seats in order to wager. Also on hand was a waitress eager to take their food and drink orders. Little Chris Carson had the winner of the first race and was alive in the double, so he was somewhat distracted as the field for race number two pranced onto the track. The rest of the men gave Arnie Rison their complete attention.

"Everybody's done their homework on trainers. We've exchanged notes or phone calls. I'm ready today to recommend Ralph Tenuta as our trainer. He's a local guy with a great record for performance and honesty."

Judge Toomey said, "I'll go along with you, Arnie. Tenuta is a brother-in-law of an old law school buddy of mine, Bud Dorsey, who's been an FBI agent for years. He says Tenuta is the straightest shooter since William Tell. Gives him big high marks."

"I went over his training records," Chris Carson said. "Very impressive. He led the Heartland Downs trainer standings the last three years in both total winners and winning percentage. And he doesn't have that big a stable. He's an ex-jock, a little guy, very sharp where he places his horses. And, as Henry mentioned, he's got a great reputation for honesty."

"A major factor," said Marty Higgins, "in picking a trainer." They laughingly agreed.

Rison said, "A retired trainer named Robby Voelkner was very candid a couple of years ago, talking to our friend Ira Kaplan, who quoted him in *Racing Daily*. Voelkner was furious because another trainer, a real slick operator, had apparently outmaneuvered him. Ira identified him only as Trainer X, but everybody knew who he was talking about. He had signed up a new owner that poor Voelkner thought was all set to hire *him*. Voelkner told Ira, "That new owner has the money, Trainer X has the experience. Within a year, that will be reversed.'

"We can laugh," Rison said ruefully, "but I'm sure there's a helluva lot of truth in that statement."

Steve Charous raised his hand for attention. "You remember what that writer William Murray said about trainers?"

"What?" Judge Toomey said.

"Murray said it doesn't do any good to ask a trainer if his horse has a good chance of winning. Because the bad ones don't know, and the good ones won't tell you."

Rison said, "Guys, I got to laugh and pinch myself thinking of the seven of us here today, talking about hiring a trainer. Us, guys who most years left the track beaten and bowed. This is fucking great! Furthermore, I think we'd get a real quality guy in Ralph Tenuta. Even Kaplan, who's a practicing skeptic when it comes to some of the current training talent, gives Tenuta very high marks."

"Beaten and bowed. That's an understatement for some of our worst days," Zabrauskis said. "Remember when we all bet that horse at Monee Park that jumped the railing into the lake and drowned? I took some abuse from my wife about that one."

"You're talking verbal, right?" Carson grinned.

"Naturally. My wife is a saint. She'd have to be, living with me."

"But they can be brutal," Charous said. "Irene never failed to greet me with, 'Where's the money, Big Time?' Well, I don't face that question anymore from my sweetie. Not after Saratoga."

Rison signaled the bet taker. "Race Four, Number Three, $25 to win, $15 to place." The young woman punched in the numbers and the machine produced Rison's mutuel ticket. "You guys want anything in here?" he said. They indicated not.

Judge Toomey said, "To get back to our discussion. My wife's favorite line? When I used to come skulking in the back door, heading for the liquor cabinet, hoping I'm not spotted for at least a few minutes? Maureen almost always quickly appeared in the doorway. This woman can hear ice cubes hit a cocktail glass from blocks away. She says, '*Another* tough card, dear?' Not mean spirited, just packed with irony. I'm not going to have to hear *that* anymore!"

"My Rita," Carson said, "asked me once, 'Did you *really* dump Billy's tuition payment in that stupid fourth race trifecta you said you *loved?* I had to tell her, 'Yes.' There's no lying to that woman. But, like the Judge said, no more worries along those lines."

Barnhill said, "I came home one time after a terrible, ball busting day at the track. 'How'd you make out?' Peggy says. 'Ran into an off track,' I said. 'Didn't do too good. It rained all afternoon. The mud was like gumbo.' Peggy says, '*Every* dodo there had to deal with the muddy track. Unless they had sense enough to go home early.' Then she flounces off and goes upstairs to watch TV and order pizza for herself and the kids. No dinner for yours truly that night." He drained his beer cup. "But those days, boys, are *over.*"

They'd gone around the box with their pari-mutuel war stories. Rison's horse won the third by open lengths. "I'll get this tab today, boys," he said, before adding, "One time I came home from here. I'd lost two photo finishes. In consecutive races. Also had a winner of mine disqualified in the nightcap. Lucy sees me coming in the door, like I said before, 'beaten and bowed.' Smart ass that she can sometimes be, Lucy says to me, 'Oh, honey, did you have another pari-mutuel learning experience?' I had to charge across the room and rush her off her feet and give her a big kiss, make her laugh, make *me* laugh. What else could I do?

"Once," Rison said, "I'm not kidding, I dreamed that I got home from Heartland Downs and Lucy greets me at the door and says, 'Darling, exactly how did the races unfold this afternoon? Please, give me all the details. And let me make you a good strong old-fashioned, my big, brave, betting man.'"

They all laughed along with Rison. "Anyway," he said, "no more of that talk, men. Now, whenever we come home from the racetrack, we walk in like kings! Am I right?"

Chapter Four

April 19, 2009

Moe Kellman leaned across the table in Dino's Ristorante and looked at Doyle in disbelief. He said, "Jack, it takes a lot to surprise the shit out of me. I guarantee you that. Not even Madoff took me by surprise. But you've managed. *You,* going back into the clutches of the Feebs? Are you fucking crazy?"

They were in Kellman's usual cushioned booth at the back of the restaurant's large main dining room, its walls adorned with huge photos of Sinatra, Bennett, Damone, Tommy LaSorda, and several lesser Italian-American luminaries who'd been hosted here by owner Dino Nigro. The large, bustling restaurant, a favored spot for Chicago's movers and shakers, had been a frequent meeting place in recent years for the sixty-nine-year-old Kellman and Doyle. The two men had first met while working out in the small boxing room of the Fit City Health Club, Kellman ripping off sit ups like the U.S. Marine he had been during the Korean War, Doyle pounding the big bag with a vicious energy. They became friends. Doyle had reluctantly accepted a commission from Kellman to fix a horse race. Since then, in a legitimate venture and again at Kellman's behest, Doyle had helped rescue Monee Downs, a failing suburban racetrack, from financial ruin. He was now, at age forty-three, unemployed and resting on his assets, as he put it, assets gleaned primarily from recent Kellman-inspired adventures.

As usual, Kellman was immaculately dressed, this day in a tan suit, black linen shirt, and white tie. With his trademark Don King-like head of white hair and his sly smile, he looked, as was always the case in Doyle's experience, absolutely at ease, ears open for perhaps some new gift from life's supply of welcome surprises. "It's good to see you, Jack. I can usually count on you to bring some elements of interest into my life." Kellman reached for his Negroni. Doyle pushed his Bushmills and water to the side and leaned forward. Kellman drained his maroon-colored cocktail and signaled their waiter for a refill.

"Moe," Doyle said, "all that happened was that your name came up in our conversation. But this has absolutely nothing to do with you. Tirabassi and Engel know all about you and me, our friendship. You've been outside their reach for so long, I think they've pretty much given up trying to tie you to your old Taylor Street buddies. They're working this horse sponging case. Since it involves betting, and interstate commerce because of simulcast wagering, it's a big case for them."

Kellman snorted in disgust. "My taxpayer dollar looks like a piece of one-ply Charmin floating down the gutter to the sewer. Why aren't the Feds going after the mortgage fraud monsters? The Iraq war profiteers? I had a guy argue with me that one of the big war suppliers was doing it on a *pro bono* basis because that's what the company president claimed. The guy was serious, otherwise a pretty smart guy. I said 'they're about as *pro bono* as bail bondsmen.'"

Doyle sat back, enjoying Kellman's tirade. The little man was usually a paragon of cool calculation, but once in a while something could strike a dormant nerve in him. Moe signaled for another round of drinks. Doyle said, "Skip me this round. I've got some homework to do."

"I'll say this, Jack. I'm kind of relieved. For awhile there, I was starting to feel like I was operating an employment agency with you as my only client."

Kellman settled the bill as he always did, with a wave at Dino. They had some kind of tab deal going that Doyle had

never been told about, and really didn't care to know. Kellman
had many such dealings, Doyle was sure. He just enjoyed the
crafty little businessman, product of a Chicago neighborhood
where he had grown up Jewish among what would become the
Chicago Outfit's current elite.

They walked outside. Doyle waved at Pete Dunleavy, Moe's
driver, who had the black Lincoln town car nestled against the
curb. Dunleavy was one of several retired Chicago policemen
now in Kellman's employ whom Doyle had previously met.
"How goes it, Pete?" Doyle hollered.

"Good and good again," smiled Dunleavy.

The three men turned when they heard a female voice say,
"Mr. Kellman, Mr. Kellman." Moe smiled broadly, opening
his arms for a hug from one of the young women approaching
him. Moe, Doyle thought not for the first time, was one of the
busiest huggers of women he'd ever known.

She was about Kellman's height, five-one or so, late twenties
maybe, with a body that hinted younger, eyes that indicated
otherwise. Her black hair was cut short. Her widely set eyes
were large and black, making for a strikingly attractive face.
She was wearing an expensive-looking black business suit over
a white camisole. Her self-assured half-smile reminded Doyle
of Charlotte Rampling in an old Paul Newman lawyer movie.
She gave Kellman a hearty squeeze. The little furrier loved it.
They separated, and Kellman said, "Jack, Pete, say hello to
Renee Rison. She's the daughter of my old client and friend
Arnie Rison, the horse racing guy. Although Renee pretty much
stands back from the racing."

That the little furrier would know Rison, "the horse racing
guy," did not surprise Doyle. Kellman seemed to know almost
everyone famous, or notorious, in Chicago. He was friendly with
many present or former aldermen and alderwomen, incumbent
or incarcerated; influential judges, leaders of the Board of Trade,
clergymen close to the cardinal, officers of the Jewish Council on
Urban Affairs, and the element he'd known in his youth, main
men of what remained of the Chicago Outfit. In considering

Kellman, Doyle could not help but measure him against other small men of major impact. Attila the Hun. Napolean. Houdini. Sammy Davis, Jr.

"Renee runs her own boutique travel agency here in the city," Kellman told Doyle before asking, "Now, honey, who's this charming woman with you?"

Renee said, "This is my business associate, Teresa Chandler. Teresa, meet Moe Kellman. And Mr. Dunleavy, and Mr. Doyle.

"Nice to see you again, Pete," Renee said to Dunleavy before extending her hand to Doyle, who said, "My pleasure, Ms. Rison. I've read a lot about your father and his buddies, The Significant Seven. What does Moe mean, that you 'stand back from that?'"

"Oh, I'm not much of a horse person anymore, Mr. Doyle. I jumped them when I was a kid, and I still like watching them run, but I'm not involved in the business itself, no matter how often Daddy asks me to get involved. I like to make my own way, *in* my own way." She smiled, looking up at him from the top of her eyes, a playfully cool stance that couldn't help but impress Doyle. That's a very practiced move, he thought, and the practice pays off.

Teresa, two or three inches taller than Renee, a brunette with a self-contained look and the body of a long-distance runner, let Kellman take her hand. Her features were as sharp as the stiletto heels she wore. "Great to meet you, Teresa," Doyle said. Renee stepped back a half-step. She looked at Doyle inquiringly. "Are you the man who almost got killed in the crash of the helium balloon at Heartland Downs a few years back? Who helped crack the insurance fraud ring?"

Doyle said, "Modesty becomes me. But honesty forces me to say, yes, 'twas I."

"He did some nice work a year or so ago at Monee Park," Kellman added. Doyle feigned surprise. "Ladies," he said, "I've been paid about as many public compliments by Mr. Kellman here as the Cubs have won pennants. I am shocked." Renee laughed. Teresa allowed herself a half smile as she looked Doyle up and down. She must be the money manager in their business, Doyle thought.

"Honey," Kellman said to Renee, "you here for lunch?" The little furrier was the only urbane man Doyle knew who could get away with calling a contemporary urban woman "honey" without risking injury.

"Just for a drink with Gordon Zenner, the hotel man. He's going to be a major new client, I hope." Zenner, Doyle knew, was one of the Chicago's wealthiest businessmen. "Daddy's known Mr. Zenner for years," Renee added. "Daddy helped arrange our luncheon meeting today. Now, it's up to Teresa and me to sell him the deal."

Just keep batting your coal black eyes like that, Doyle thought, and you'll have Zenner on the dotted line before the first cocktail arrives.

After a few more pleasantries, the women said goodbye. The men watched them walk to the restaurant door. "Now, that's a pair of lovely movers," Doyle said. Renee stopped at the door to turn and give them a final wave.

"Nice girl," Kellman said. "I wish her luck." He opened the back door of the Lincoln Town Car as Pete walked around to the driver's side. "Am I right, Jack, or am I right, that this town has got as many knockout broads as anywhere on the planet?"

Inside Dino's, as they waited for the hostess to escort them to their table, Renee said, "I do remember reading about Jack Doyle. Cool-looking guy."

Teresa Chandler said, "I don't know. He reminds me of one of the men I sometimes dream of having known in a past life."

"So?"

"They were never lives that turned out well."

Chapter Five

January 11, 2003

The coming together of The Significant Seven and the penny-colored chestnut colt they would name The Badger Express occurred on a cold, dark, winter night at the Keeneland Sales Pavilion outside of Lexington, KY. The area had been battered by a serious ice storm the previous day, and the wind from the northwest scooted across the piled ice and snow with a vengeance. Nearby roads had been cleared after long delays. Several sections of the area were still without power. It was obvious that the crowd on hand for this auction of "Horses of All Ages" was much smaller than usual.

Of The Significant Seven, only Arnie Rison was on hand. He'd flown down from Chicago with trainer Ralph Tenuta, the man they had chosen to work with the horses they intended to purchase. Tenuta was a swarthy, pleasant-looking man in his early fifties with a long and impressive training record. He had emerged from the group's list of "contenders," as Joe Zabrauskis termed them, bolstered by his good nature, willingness to communicate with owners without being begged, and reputation for honesty. The tall, lanky Rison and the short, stocky Tenuta made an odd couple as they hurried through the weather from Rison's rental car and into the sales building.

Rison's long strides carried him ahead of Tenuta, who hurried to keep up. "Damn, Ralph," Rison said, "this is some brutal weather to go buying horses in."

"You want good weather," came Tenuta's answer, "go to the summer sale here. But be prepared to pay big summer prices." Rison slapped him on the back as they neared the pavilion door. "Heard that."

It had been the week before Christmas that The Significant Seven hammered out their horse ownership plan. Their primary objective was finding a successful trainer they could trust, one who would want to work with a bunch of new owners. As he was being interviewed by Rison, Tenuta had recounted the story of a previous owner who had employed him, a very rich and controlling Chicago heiress who would bring hand-drawn maps to the paddock indicating what path her steed should follow during that day's race.

"I can't get along with people like that," Tenuta told Rison. "If I'm going to be your trainer, I'm going to *be* your trainer. I'm not saying I'll make all the decisions. Hell, you're paying the bills. But I don't want to be interfered with or second-guessed when I make a decision about the best thing for the horse or how the jock should ride him."

Rison reported this conversation at The Seven's dinner meeting in Ruffalo's, a Kenosha restaurant that had garnered great reviews for its "top-class Italian cuisine." It wasn't just the food recommendation that drew them; it was the convenience. Judge Toomey could drive there from Madison in less than three hours, Carson from near Milwaukee, the Chicago area partners coming just sixty miles north into Wisconsin. Over platters of antipasto, Rison said, "I think Tenuta is our guy. I've had him checked out six ways from Sunday. He gets A-pluses all the way down the line.

"Also," Rison continued, "and this is the best part: Tenuta will not charge us a day rate per horse, which is now $65 or $70 per horse per day at big tracks like Heartland Downs. Tenuta says that if we let him get involved in selecting horses to buy, he'll settle for fifteen percent of the horses' earnings. If they flop, he doesn't get a nickel. Tenuta seems very confident that he can make money both for himself and for us. I find it hard to argue with a deal like that."

Chris Carson said, "Tenuta must have a hell of a lot of confidence in himself. But I'll tell you, I looked up his training record for the past ten years. The majority of his clients have made money each year during that span. That's a powerful endorsement of this guy."

"Let's hope we wind up with the majority," Steve Charous said, lifting his cocktail glass. "Hear, hear," said the others. Their decision was unanimous. Ralph Tenuta would be signed up as the first trainer ever employed by the old friends from Madison.

Tenuta was hailed by several people as he led Rison to the rear of the large Keeneland Sales Pavilion, back to the area where horses were walked in what Tenuta termed the show ring. "There's a couple of thousand horses in this week-long sale. It takes a huge staff of workers to manage all these animals, and their sellers and buyers, for that matter. They do a great job here. Watch, Arnie, when one horse leaves to go into the sales ring section of the building, another one is brought in from a barn outside to replace it. They keep ten or so horses in this ring at the same time all night, moving them in and out. Their handlers are real pros. Some of the young horses get damn skittish. They've never been in a place like this before."

Rison and Tenuta watched dozens of animals enter and leave their part of the building. Tenuta had said that afternoon during the plane ride that he would "like to take a real close look at four, maybe five, of the two-year-olds in the sale tonight. I know their pedigrees. I think a couple of them might fall into our price range." That range, it had been established, was a total of $150,000 to be spent, maximum, for whatever the syndicate acquired.

Two hours, several cups of coffee, one Irish for Rison, and the men had looked at the first of Tenuta's two catalog picks. Only one was appealing to the little trainer, who was assessing these animals with the practiced eye of a jeweler using a loupe to examine uncut stones.

At 9:30, they moved into the main body of the pavilion and sat in stadium seats to observe the bidding for an hour or so. Rison gulped several times, when what he thought were nondescript looking horses were hammered down for $200,000 and $300,000. Tenuta said, "Arnie, let's go back to where they come in. I want to see Hip Number 1,106." Rison followed along, took his place at the railing, and looked at Number 1,106.

They returned to their seats inside the pavilion. Ten minutes later, Number 1,106 entered the sales ring, very well mannered, and struck a picture pose without his handler even having to urge him. Before Tenuta could raise his hand, buyers in front of them went back and forth in a flurry of bidding that saw the colt sell for $160,000 in ninety seconds. "Nice looking colt," Tenuta shrugged, "but too rich for us."

At 10:45 they returned to their spot on the railing at the walking ring. They'd spent so much time there that the sales personnel were starting to kid them. One hollered out, "Hey, Ralph, when are you going to open the check book?"

"When the time is right, Beasley," Tenuta shouted back. "When the time is right."

Rison said, "Ralph, I'm getting tired. What other horse do you want to look at tonight?"

"She's coming right up, Arnie. It's that leggy bay filly, Hip Number 1,203, just walking there on the other side." Tenuta leaned forward. "Man, she looks good, Arnie. She looks good."

Rison didn't answer. Apparently he had not heard Tenuta. His eyes were riveted on the chestnut colt that walked along behind the filly, Hip Number 1,204. The youngster had his head turned and seemed to be staring directly at the spot were Rison and Tenuta stood.

The colt's groom attempted to pull his head forward when they passed the two men, but couldn't. Hip Number 1,204's eyes were riveted on Rison, who gripped Tenuta's arm. "That horse there is trying to say something to me, Ralph." Rison spoke without taking his eyes off the colt. "He's looking at me like he knows me." Rison took a deep breath. "Ralph, the way he looks at me reminds me of the way my old man looked at me when he was wheeled away into his final surgery. Jesus!"

Tenuta looked away, pretending not to have heard this. Then he felt big Arnie Rison's iron grip on his arm, pulling him away from the railing. "Ralph," Rison said, "hurry, man. We've to get in inside and buy this horse. Let's go."

As they walked, Tenuta flipped hurriedly through the catalog pages. "Not a bad pedigree on this one," he admitted. "First foal of his dam, who won a few small races. He's from his sire's first crop. His sire was well bred, but only raced at two. Must have got hurt. Actually, his ped's pretty damn good. And he's a nice moving little guy."

They took their seats. Rison grabbed Tenuta's arm again. "Ralph," he urged, "buy this horse. *Buy* this horse.

Rison made the opening bid of $6,000. Silence. Then one of the bid spotters in the back of the pavilion shouted "I've got ten." A series of small escalations followed, just between Rison and the sole party who was competing against him.

"Arnie, how high do you want to go on this horse," the worried Tenuta whispered thirty seconds later. "We're already past the half-way mark on your budget, all on this one horse."

Rison, jaw tight, concentrating on the chestnut colt, replied, "We'll go to the whole $150,000 if we have to. And beyond. If we do, I'll make it good to the other six. I *have* to buy this horse."

To Tenuta's relief, bidding on Hip Number 1,204 ended at $95,000. "Sold," hollered the auctioneer as Rison sat back in his seat, exhaling. He shook his head. "I don't know what happened there, Ralph. Something I can't explain. I just knew we had to have that colt. That he was the horse for us."

When Rison came out of the sales office, having signed the purchase slip and written a check for $95,000, he was approached by a young dark-haired man wearing worn work clothes and a harried expression. Believing him to be a stable worker, Rison started to step around him when the man said, "Mr. Reason?"

"It's Rison."

"Oh, sorry, sir. Ah, I'm Chip Wadsworth. I'm glad to meet you." He extended his hand. Rison took it, looking quizzically at Wadsworth, saying, "What can I do for you, son?"

Wadsworth took off his University of Kentucky Wildcats ball cap and smoothed his tousled brown hair. "That colt you bought, Mr. Rison? I bred, raised, and consigned him. I was kind of sorry to see him sell. I had a reserve price of $85,000 on him. But when he went past that, and you got him, I was happy, because we need the money badly. Still, I was sorry to see him go.

"I wanted to tell you," Wadsworth continued, "that I believe this colt is real special. I've been working on Kentucky horse farms since I was a kid. I'm thirty-two now, with a growing family to feed. I know horses. What the good ones look like, how they act. How the ones that look good won't ever turn out to be nothing because they don't have heart for it.

"I just *hated* to sell this colt, Mr. Rison. But I sure wish you the best with him. I'll be watching for him and rooting for him, I guarantee you. And, you watch, he'll surprise a lot of people. So long."

Wadsworth started walking off, then stopped. "Sorry, Mr. Rison, I forgot to ask. Who's going to train your horse?"

"This is the first horse me and my friends and I have owned," Rison said. "Ralph Tenuta will train for us. Ralph is here at the sale with me."

Wadsworth grinned and said, "Well, that's good news. Mr. Tenuta has a great reputation. Where are you shipping my colt— sorry, your colt— from here?"

"To Hill 'n' Dale Farm up in Illinois. Ralph will pick him up there in the spring and put him into training at Heartland Downs."

Rison watched Wadsworth hurry down the long corridor toward a small dark-haired woman with two toddlers in tow. He and the woman embraced. Wadsworth picked up the heaviest and oldest of the children, and the family walked out into the January night.

Tenuta reappeared carrying two large, steaming containers. "I asked them to make us Irish coffees," he said. "No problem, especially at these prices. Who was that young guy you were talking to?"

"Chip Wadsworth. He bred our colt. He said he wanted to wish us well, tell me what a nice horse we bought." He sipped his coffee. "Seemed real sincere."

Tenuta said, "I've heard of that young man. His father was a well known farm manager here for years. The son's got an excellent reputation for recognizing talent and breeding sound horses. Here's to young Mr. Wadsworth," Tenuta said, raising his drink.

An hour after buying Hip Number 1,264, Rison signaled that he would pay $33,000 for a nearly black filly, Hip Number 1,376, who despite her handler's efforts was skittering around the sales ring like, as Tenuta put it, "a pig on ice. But I like her spunk," he added.

Rison rose from his seat and stretched. He was tired but jubilant. "We got the horse we need in that colt, and a filly, too, Ralph," he said. "Good night's work as far as I'm concerned. Let's go downtown. You drive. I'll call Judge Toomey from our car, he can e-mail the other guys as to what we did here tonight. Then I'll buy you a good steak dinner at Malone's."

As Tenuta and The Significant Seven would discover in the year ahead, the black filly "couldn't run a lick." Hip Number 1,204, however, was another story.

Chapter Six

It took Doyle nearly ninety minutes to drive out of Chicago and up the Kennedy and the Edens and turn west on to Willow Road and, finally, arrive at the stable gate at Heartland Downs, the showplace facility renowned as one of the world's most beautiful and well operated racetracks. However, he found the stable gate guard to be a less impressive model of efficiency.

"Sir, do you have a pass to come in here?" asked the chubby, serious-looking young man. He wore a khaki uniform, dark sunglasses, a Smoky and the Bandit hat, and an expression of extreme suspicion. His badge identified him as Alvin Boemer Jr.

"No," Doyle said. "I don't have a badge. Yet. I'm here to see trainer Ralph Tenuta. I'm going to start working for him. But I can't start working for him until I'm licensed by the Illinois Racing Board. And I can't get Tenuta to take me to the licensing office until I meet him at his barn."

The young man shook his head. "You should have a letter or something. So I could authorize your entrance. Without a badge, I can't let you in."

Doyle lowered his forehead onto his steering wheel. "I suppose, Alvin," he said, "you've never heard of Catch 22?"

"Catch what?"

"Never mind. Let's try another tack. I'm trying to go to work here, Alvin. I mean, Alvin, Jr. Take a look at me. Do I look like

I'm about to set fire to the stable area? Please, just call Ralph Tenuta. He'll tell you about me."

Alvin Boehmer, Jr., slowly retreated to his security booth. Doyle tapped his fingers on the steering wheel as the young man laboriously worked his way through what appeared to be a book of stable area phone numbers. Alvin licked his right thumb before applying it to every page he examined. Finally, he picked up the phone.

Ten minutes later, Doyle pulled his Accord into a parking place at the far end of Barn C. He was careful to sidestep a pile of horse flop at the entrance to the long, dark, dusty, musty barn. He asked one of the female Mexican hot walkers who was passing by on the end of a shank where he could find Ralph Tenuta. She smiled and, pointing behind her, said, "Down there, *Señor. Va a numero viente-seis.*"

Carefully staying out of the way of the procession of sweating, recently exercised thoroughbreds that were being cooled out by their hot walkers or grooms, Doyle made his way to the stall numbered twenty-six. He could hear a racket erupting from it even before he'd gotten there. There was the sound of hooves crashing against the wooden stall walls. Loud exclamations in both English and Spanish. Even louder vocal horse noises. It was a rumpus of magnitude.

Doyle peered into the gloom of the stall. Two men were attempting to manage a large, very active and uncooperative bay horse, trying to put protective bandages on his hind legs. The horse was wearing a metal contraption that covered his mouth and nose. He didn't appear to want any part of the mens' plans for him. He pulled back against the shank, the whites of his eyes almost popping out of his head. Every thirty seconds or so, he unleashed a vicious hind leg kick. The little man working to bandage those back legs, dodged artfully each time, as if he and the animal were working on a shared, dangerous choreography. After kicking, the horse reared up, front hooves climbing toward the ceiling, as the taller man pulled down on him. It was an awesome concentration of energy in a confined space, making Doyle wince as he watched and listened.

When, finally, there was momentary lull, Doyle said, "I'm looking for Ralph Tenuta."

"You're looking at what's left of him," a voice came back from the rear of the stall, followed by the appearance of a short, compact man wearing a tan windbreaker, jeans, worn boots, and a ball cap that read "Keeneland Sales." His dark complexioned face had exertion-caused small patches of crimson below each cheek bone. He opened the stall door and stepped outside before turning back and saying, "Jose, just let that sumbitch go unbrushed if you have to. He don't deserve to get brushed, and you don't deserve to get stomped by that mean bastard."

"*Sí, Señor* Ralph," the groom replied. "No worry now. I handle *mi grande caballo*."

Tenuta said, "Good luck, *amigo*."

Doyle introduced himself. "I knew you were coming," Tenuta said. "I had a call from my brother-in-law, Bud. I sure as hell hope you can be some help back here, trying to catch this damned sponger."

"That's the idea."

Tenuta said, "Let's go into my office." As they walked down the shed row, Doyle said, "What horse was that back there? A helluva handful, whoever he was."

"What do you know about horses, Jack?"

"Enough to stay out of their way. Especially that one back there." He didn't mention his backstretch adventure a few years back on behalf of Moe Kellman.

Tenuta opened his office door. He motioned Doyle to take the only chair that fronted a battered desk almost covered in old track programs, condition books, horse business magazines, copies of *Racing Daily*. Tenuta had to shoo an old black-and-white cat off his own spring-blown chair before he could sit down. "Move, Tuxedo," he ordered. The cat gave him a baleful look and took her feline time. Tenuta's chair creaked like a Halloween fright house door when he plunked his chunky form into it.

Leaning forward in his noisy chair, Tenuta looked at Doyle. "Aren't you the fella that worked at Monee Park when Rambling Rosie was running there?"

"That's me. That was a great summer and fall."

Tenuta's look was now more respectful. "My old friend Tom Eckrosh, who trained Rambling Rosie, told me about you. Didn't you save his life?"

"His, mine, and several other peoples'."

"You had to kill somebody, right?" Tenuta said softly.

"Right," Doyle said, then changed the subject by walking over to examine the photos on the wall behind Tenuta. He said, "You must have had a lot of fun training The Badger Express for that partnership." The largest photo showed all of The Significant Seven surrounding their wonder horse in the Keeneland winner's circle. Tenuta was dwarfed by most of the men, as was jockey Davey Morales.

"That was The Badger's sixth straight stakes win. He had a dozen stakes win all told when he was retired the following year."

Doyle said, "That's a happy-looking bunch of owners."

"They were that, all right," Tenuta said, "and real, real good guys. They always staked my barn help when the horse won. And he won enough money to make my fifteen percent of his earnings into a pretty good pile. Enough for me and my wife to buy a small farm down in Florida. We'll retire there some day."

Doyle continued to examine the frame containing The Badger Express' lifetime past performances. The horse's career earnings were slightly more than $3 million. He whistled softly, calculating that Tenuta had gleaned some $450,000 from his trainee's heroics.

"And they paid how much for him? A hundred thousand?"

"Ninety-five," Tenuta said proudly. "One of racing's greatest bargains. And I helped pick him out at the Kentucky sale."

Doyle returned to his chair in front of the desk. He said, "What horse is that back there that you were working on?"

Tenuta said, "The meanest creature to come on the racetrack during my time. His name is Editorialist. Great-looking horse.

One of the fastest milers in the Midwest. And one with the worst temperament. Editorialist doesn't like people, he doesn't like other horses, he probably doesn't like himself. But he loves to run. And he *can*. I won three stakes with him last year and one already here at this meeting."

"I remember reading about him," Doyle said. "He was a fairly expensive sales yearling, wasn't he? With good breeding?"

"Yeah, but all his 'good breeding' is in his pedigree, not in his nature. If it weren't for that groom back there with Editorialist, Jose Ruiz, I don't believe I could keep the horse here. Some grooms can communicate with horses like nobody else. They have a gift for it. Jose is one of those, thank God. I go to take a look at Editorialist in his stall and he stands in there in the corner, baring his teeth at me. Other times, he turns his back on me, and drops a load.

"But with Jose, it's a whole different story. Jose comes up to Editorialist's stall door and the horse's ears are pricked, standing straight up, he's happy to see Jose. A horse is like a person. You don't need words to figure out what they want, what they don't want. You just have to take your time with them. And, of course, if you're lucky enough, have a guy like Jose Ruiz working for you."

"Who owns Editorialist?" Doyle said.

"The Significant Seven, that syndicate. You just missed one of the owners, Arnie Rison. He came out to watch Editorialist work this morning. Came with his daughter Renee. Look, they're over there at their car, talking to one of my grooms."

Doyle saw a tall man in a blue golf shirt and khakis, sunglasses up on his head. He recognized the woman. Renee had on a tight white tee shirt and tighter beige slacks that emphasized the admirable contours of her ass. Her sunglasses were down on her face.

"You want to say hello to the Risons?" Tenuta said.

"Naw. I've met the girl. I'm sure I'll meet her father some other time if he comes out here often," Doyle said. "Ralph, can I ask you something? Did they ever think about gelding Editorialist? I know that's supposed to calm down a lot of stud horses."

Tenuta laughed enough to make his chair creak. "Doyle, that ferocious creature in there *was* gelded. A year and a half ago! Think it improved his disposition. Hah!"

"Why do you put up with a horse like that? One that is so hard to handle, so much trouble? Hell, so dangerous?"

"Because he can flat out run."

Doyle smiled. "I guess that's a good reason. But what's that mask, or metal thing, or whatever it is, over Editorialist's mouth? He looks like an equine Hannibal Lecter."

"Who?"

"Never mind. What is that contraption anyway?"

Tenuta said, "Right after he first came to the track, Editorialist turned into a cribber. He'd grab the top of the stall door with his front teeth, arch his neck, pulling back on the door and sucking in air. The veterinarians say horses get a kick out of this, some endorphin or some shit, makes them feel good. But it's bad for the door, for their teeth, for their energy, screwing around like that. Editorialist would spend hours doing that if I let him."

Tenuta stopped to take a phone call from an owner whose mare was to run the next afternoon. "All is well, Mr. Steiner. Bring betting money. Your horse is sittin' on ready.

"Where was I?" he said to Doyle.

"That device you've got on Editorialist."

"Yeah, well, it's not just to prevent that son of a bitch from cribbing. It's to protect me and my help so he doesn't bite our arms off. You've got no idea, Jack, what that devil can be like. We take the mask off only when he eats, drinks, and runs. It goes on right after each of those times, usually taking three of us working together on him."

After Tenuta fielded another phone call, he said, "People will put up with a lot if the animal produces. There was a stud horse down in Kentucky several years ago named Ribot. He was a genuine terror. They had to build him a padded stall and even put padding on the ceiling, because he'd get up on his hind legs and try to tear the roof off from the inside. They had special equipment to control him going to and from the breeding barn. Those poor stud grooms that had to deal with Ribot, they had to be pretty damned quick on their feet. But the horse sired tons of stakes winners.

"Now, Editorialist is right up there with Ribot for being hard to handle. But my daddy years ago trained a mare that'd make either one of them seem like angels. Her name was, believe it or not, Sweet Girlie. You had to fight to rub her, to bandage her, she hated just about everything that you had to do with her. And she didn't like anybody on her back. She tossed off so many jocks, my Dad had to pay extra to the rider who would take her on. But she could win races for you."

Doyle grinned. "On the Meanness Meter, where would you rank Editorialist and Sweet Girlie?"

"Sweet Girlie. Not even close."

"Really? Why?"

Tenuta said, "She had one habit worse than the regular ones that came out of her rotten disposition. Sweet Girlie hated to be whipped. You'd never dare use it on her. And my Daddy always had to instruct the riders about that.

"Sometimes, though, in the heat of the race, a rider would forget and give her a few whacks. Sweet Girlie would then start pissing while she was running. If she was hit again, she'd let go with another spray.

"This," Tenuta said, "was awful tough on the horses and riders behind her, as you could imagine. That's what I call real mean."

Chapter Seven

April 22, 2009

Orth was splitting logs for firewood in the yard behind his cabin when the call came on his cell phone. It was barely an hour and a half past dawn, but he had already run his four miles through the adjacent forest, taken his daily two-mile swim in the cold waters of the spring-fed lake bordering his property, and was enjoying the exercise with axe and awl.

These spring mornings began misty, then cleared into a radiance beneath the tall pines that Orth had treasured since growing up in these woods. He looked at the cell phone screen, saw the number, said into the phone, "I'll be there in twenty minutes."

He cleaned and put his tools in the woodshed, got into some town clothes, and drove his black Jeep Cherokee to Boulder Junction, the town nearest to his backwoods home. He pulled into the parking lot of the Qwik Stop service station and walked to the outdoor phone at the east end. The phone rang almost at once.

"Got something, something primo," said the familiar voice. It was his fellow ex-Navy SEAL, ex-private security worker in Iraq, and continuing "asshole buddy," as Orth liked to refer to Scott Sanderson.

Orth and Sanderson met at the U. S. Navy's Special Warfare Center in Coronado, California. The two Midwesterners and enlistees bonded during the course of the extremely demanding twenty-six weeks spent training to become members of the Navy's elite SEALS program. On the surface, they seemed an unlikely pair. Orth was a paragon of reticence, Sanderson a voluble, sociable young man. What they had in common was great aptitude and liking for the training they were receiving. Unlike more than 60 percent of their carefully selected entering class, they passed, Orth ranking second, Sanderson third, and began fulfilling their fifty-one month obligation to their government. More than eighteen of those months saw them together in the same unit, engaged in reconnaissance, then direct action, in various dangerous sections of Afghanistan. Their efficiency was noted and rewarded with medals and promotions. They were born killers.

Before putting in for their discharges in the summer of 2002, Orth and Sanderson discussed their futures. Sanderson had a young family, no job to go home to, and major financial issues courtesy of his free-spending wife. Orth had no obligations, except to himself, and hoped to find something he enjoyed doing while making good money. Stateside, they arranged to be interviewed by the president of a rapidly growing private security firm headquartered in northern Alabama. The young, politically connected firm had won lucrative contracts from the U. S. government to provide security for private contractors in Iraq. Sanderson's eyes widened as he listened to the conditions of the contracts they were being offered, especially the pay scale. Even the normally stoic Orth could not hide his surprise at the terms. The two ex-SEALS looked at each other, then rose to shake the hand of their new employer.

Two months later, Orth and Sanderson arrived in Baghdad to join their division of the Aqua Negro Company. They found themselves among men much like themselves, ex-military personnel in some branch of special forces, many with shaven heads and muscled up like products of the weight rooms of American prisons. Some were fleeing bad marriages, or debts. Others, like Orth and Sanderson, were seeking work they loved and more money than they could make anywhere else that they knew of.

For riding shotgun in armored SUVs for various contractors, or providing personal security for chosen individuals, they each drew down $5,000 a week. Some weeks, swimming smartly in the ocean of loose U.S. cash washing over Iraq, their rewards were much greater.

Since the two men's rapid and secretive departure from Sadr City in the winter of 2006 and the subsequent dustup over the disaster they'd been involved with that led to the death of several innocent citizens, Orth and Sanderson had gone their separate geographical ways while maintaining low profiles and a strong thread of common interest in violence and money. Sanderson now lived in a Dallas, TX, suburb with his wife and three children. The lifelong loner Orth had gone back to his roots in the northern Wisconsin woods, just a few miles from where he'd been raised. Orth bought a dilapidated fishing cabin and spent four months meticulously renovating it. He worked alone, patiently awaiting the next thing life might bring to him. At thirty-eight, he had a decent bank account, tremendously good health, and no inclination to engage in anything other than lethal work.

It was the resourceful Sanderson who had discovered a network of American enterprises looking for talent to do what he and Orth were so good at. He learned that a great portion of the U.S. underworld, for decades dominated by Sicilian-Americans, was experiencing a shortage of trusted, trained, efficient killers.

"They just can't come up with enough of their own guys," Sanderson gleefully told Orth. "The young talent is going into banking, or lawyering, or politics, not murder. I see us as filling a need." Even his humorless buddy chuckled at that. "And," Sanderson said, "some of the guys we were with in Iraq can steer us other business. They take a percentage for doing so, but so what? The money is still great."

Beginning with the discreet suffocation of a St. Louis accountant who had learned things he shouldn't have, Orth and Sanderson worked efficiently and profitably. Typically, Sanderson would either conduct surveillance of the intended target or hire a member of the Agua Negro alumni to do so. Armed with the target's daily schedule, habits, addresses, vices, virtues if any, Orth then carried out his deadly work. He and Sanderson were rarely in the same city at the same time, communicating mainly via cell phones that they purchased cheaply and changed often.

Sanderson took pleasure in paraphrasing the long dead baseball magnate Branch Rickey, who had famously declared that "luck is the residue of design."

According to Sanderson, the work that he and Orth did was indeed the product of cautious and thoughtful design. The jobs Sanderson found for them were at various places throughout the Northern Hemisphere. Not once had they ever been close to being caught.

On the phone this afternoon, Sanderson said, "We'll have to meet to get this deal set up."

"Shit. Why?" Orth said. "The last one was straightforward." A woman walking toward her car at the Qwik Stop saw the look on Orth's face and moved faster.

Sanderson said, "This is a deal on a different level for us. We're just going to have to talk about this *mano o mano*. Copy?"

"When. Where?"

"I'll meet you tomorrow night in Madison. The Holiday Inn Express on John Nolen Drive. I'm flying into O'Hare, then I'll drive up. I've reserved the rooms. You register as Ray Warren. I'm there under Jay Winston. Like always, pay cash."

Orth said, "This must be big, you coming up that far."

"You got it, brother," Sanderson said. "It's big."

Before ringing off Sanderson said, "Hey, bro, let me ask you something. Are you feeling your usual fine self?"

"Sure. Why wouldn't I be?"

Sanderson said, "I saw on the Internet last week that Al Casey, the guy who was with us that summer in Kabul, died. They said the cause of death appeared to be from natural causes. How about that? Casey was as fit as we were when we started there. He was what, thirty-four, thirty-five. Just like us, ex-mil trying to make good money. His wife insists Casey died of cancer. She's trying to sue Agua Negro, which had cremated him and shipped him home to Tulsa. And quickly."

"Scott, I don't get it. Sue Agua Negro for what?" Orth said.

"Casey's widow has a lawyer who claims that Agua Negro employees were, I am quoting now from the story on the Net, 'Knowingly exposed during their work to a toxic chemical, a carcinogen, which is known to cause cancer.'"

Sanderson said, "Hold on a second." Orth heard him hollering, "You kids, keep the damn noise down in there. Hear me?" Back on the phone, Sanderson said, "Sometimes here in my house, it sounds almost louder than one of our war zones."

"No way," Orth said. "What was this toxic crap that we were supposedly exposed to?"

"I was getting to that. It was at the water pumping station we guarded that summer. Remember? A gazillion degrees hot. We were breathing in all that bad air. Mrs. Casey's lawyer says his research shows that water plant was, quote, contaminated with sodium dichromate, a known carcinogen. Unquote."

A silence. Orth said, "Maybe Casey got sick some other way."

Sanderson said, "Maybe." Orth could hear the snapping open of what was undoubtedly a pint of the Australian lager his buddy had favored during their years in Iraq. "But maybe Casey didn't," Sanderson said. "Take care of yourself, bro. Let's get going with this big project, and get the green, and hope for a long, healthy retirement."

Sanderson heard Orth say, "I remember Casey real well. Good man. You think Casey's wife will get any money?"

"Doubt it. The Agua Negro lawyers will fight her claim for years."

There was a pause before Orth said "Scott, you think we got fucked over over there? With this cancer shit? While we were protecting this country?"

Driving the two hundred and thirty miles south the next day, Orth thought, not for the first time, about the unlikely partnership he had entered into. Orth was the only child of a Wisconsin lumberjack who drank himself to an early death and a woman who quickly followed her husband's path once her son had joined the service out of high school. Orth neither had nor saw the worth of social skills beyond that elementary level needed to move unobtrusively through life.

Scott Sanderson's background was very different. He was the third of five children of a South Dakota couple who doted on their offspring. Scott's three sisters became teachers, his brother went into the family drugstore business. Scott enlisted in the Navy after two years at the University of South Dakota, where he'd majored in drinking and raising hell. He was loud yet likeable, and very ambitious. Once admitted to the SEALS program, he thrived in that ultrademanding organization. When they met early in their training, Sanderson and Orth sized each other up, competed fiercely against each other, and eventually bonded. Their Afghanistan action taught to them to trust each other in a way few other members of their unit understood.

Orth checked into the Holiday Inn late in the afternoon. There was message for him, a note saying only "three eighteen." He went to his room, unpacked his light gear, and walked next door. Sanderson opened his door, grinning, a can of malt liquor in one hand. "My man," he said, "come the fuck in." They gripped hands.

Sanderson had ordered room service for them both. They ate as they talked casually about Sanderson's family, about the respective chances of the Dallas Cowboys and Green Bay Packers in the next football season, about what they agreed was "the shit war in Iraq."

Orth ate everything on his dinner tray: a half-pound cheeseburger, shrimp cocktail, fries, salad. He drank two bottles of water from the minibar. Sanderson only took two or three bites of his turkey club, which was unusual for him. He opened another Malt 45 from the pack he'd brought with him. When Orth's plates were empty, Sanderson said, "Ready?"

"Go on with it."

Sanderson leaned forward. "This," he said, "is our biggest project yet. It's going to have to be very, very carefully thought out. Main reason is, we're getting paid on a sliding scale. I've met with the money person. The deal looks very solid. The money's there. I got a down payment forwarded to our off-shore accounts yesterday. But it's not going to be easy."

Orth frowned, awaiting an explanation.

"There's six targets," Sorenson said. "We eliminate them all, one at a time. Different methods. Different locales. Nothing you can't handle. I got the whole schemata worked out, you know? Like always, we're the fucking stealth team. Yeah, it's going to get harder to do as we go along through the list. That's why I negotiated an increasing pay scale. It got complicated. It took some doing. But I did it."

Orth hated complications. "Keep talking."

"Like I said, we've got to do six. These people, all men, all know each other. After one or two go down, the rest, if they have any fucking sense whatsoever, and I'm sure they must, are going to be plenty nervous. Harder to get to."

"What numbers are we talking?" Orth said.

"We get fifty for each of the first two. Next one, seventy-five thousand. One after that, a hundred. Another hundred for the fifth one. A hundred and a quarter for the finalist."

Orth said, "Where are these guys?"

"Pretty well clustered," Sanderson said, "all in the Midwest. You'll be able to reach them easily. Did I say expenses are included?" he grinned, before draining his Malt 45. "So, what we're talking about here…"

Orth interrupted him. "Scotty, I can still count. Five hundred grand, forty percent to you." He stood up to stretch. Sanderson watched him, thinking that Orth looked like he'd even further tightened up his muscular body in the north woods. "One dangerous fucking cat," is how Sanderson had described him to his wife.

"Not a bad summer's work, bro," Sanderson said.

Orth said, "Not bad at all."

Chapter Eight

April 24, 2009

Trainer Larry Lambert's top two-year-old filly, Princess Croft, came out of her sleep with a jolt when she heard some of the other horses down the line in the barn nicker nervously in the early morning darkness. She shook her head and pricked her ears. A voice was saying, "Quiet, quiet, now. It's only me."

Wide awake now, Princess Croft poked her gray head out the stall door. Almost immediately, familiar hands were stroking her neck and a familiar voice was pouring over her in soft but insistent tones. "Easy does it, babe. It's only me. Just relax, baby."

Princess Croft shuddered with pleasure at this most unusual nocturnal happening. She was a very sociable sort as horses go, especially young fillies, and she reveled in this unexpected attention. She sniffed the peppermint candy pieces in the visitor's hand, snuffled them up with rapidity.

The familiar hands moved to Princess Croft's jaw. Her head was pushed up a few inches. Suddenly there was the thrust of something alien into her left nostril. The filly whinnied in fear, raising her head. But the strong hands held her nose down. The soothing voice continued. A small probe forced the wad of sponge even deeper into her nasal passage. Then it was over. For Princess Croft, there was no real pain accompanying this intrusion, just the uncomfortable sense that something terribly unnatural had been placed in her body.

The soft voice took on a regretful tone. "Sorry, babe. Hated to do that to you, but…" There was a final soothing rub of the filly's neck. "Good going, girl, you've handled this fine. Here, take this." Princess Croft, wary now, nevertheless tentatively reached out and nibbled up the last pieces of peppermint candy. Finished, she snorted in appreciation. She watched as her visitor briskly, silently walked around the corner of the barn and disappeared into the night.

Two days later, in Heartland Downs' fifth race, a maiden event for two-year-old fillies, Princess Croft was made the 3-to-5 favorite. She had been a strong second in her only start, impressing observers with the strong way she finished.

Princess Croft broke sharply and gained the early lead. She buzzed along in front for the first quarter-mile. Then, suddenly, she began to shorten stride. When the winner crossed the finish line, Princess Croft was dead last, nearly twenty lengths in arrears. There were scattered boos from the crowd aimed at her disgusted jockey.

The winner paid $28.40. She topped a $382 exacta and a trifecta worth $1,420 on $2 bets.

Trainer Larry Lambert, baffled by Princess Croft's dismal performance, called Doc Jensen two mornings later. Using an endoscope, the veterinarian found and then extracted a foul-smelling sponge. "Well, at least I know why she ran so bad," said Lambert. "Goddam, I'd like to get my hands on whoever would do something like this to a horse."

That same night, the sponger collected a thick pay packet.

Chapter Nine

Autumn 2005

The seven old friends met for dinner at Hobson's, an extremely popular steak house in the heart of Chicago's so-called Viagra Triangle, where young women and older men sought connections over expensive drinks and lavish meals. That was not the case with these seven. Arnie Rison had called them together, Judge Toomey and Chris Carson driving down together from Wisconsin, on short notice. Their meal was excellent, but their mood gloomy.

"I got the call from Ralph Tenuta early this morning," Rison told them. "He said The Badger worked beautifully about six o'clock. A half hour later, when he was being walked and cooled out, the groom saw him limping noticeably. Ralph called our vet, Jensen. X-rays were taken. The Badger has bone chips in his left front ankle."

Rison was gently interrupted by a tap on his shoulder. Looking up, he said, "Moe, good to see you. These are my partners in the horse business."

"Looks like serious business tonight, Arnie," Kellman replied. "I'm on my way to a dinner upstairs in the private room. I just wanted to say hello." He nodded at the rest of the men and walked to the nearby stairway.

Mike Barnhill said, "Bone chips. I've had those, when I was playing ball. How serious are they for The Badger?"

"According to Doc Jensen," Rison said, "they could be operated on. The Badger would miss maybe half the year. But, as Tenuta pointed out, what's the point? The horse would have to undergo surgery, and he might not come back as good as he was."

Steve Charous said, "I'm sure we always figured that The Badger, like any racehorse, could get hurt. Funny, it just never seemed to me that would happen to him. Not the way we've been so lucky. Well," he said, raising his cocktail glass, "here's a toast to The Badger. He's been awfully damned good to us."

Judge Toomey was about to signal their attentive waitress, Mary Joyce, for a repeat round of predinner drinks, when she arrived with a tray full of glasses. "I figured you fellas for a second round," she grinned, and set their glasses before them.

"We have indeed been lucky," Rison said. "But, fellas, believe it or not, our luck with this animal may not be finished." He took a piece of paper from his pocket. "This is a fax I got late this afternoon," he said. "It came from Fairborne Farm down in Kentucky."

Carson whistled. "Fairborne is about as big time as big time gets. What's up with them?"

"They heard about The Badger's retirement. They want him to stand at stud at Fairborne. They offer to manage his career as a stallion, find the best mares they can to be bred to him, and take a percentage of the profits from the sale of foals resulting from the breedings."

"*If* there are any," interjected Judge Toomey. "A hell of a lot of good racehorses turn out to be duds as studs."

"True enough," Rison said. "But I don't see how we have anything to lose with this proposition. The Badger has a decent pedigree, excellent conformation, and a terrific racing record. He's got to live somewhere nice, and my back yard is spoken for. Why not Kentucky, where he can conceivably, and yes, I use that word advisedly," he said to the laughter it elicited, "make us some more money? And have some fun while he's doing it? Remember how he used to call out to all the fillies in his barn last summer. Strutting along with his hose hanging down? He's got a libido as big as his heart."

"So you're saying there's no downside to this plan?" said Barnhill. "What if he winds up shooting blanks, like the great horse Cigar?"

"That's always a possibility, though a remote one. But c'mon, Mike," Rison shot back, "do you know any plan that doesn't have a possible downside for somebody? Look, it'll be a couple of years before The Badger's first foals hit the racetrack. The usual practice in this business is to give a new stallion at least three crops of runners before he pretty much defines himself in the stud league. We won't really know if The Badger is going to be a success until then. But his stud fee stays the same for at least two of those first three years, depending on how the foals look and how they do at the big Keeneland and Saratoga sales."

"What's his stud fee going to be, Arnie?" Carson asked.

Rison looked at the fax in his hand. "The Fairborne people say that they want to, quote, price him realistically, unquote, in order to make him attractive to breeders. His fee will be $12,500 per live foal. That's damn reasonable for a horse with The Badger's record.

"How many mares can he be bred to each year?" Barnhill persisted, still somewhat skeptical about this venture.

"One hundred the first year," Rison said.

Carson scribbled some figures on his napkin. "Holy shit. That's a million and a quarter in stud fees."

"Wait," Rison said. "Probably only eighty percent of those hundred mares will produce a live foal. So the gross won't be that high. But, still, it'll be around a million. And," Rison added, "remember that if The Badger turns out to be a success as a stallion, that stud fee will be increased."

Talk erupted around the table as Rison reached for his nearly empty martini glass. He drained it, then tapped it with a spoon. "One more major item, gentlemen, so listen up. Judge Toomey, drawing on his vast legal experience, recommends we have a partnership contract drawn up to cover The Badger's stud career. He can't do it because he's involved. A friend of mine you just saw, Moe Kellman, recommended a Chicago attorney named Frank Cohan. Supposedly the city's top contract lawyer. Cohan drew it up. I've read it over, and I think it's just what we need. Just as with the racing partnership corporation, any profits will be divided equally among the seven of us after expenses and taxes.

"But this new contract goes further. At my recommendation, it calls for a new pattern of distribution. If, God forbid, one of us dies during The Badger's years at stud, that person's percentage of the profits, or losses, goes not to his heirs but to the remaining members of the corporation. The Badger's production proceeds stay in *our hands only* until the last of us goes. We're not ever going to sell this horse that has been so good to us. The final survivor's heirs will be in charge.

"Now, here's the kicker. If The Badger is still producing when six of us have died, the lone remaining heir must use the monies for charity. Specifically, a retirement foundation for retired and rejected thoroughbreds."

They debated the merits of this plan, but not for long. Chris Carson said, "I'm all for this. Count me in." The others followed suit. Rison said, "I'll send copies of the agreement to everybody to sign." He raised his replenished martini glass. "Here's to The Badger Express. If he's even half the stud he was as a runner, we'll all be farting through silk."

After dinner they walked a few blocks to Butch McGuire's saloon for a nightcap. Joe Zabrauskis stopped them, holding his big arms wide and smiling. "Honest to God, you guys, can you believe this? We're stallion owners? The seven of us, who could hardly scrape up $2 daily double bets with bookie Doherty back in Madison. Unfucking believeable?"

Ira Kaplan's story appeared two days later in *Racing Daily*.

```
CHICAGO, IL—One of thoroughbred racing's
most popular performers of recent years,
The Badger Express, will race no more, this
```

publication has learned exclusively. The
four-year-old multiple stakes winner suf-
fered a career-ending leg injury following
a workout earlier this week, according to
Arnie Rison, spokesman for The Significant
Seven, the syndicate that campaigned The
Badger Express

The Significant Seven acquired The Badger
Express at the Keeneland January Sale of 2003
after winning a huge Pick Six at Saratoga
the previous August. Their story, involving
old friends who were veteran horse players
who hit a pari-mutuel bonanza, became a
familiar one to the racing public. Trained
by Ralph Tenuta, "The Badger," as he was
known to his many fans, was named in honor
of the owners' alma mater, the University
of Wisconsin-Madison.

Under Tenuta's guidance, the chestnut colt won thirteen of his twenty-four
career starts over three seasons, including eight graded stakes, for total earnings
of $3,213,048, a remarkable return on his
purchase price of $95,000. This model of
consistency finished in the money in all but
one of those two dozen starts.

Said Rison, "We've had a remarkable run,
me and my friends, first hitting the Pick Six
jackpot, then buying this wonderful racehorse, who gave his all in every start he
made. We will retire him to stud. We hope
he can pass on his physical attributes and
his will to win to his offspring. That's
the idea, anyway. No matter what happens,
The Badger has already given us more fun
and money than we ever could of hoped for."

Details of The Badger Express' future are
expected to be made public in a few days.
"We are finalizing a contract with a major
Kentucky farm," Rison said. That farm is
rumored to be Fairborne, home of some of
the world's top stallions.

Chapter Ten

April 27, 2009

"Damn," Doyle said, admiringly, "who's that fine-looking girl with the Doc?"

Ralph Tenuta was standing next to Doyle in front of his stable area office on this bright summer morning. The veterinarian for the Tenuta-trained horses, Ron Jensen, had gotten out of his truck and begun walking toward them. Accompanying Jensen was a tall, slim blond woman carrying a medical satchel. She wore jeans, a yellow tee-shirt that revealed her tanned arms, and a black ribbon tied to hold back her long pony tail. She smiled and said, "Good morning, Ralph. I'm back."

"Always good to see you, Cindy," Tenuta said, "early or later. This is Jack Doyle. He's my new stable agent. Jack, say hello to Cindy Chesney and Doc Jensen. After Cindy works as an exercise rider, some mornings she helps the doc on his rounds."

Doyle said hello to the two of them. Tenuta asked Cindy, "How did that black filly go for you today?"

"Good mannered, just not much interested in running along with other horses. She's kind of an out-of-place baby at this stage."

"That's what I'm starting realize," Tenuta said. "We might have to send her back to the farm to grow up a little. How did the other three go?"

"Went great." Cindy moved off with a wave to join Doc Jensen down the shed row.

Doyle watched intently her graceful, athletic walk. "*Damn* nice-looking woman," he said. "Tell me about her."

Tenuta said, "She's one of the best exercise riders around here. She's worked for me first thing in the morning, five-thirty or six o'clock, for the last three years. Then she has other trainers she rides for. Some days of the week, she assists Doc Jensen."

"Hard-working woman," Doyle said.

"That's for sure. And one of the nicest people you'd ever meet."

Doyle said, "Married?"

"No. Widowed. Like her ma, who lives with her. Cindy's got a little boy. There's something wrong with him, I understand, but she's never said anything to me about that."

"Working two jobs like that, pretty tough."

Tenuta said, "Yeah. I guess she needs both incomes. Her mother's in the senior ranks. I think she looks after Cindy's kid during the day."

They heard the crackle of the track's barn-area loud speaker being turned on. "All horsemen are reminded that entries for Saturday's program close today at ten-thirty a.m." said an assistant to the Heartland Downs racing secretary.

Walking back into his office, Tenuta said, "You been married, Jack?"

"Oh, yeah." They kept walking.

"That's all you've got to say about it?" Tenuta laughed.

Doyle said, "Well, Ralph, as if it's any of your goddam business, which I would tend to dispute, I've been married twice and divorced the same number. Been in love more often than I should have. I'm not exactly a big favorite for the matrimonial derby."

Tenuta said, "Okay, okay, Jack. I didn't mean to raise your hackles."

"What the hell is a hackle anyway, Ralph?"

"Never mind. It's just something my old man used to say. I meant to say I didn't want to get you pissed off, like I did."

Doyle laughed. "Raise my hackles. The other morning, you told me you slept like a log. How the hell does a log sleep? Last week you said the new groom was smart as a whip. What the hell is smart about a whip?"

"Could we just talk about Saturday's entry schedule, Jack?"

Chapter Eleven

April 29, 2009

Cindy Chesney parked her faded black '94 Geo Prizm next to her leased, faded green weather-beaten home in the East Meadow trailer park ten miles from Heartland Downs. She was exhausted after her four-hour shift the previous night at the nearby Qwik Stop cash register, one of three such shifts she worked each week. She'd exercised eight horses at Heartland Downs this morning, starting at break of dawn. She'd earned $88 from those efforts, $30 from her two hours accompanying Doc Jensen and aiding him on his rounds. Now, Cindy had an hour to shower, eat a quick dinner with her mother Wilma and five-year-old son Tyler, before returning to the Qwik Stop four miles down the road, part of the chain of service station/convenience stores that enabled her to pad out her tenuous income. Her reward for the latter effort was $36.50 per three-hour shift. All this effort added up to a weekly income that varied between $500 and $600 before taxes, since some mornings there weren't many horses to work, some afternoons no clients to help Doc Jensen with. What Cindy brought in, coupled with Wilma's monthly Social Security check, enabled them to survive.

"Hey, Mom," Cindy said, entering the small kitchen area of the modest-sized trailer. Seated at the table, Wilma Morton smiled up at her only child, then continued preparing the vegetable soup they would have for dinner.

"Hi, honey," Wilma said. "How'd it go today?"

"Worked four head for Ralph Tenuta, two for Larry Lambert, couple of two-year-olds for Carlos Yanez. Both of the two-year-olds were half crazy."

Cindy took a container of orange juice out of the small fridge and poured herself a glass. "I don't know what kind of idiots they've got prepping some of these young horses to get to the track, but they are doing lousy work. It's like climbing on wild horses, some of them. Mama," she said with a tired smile, "I am muscle sore and leg sore and worn out. I got to lie down for awhile after I shower and before I go to work."

Wilma reached out to her daughter. "Aw, honey," she said, "I wish to God you didn't have to work so horrible hard. After you lost Lane, I thought you and Tyler could come and live with me and your Dad. Then the black lung took him." She poured herself a small glass of orange juice. "Wish I had me some vodka to go with this," Wilma grinned. Then she turned somber. "I never in my wildest fears saw myself wind up in a trailer park with my daughter, a widow along with me, miles from West Virginia."

"Mama," Cindy said, "this isn't exactly what I had in mind for a life, either."

The two women sat in silence for minutes. On the wall behind them were two photos, one black and white, the other in color. The first was of a tall, husky, dark-haired man, shy grin crossing his long face, Cindy's father. Next to that was a winner's circle photo from Charles Town racetrack. Poised proudly on a dark bay filly was a handsome young man who sat erect in the saddle, grinning at the camera. It was Cindy's late husband, Lane Chesney. The picture had been taken two weeks before Lane tumbled under a horse's hooves during a race at the same track, incurring fatal head injuries. Lane Chesney had been called Little Dynamite for the way he could blow through on the inside rail with his mounts, taking chances by the hundreds. It only took one wrong one to kill him.

Cindy said, "Is Tyler watching *Barney?*"

"Yep. Guess he doesn't know you're home." Wilma stuck a couple of fingers into her mouth and produced a whistle that overrode any nearby audio. Seconds later a chubby, bespectacled boy of eight bounced through the connecting doorway. "Hey, Mama. Hey, Mama," he said, reaching for Cindy. She hugged him long and hard. "Good day, Tyler? Did you have a good day?"

"Good day, Mama? Did you have a good day?"

Cindy looked lovingly at her boy, whose brown eyes slanted upward behind the thick lenses of the glasses that rested somewhat precariously on his flat nasal bridge. His little mouth could hardly contain his tongue as he smiled at his mother. She clutched Tyler to her breast, her fatigue eradicated by the strength of his love.

"Mama's going to take a shower, Tyler. Then, when *Barney* is over, we'll have dinner with Grammy. Okay, Tyler?"

"Okay, Mama, okay?"

After Tyler waved at her and trotted into the television room, Cindy's thoughts went back to the day her son was born, when the obstetrician took her hand and said gently, "Your son weighs almost six pounds. He's twenty inches long." He paused. "But he is a Down syndrome child, from what I can see. I've delivered a few in the past. I've also known mothers whose pediatrians advised them to abort."

The shock of what he'd said rippled through her. Down syndrome? Of course, Cindy had heard of it. Of course, she never thought a child of hers would emerge so burdened. She was to learn that her son's physical growth and mental development would be impaired by this chromosome disorder.

In the early months of Cindy's pregnancy with Tyler, Wilma said one night, "Are you going to take that test they give pregnant women? Called an amniotesis or something. They didn't have them during my child-bearing time," she added, "and you turned out perfect anyway."

Cindy had responded, "I know what test you're talking about. It's called amniocentesis. My pediatrican, Dr. Atkinson, mentioned it to me. I told her, 'I'm not interested in that. I'm having this baby no matter what. Period.'"

When Cindy was sixteen, unwed, she had given birth to a girl. Shortly thereafter, she put the child up for adoption. She had regretted that decision ever since. Cindy had never regretted her decision to give birth to the damaged boy she named Tyler, the love of her life.

Cindy slumped back in her chair and sighed. She looked around the small kitchen. "A couple of widows in a dumpy old trailer, Ma, that's what we are. I'm sure there's a country song in there somewhere."

Chapter Twelve

April 23, 2006

Arnie Rison sent an e-mail to the other members of The Significant Seven. It read, "Men, we can all ride down to Kentucky together. I'll pull one of the eight-seat Chevy vans off the lot. Joey Z can put his large self on the rear seat next to the cooler with the beer and sandwiches. The drive to Lexington takes about seven and a half hours. We're all set for accommodations at Scottwood Bed and Breakfast. Come to my Western Springs dealership by ten o'clock Tuesday morning. I'll have the coffee and Krispy Kremes ready. The folks at Fairborne Farm will be ready for us on Wednesday morning."

Theirs was a convivial trip to the Blue Grass State. Signs of hunger were evidenced as the van neared Indianapolis, so Rison pulled off Highway. 65 and parked in the Shapiro's Delicatessen lot. Zabrauskis ordered for them all at the takeout counter. Minutes later, Joey Z toting a shopping bag full of corned beef and pastrami sandwiches, they resumed their journey.

Of the seven, only Arnie Rison had previously been to the Lexington area, a part of the country perhaps at its most striking in the spring when the redbud trees were in bloom and the new foals followed their dams around the bright green pastures. Chris Carson, noting the extensive and expensive fencing surrounding the horse farms, most of them hundreds if not thousands of acres each, was awed. "It must cost these people thousands a month just to cut the grass," he calculated. "Upkeep on all those fences is probably another small fortune."

Similarly impressive to Judge Toomey was their B&B, a Federal brick house built in the nineteenth century and nestled on a six-acre property overlooking Elkhorn Creek. The owners, a young couple named Grahl, warmly greeted the travelers. "We've read about you fellows," Annette Grahl said. "I guess you're down here to visit your famous horse."

"That we are," Steve Charous said. "It's a new experience for us. We're all old horse players. But none of us has ever seen a mare being bred, especially not to a horse we own." He nodded appreciatively at the beautiful dining room in which they stood, with its antique furniture, restored fireplace, and checkerboard floor.

"I wish," Rison said, "I had known about this place before, when I came down with our trainer to buy The Badger on my first Kentucky visit. This is wonderful."

Annette's husband Tim said, "Thank you very much. I hope you'll enjoy all of your stay."

"We'll need an early breakfast, Tim," Rison said, "so we can get over to Fairborne."

"No problem," Tim said. "Seven early enough for you?"

"That would be fine," Rison answered. The others agreed.

Annette said, "Cheese omelets, French toast, ham biscuits, fruit plates, three kinds of juice. Sound all right?" She was smiling.

Joey Z smiled back. "I'll be down before seven," he said. "I'm the partner with the appetite."

The Chevy van was buzzed through Fairborne Farm's imposing front gate a little after eight the next morning. Rison drove slowly up the long, tree-lined drive toward a cluster of barns positioned behind a huge main residence. Pastures on both sides were dotted by thoroughbreds of various ages, most of them grazing on the lush grass. This was the home of several of the nation's most prominent thoroughbred stallions, the "capital of equine copulation," as Chris Carson termed it.

"The mansion looks like Scarlett O'Hara could pop out the front door," Carson said. "*Look* at it."

Rison parked carefully in an area marked for visitors between a blue BMW and a red Maserati. "Hope we don't get towed away for being nondescript."

The Seven were immediately hailed by a fortyish, very fit-looking man wearing a Fairborne Farm windbreaker, jeans, and a ball cap with "The Badger Express" emblazoned on it. "Morning men," he said, "welcome to Fairborne. I'm Arthur Logan. Great to see y'all here this morning."

Rison said, "Our pleasure, Arthur. These are my partners." He introduced them all to the Fairborne Farm owner, who shook each man's hand enthusiastically. Mike Barnhill said, "How's The Badger doing? We haven't seen him since he left the racetrack."

"Mr. Barnhill," Logan said, "your horse is a real pleasure. Very well mannered, even gets along with the older studs in the stallion barn. Looks good and is feeling good. We're mighty happy to have him here at Fairborne." He turned and motioned them forward. "Gentlemen, please follow me."

Logan led them up a red brick walkway to what he said was "the breeding shed." It was a large, two-story brick building with rubberized flooring, a couple of walnut-paneled stalls, and several walnut-trimmed windows. "Some 'shed,'" Barnhill said.

"You should see the stallion barn," Rison answered. "Mr. Logan sent me a color video about Fairborne. You could move your family in there and invite people over."

Inside the wide doorway, they were met by a large, red-haired man wearing clothes and cap identical to Logan's. "This is our stud manager, Harley Livingston," Logan said. "Morning, men," Livingston said. "We're about all set for your horse. The teaser has done his job."

To a puzzled looking Marty Higgins, Livingston explained, "The teaser is a stud horse, not real well bred, that is used to get the mare revved up and ready. He has equipment on him so he can't ejaculate in her."

"What a rotten damn job," said Joey Z.

The Fairborne owner directed them to a stairway leading to a balcony overlooking the breeding area. An elderly couple was already there. Logan said, "Mr. and Mrs. Berns, I'd like to introduce you to The Significant Seven. The men who raced and own The Badger Express."

Logan went on to say that Peter and Barbara Berns owned the mare that would be bred that morning to The Badger Express. "We try to be here whenever our girl is bred," Mrs. Berns said. She was wearing a stylish tweed jacket and pants, which made for an incongruous contrast to her black ball cap that read "Go Dee Dee." After shaking hands with each of the Seven, her gray-headed husband turned to concentrate on the scene below. "Mr. Berns acts like a worried father in the maternity waiting room," Judge Toomey whispered to Rison.

"That's the Berns' mare," Logan said, "Dainty Dee Dee. She'll be Badger Express' first mating. She's fifteen now, knows what she's doing. And likes what she's doing. She's never been barren or slipped a foal. One of the best producers we've ever had here."

"That's our girl," said Mrs. Berns proudly.

Suddenly, from outside the barn, came the resonant, trumpeting call of a horse in a hurry. The Badger Express was not being led but was almost dragging his stud groom to the breeding shed. He was tossing his head, nostrils flaring in the exciting air he was experiencing for the first time, swinging his already extended penis, which looked like a yard and half of slightly slimmed down fireman's black hose. His attention was lasered on Dainty Dee Dee. "That's Baily Williams with your horse. He's our best stud groom. Been here almost thirty years. But he's got his hands full today," Logan said.

Mrs. Berns observed The Badger's entrance with a mixture of repugnance and awe. Her husband glanced at his watch. Nodding toward the scene below, he said, "This shouldn't take long."

"Our boy is ready to go," Carson said.

"They won't have to put any Viagra in his oats," Rison answered.

"Maybe you should get some of *his* oats for your breakfast cereal," Joey Z said, bumping Barnhill's arm with his elbow."

"Speak for yourself," Barnhill barked back.

The Badger Express shuffled about anxiously while Dainty Dee Dee was being positioned for him. Once the mare was in place, The Badger needed no urging. He mounted her eagerly, his front hooves resting on Dainty Dee Dee's shoulders that were covered with protective pads. Livingston adeptly guided The Badger's penis into her vagina, the mare standing firmly, her flanks trembling. The Badger ejaculated almost immediately, the process taking less than a minute. Dainty Dee Dee's handlers tucked a small bag under her rump to catch any expelled semen, which would be discarded.

The Significant Seven looked around at each other. "Holy shit," said Marty Higgins, "that's how they fucking do it? I mean, do it, horses fucking? I'll be damned."

Livingston led their horse to the doorway. The Badger Express pranced down the walkway toward the stallion barn, tossing his head, a picture of physical pride. "He'll be back at work this afternoon," Arthur Logan said. "He's going to be a real pro at this."

The Significant Seven whooped as if they'd just witnessed a Chicago Bears touchdown.

On their way back to the parking lot, Steve Charous said to Rison, "Straighten me out on this. When will his first sons and daughters be born?"

"Offspring, they call them," Rison laughed. "A mare's gestation period is eleven months. The Badger's babies will hit the ground, running we hope, starting next March. They'll go to the races two years later. I can't wait."

Chapter Thirteen

May 2, 2009

Judge Henry Toomey slipped out of his bed, careful not to disturb his sleeping wife, Janie, at this early hour. Whenever the Toomeys were vacationing at their Lake Geneva second home, the judge, a former swim team captain at the University of Wisconsin, began his day with an hour's exercise in the very cool, spring-fed blue waters, usually spending at least half of that time on what had been his collegiate specialty, the back stroke. Other early risers on this beautiful southeastern Wisconsin lake were used to seeing the lanky Toomey's long arms churning paddle wheel style across this body of deep water from his pier on the northern shore.

Toomey put on his black trunks, flip-flops, a sweat shirt, and picked up a towel. Before walking out the back door, he started coffee brewing. On the pier he spent several minutes stretching and breathing deeply.

Toomey started out a strong, level pace. Looking up at the cloud-cleared sky, he anticipated another beautiful spring day in this pleasant town. Probably nine holes of golf with Janie after breakfast, then some fishing with his neighbor, Chuck Siebert. At the mid-point of his lake crossing, back of his head in the water, face turned to the morning sky, he did not spot the figure directly in his path, awaiting him, a figure in a black wet suit, diving gear, diver's mask just above the water as Toomey churned closer.

Seconds later the judge felt powerful hands grasp his ankles from below the water. He did not have a moment to speculate as to what was happening before he felt himself being pulled downward, his body held two feet below the lake's surface.

Mouth closed, attempting to conserve breath, Toomey frantically tried to kick free. He reached forward and managed to briefly touch the shoulders of his attacker. He felt himself running out of air, out of strength, but not out of astonishment. *"What the hell?"* was the last thought that crossed his mind as the water rushed into his now open mouth. His struggle to escape the iron grip of the diver dwindled, diminished further, then ceased.

Judge Toomey's floating corpse was discovered an hour later by one of the first sailboats to come out onto the lake. Resultant shock and horror registered in Lake Geneva, in Madison, throughout Wisconsin's legal fraternity, when it was announced that the popular Toomey, a powerful swimmer, had died of an apparent heart attack at age fifty-three.

That evening, back in northern Wisconsin, Orth unpacked his diving gear and set it out on the bench in front of his cabin's front door. He went inside and grabbed a Leinenkugel before getting into his Jeep Cherokee for the drive to the outdoor phone he always used.

In Dallas, Sanderson picked up on the first ring of his cell phone. Orth could hear childrens' voices in the background, the blare of a television cartoon show. "It's me," Orth said. Sanderson said, "I can hardly hear you. I'll go out on the patio."

Seconds later, Sanderson said, "Yeah?"

"All done, *amigo*. Let me know when the money transfer is headed to my account."

"Will do. Hey, great work, bro. We're on our way."

Chapter Fourteen

May 7, 2009

"A damned shame, Jack. That's what it is," said Ralph Tenuta.

The two men were standing outside Tenuta's office on the Heartland Downs backstretch. The subject was Judge Henry Toomey's death, which had been widely reported the previous day.

"I only met him a few times," Tenuta said, "when he came out with the rest of the syndicate members. Seemed like a class act. I talked to Arnie Rison this morning. He and the other five are all planning to go up for the funeral in Madison on Monday."

They finished their coffee. It was a little after ten a.m. Tenuta's trainees had been excercised, cooled out, and put away. The stable's morning work was finished.

"Jack, you might want to bring some betting money when you come back this afternoon. Forget about the two-year-old filly in the second race, she's in there just for the experience. But Editorialist should blow them away in the stakes race, even if it is on the grass."

"I'll meet you in your clubhouse box," Doyle said.

Two mornings earlier, in his role as Tenuta's stable agent, Doyle had walked into the Heartland Downs entry clerk's office after Tenuta had instructed him to enter Editorialist "in Saturday's turf course stakes." It was a $150,000 event, Doyle knew. He said to Tenuta, "Has that nut case ever been on the turf?"

"Only when he was a baby, roaming the Kentucky pastures. But I want to give him a shot. His granddaddy was Theatrical, a helluva grass runner. Maybe those genes will transfer. And the way he moves, I think he'll like the turf. Anyway, there's no other race for him here for several weeks. So, we'll experiment."

Personnel in the entry clerk's office had come to know Doyle. Clerk Chris Polzin looked at Doyle in surprise when he had read the entry slip. "Jack, you putting Editorialist in the grass stakes?"

"Just doing what the boss says, Chris."

After getting a haircut, Doyle arrived back at Heartland Downs a couple of hours in advance of Editorialist's race. He had a Chicago-style hot dog ("drag it through the garden") before he rode the escalator to the second floor of the clubhouse where he bought a Heineken from his favorite racetrack bartender, "Las Vegas Lou."

Lou DiCastri worked at Heartland Downs in the summer, a bar at McCarron Airport most of the rest of the year. He was a big, bluff, fifty-eight-year-old man with an engaging line of patter and an impressive memory for his regular customers' drink choices. He also touted horses a bit, and evidently fairly well, for Doyle had seen many of Lou's clientele tip him lavishly.

Lou was chatting up two heavily made-up, fortyish women, both dressed as if they were in their early twenties, with tanning bed hues and bleached hair. They laughed loudly at something he'd said, the bracelets jangling on the shorter one's wrist as she lifted her margarita to her lips. When Lou noticed Doyle standing behind the two women, he winked over their heads. He began to draw a plastic cup of Heineken. "Jack," he asked, "what's the word on Tenuta's horses today?"

"Pass on the filly in the second. That screwball Editorialist? Lou, nobody ever knows what he'll do. He's been disqualified four times in his career for attacking other horses. If he runs straight, he wins. That is, if he doesn't decide to take a bite out of the starting gate." Doyle paid for the beer, left a tip, and started moving away from the bar. "For what it's worth, Lou, I'm betting him," he said over his shoulder.

"Thanks, Jack."

The taller woman, whom Lou always flattered by calling Lucky Linda, said, "Who's that guy, Lou?"

"He works for the trainer Ralph Tenuta. Name's Jack Doyle. Nice guy."

"Is he married?" said the woman with the noticeable jewelry.

"Ladies," Lou said, "drawing on my long experience observing human nature from behind the wood, I'd say 'no.'"

Walking through the crowded clubhouse, Doyle again marveled at the nonhomogeneity of American horse players. There were a couple of dozen white senior citizens, female and male, sitting in chairs in front of a bank of large television screens. In the next section, all thirty-six carrels, each equipped with a small television set and writing desk, housed the most serious of gamblers present, all male, all poring over statistics and *Racing Dailys* and file folders filled with what they believed to be notable notations on horses competing this day. Three Asian men, probably Chinese, Doyle guessed, had lined up in front of the $50 betting window. Congregated on the terrace overlooking the track's paddock was a group of Latinos, all dressed as if they had just come from their demanding jobs in the barn area. Next to them, a half-dozen loud, beer-drinking college boys laughed and jived, trying to impress the two very impressive-looking coeds in their midst. Situated in the far corner of this balcony, where the hint of marijuana could often be discerned, seven or eight young men with strong Jamaican accents debated the merits of the horses in the upcoming race.

"Only at the racetrack," Doyle said to himself, "would this kind of collection collect."

Doyle bet $100 to win, $50 to place on Editorialist before joining Tenuta in the box overlooking the finish line. Arnie Rison was there with the trainer. "Arnie," Doyle said, "we were all very sorry to hear about Judge Toomey."

"Thanks, Jack." He dug a Marlboro out of his jacket pocket. "Believe me, that was hard to believe. Henry kept himself in terrific shape all his life. Who would think a heart attack would take out a guy of his age who'd never had a hint of heart trouble?"

Rison turned as his daughter came down the steps to the box. "Jack, I think you know Renee." She smiled at Doyle. Her outfit this afternoon was a cunningly cut sundress that did her shapely, petite figure complete justice. "Nice to see you again, Jack," she said. She handed her father some pari-mutuel tickets. Arnie didn't bother to look at them. He raised his binoculars to key in on Editorialist, who was bouncing up and down behind the distant gate at the start of this one-mile race.

Rison said to Tenuta, "Did you bet him, Ralph?"

"Do they keep a good kitchen in the Vatican?" Tenuta answered. "Of course. So did Jack and the rest of the stable crew."

"Let's hope he comes through," Rison said. "After we heard about Henry, the rest of us talked and talked and then decided to dedicate every dollar Editorialist wins from now on to a Henry Toomey Scholarship Fund at the University of Wisconsin law school. We'd like to kickstart that fund today."

Tenuta said, "We're kind of in luck, because Editorialist drew the one hole. With the rail right next to him on his left, he can only ram into the horse on his right if he wants to, instead of pinballing between two of them, trying to do damage, which he is very fond of doing."

The gate doors clanged open. Editorialist, Doyle saw, had come out straight and true. But the Number Two horse, outside Editorialist, almost had his feet go out from under him. Recovering quickly, and despite his jockey's attempt to straighten him, Number Two veered over and banged into Editorialist's hind quarters, almost turning him sideways.

"Christ almighty," shouted Tenuta.

Rison lowered his glasses and sank down into his seat next to Doyle. His dejection was obvious. He reached into his coat pocket for his pack of Marlboros. "*Wait,*" Doyle said, seconds later, elbowing Rison, "he's straightening out."

Unlike many previous races when Editorialist, feeling he'd been abused or disrespected and responding by trying to bite the hide of any horse within range, this time lowered his head and powered up the rail like a bullet train. He had the lead after a half mile, a lead he continued to extend. Jockey Javier Hidalgo tucked his whip away and sat still on this combustible creature. Editorialist won by four widening lengths.

Tenuta, face flushed, looked around excitedly. He said "How *about* that son of a gun? Is he something else?" Rison embraced him, as did Renee. Tenuta reached over the little woman's shoulder to give Jack a hearty high five. "Come on," he said, "let's go to the winner's circle."

Rison stood up. His sweat-soaked seersucker suit looked like it had been worn out from the inside. On his long, creased face was a look of both pain and relief. He gave his daughter a hug. "That one's for Henry Toomey," he said. "It's a start on the scholarship fund."

"That's a nice start," Doyle said to Renee as they left the box. "Editorialist's winner's share today is $60,000."

They hurried down the indoor stairs to the trackside level of Heartland Downs, where they were ushered by a security guard to the winner's circle. Editorialist was being led in by two of Tenuta's grooms. He skittered about as the photo was taken. Jockey Hidalgo cautiously reached up to remove his saddle from the fractious horse's back.

Tenuta gave the jock a hearty hug. "Nice job, Javvie. You took a serious knock there, coming out of the gate."

Hidalgo wiped his sleeve across his sweaty forehead. "That just made the 'orse mad, Mr. Ralph. Then," the jockey grinned, "he decided to run his ass off and show 'em who is the boss."

Tenuta laughed. He clapped Hidalgo on the back. "Editorialist, that son of a bitch, is *always* mad," the trainer said.

Chapter Fifteen

May 10, 2009

Doyle parked his Accord in the trailer park lot, noticing that his vehicle, a 2006 model, stood out amidst a generation of much older cars and pickup trucks. A couple of families sat under the two scraggly trees at the far end of the property. The men drank beer as they talked and and occasionally tended to the meat broiling on the battered Weber grill. The women sat at the scarred picnic table, watching their children chase each other around the dusty perimeter of the property.

The drive over from the track had taken longer than he'd expected. It was evening traffic time in the western suburbs. The previous year, Doyle had finally broken himself of his habit of reading every bumper sticker and vanity license plate that came into his view when he was behind the wheel. It was a ridiculous habit, and he knew it, but it had taken him time to change his compulsive ways. But he managed.

Unfortunately, he'd replaced those two addictions with a concentration on car names, the likes of which astounded him. At the intersection of Highway 53 and Keno Road, waiting for the very slow-to-appear left turn signal, he started saying to himself, "A car named the Equinox? There's an Avalanche over there. Whoops, don't drop onto the Canyon next to you, man."

The light changed with Doyle muttering, "The Vibe? The Stanza? The Sonata? Enclave? What the hell does an Enclave have to do with a car?"

Doyle had bumped into Cindy that morning as she was leaving the Tenuta barn, having exercised four horses for Ralph. It was a literal bumping, Doyle turning right at a corner of the barn just as Cindy veered left coming from the opposite direction. There was a moment of surprise, shock, then laughter. Doyle, involuntarily reaching out to grab her, felt the work-created strength of her arms, smelled the combination of sweat and perfume that she emanated.

"My fault," Doyle said.

"No, just as much mine," Cindy replied. "I had my mind on a couple of things besides backstretch foot traffic."

They chatted for a few minutes before Doyle said, "Hey, how about I buy you dinner some night?" He gave her what he believed was his most sincere, engaging look. For a change, it worked. "I'd like that," Cindy said. "Tonight'd be great."

Home from the track, Cindy played with Tyler, the two of them doing rudimentary puzzles at the kitchen table. Then she showered and walked into the trailer's kitchen, wrapped in a towel, blond hair damp, and poured herself a shot of tequila from the bottle on the door of the refrigerator. She heard her mother say, "Now, just exactly what knight missing his armor will be calling for you here tonight?" The remark was followed by the combined laughter of Wilma and her best friend, Doris Bush, visiting from her nearby trailer.

"I wouldn't be making fun of my date before you meet him," Cindy shot back. "You two haven't had anything to do with men for twenty years. Except the clerks you harass at Walmart. Or the old farts you bully at church bingo." She heard them cackle at that, too.

"What's he like?" Cindy said to herself. "Nice looking, good manners, good sense of humor. An interesting man." *And single*, she said to herself. She decided she'd withhold that last bit of info from Wilma for the time being. Cindy frowned, remembering that she'd heard Jack was a university grad, University of Illinois she thought, compared to her total of five spread-out semesters at three community colleges.

Showered and dressed, Cindy checked herself in the small mirror over the old brown bureau in her tiny bedroom. It was one of the several pieces of third-hand furniture she and Wilma, Tyler in tow, had hauled into their leased home two years earlier. "As good as I can get now," she murmured, tucking a still moist tendril behind her ear.

Cindy opened the door before Doyle had reached the top of the four trailer steps. "Hi, Jack. Welcome." She motioned him forward. Doyle's eyebrows lifted as he watched her proceed him. This evening Cindy was a startlingly feminine contrast to the woman he saw racetrack mornings.

She led him into the living room of the trailer, its largest room. The centerpiece was a large television set. Staring at it intently were two elderly women. They were watching *Wheel of Fortune*. Each had a half-finished highball in her hand. Both women had their feet up on a wooden table in front of the couch on which they sat. In front of the table was a floor fan, cleverly aimed to cool them up their skirts, which were pulled up knee high. They smiled merrily as Cindy introduced Doyle. "My mother, Wilma, and her friend, Doris. My friend, too."

"Glad to meet you, ladies."

Cindy went over to the left door leading to that side of the trailer. "Tyler, c'mon out here," she said. A thumping of feet was followed by the arrival of a chunky, fair-haired youngster wearing Spiderman pajamas and a Chicago Cubs baseball cap turned sideways. There was a surprised expression on his round face. He took off his thick glasses and rubbed his eyes before looking directly at Doyle. "Tyler," Cindy said, "this is Mr. Doyle. Jack, this is my son Tyler."

It was then that Doyle recalled Ralph Tenuta saying Cindy was a single mother of a child with some disability. Doyle had assumed she was just single, one of the numerous independent feminine members of the backstretch work force who'd filled out their census forms that way. He held out his hand. "Tyler, how are you. Good to meet you."

Tyler regarded the hand warily Then he responded with a quick grab and a gap-toothed grin. "Gotta finish…gotta finish… see cartoons," he said. He rapidly reversed course back into his bedroom.

Minutes later, in the car, Doyle said, "I made a reservation at Tom's Charhouse, over on Palatine Road. Is that okay with you?"

"I've never been there," Cindy said. "I've heard it's really good."

"Ralph recommended it. He takes his wife there a lot."

"Ralph Tenuta's got money," Cindy said softly, looking out her window into the advancing dusk.

Doyle shrugged. "I have, too," he smiled, "at least for tonight."

He turned north on Wilke Avenue. "How old is Tyler?" he said.

Cindy gave him a sharp look before saying, "He's eight. He's short for his age."

"Nice-looking kid," Doyle said.

They rode in silence for several blocks before Cindy said, "You must be aware that Tyler's different, right?"

Doyle hesitated before saying, "A cousin of mine has a daughter who kind of reminds me of Tyler. About the same age. She's a wonderful kid named Naomi. She has Down syndrome." He banged his horn as a tiny, gray-haired woman driver attempted to enter his lane in her old Buick. She responded by angrily raising a middle finger.

Cindy said, "Tyler was unlucky to be born with Down. But I'm lucky to have him. He's the light of my life. He's what I live for, knowing that he lives for me." She looked out her window, talking now with her head turned away from Jack. "And we were lucky he doesn't have some of the worst things that Down kids can have, like congenital heart defects. Like severe mental retardation. My husband was killed when Tyler was four. But those four years we all had together, I thank God for them."

Doyle zipped through the next intersection before saying, "Gotta be very, very tough."

Cindy laughed an are-you-kidding laugh. "Sure it's tough. How could it be any other way? Finding Tyler the right kind of schooling, near us, that I could afford. Watching him struggle with simple things. Watching people give him the strange looks that people do, for kids that look like he does. Or adults like him, for that matter. They stand out from a physical standpoint, no question."

"But then, after awhile," she said with a smile, "watching Tyler *get* stuff. That was so exciting for me. Way after most kids his age, but still making progress. The look on his face when that window opens in his mind, that makes my heart lift. And my Mom's. She's a character, had rough times of her own, but she is great with my Tyler. And she loves him like I do. We're going to get him into a great school next year."

She paused. Turning to Doyle, she said, "I'd really rather not talk about this anymore tonight, okay?"

Doyle turned on the Accord's CD player. He advanced it from the vibrant sounds of New Orleans luminary Dr. John to the quieter work of another Crescent City legend, Wynton Marsalis, playing ballads.

Cindy sat back in her seat. "What are you smiling at?" Doyle said.

"Not anything very interesting," she said. She relaxed her tired shoulder muscles, thinking how nice it was to have a rare night out with an apparently nice guy, no financial worries on her mind right now. Not another Friday night at the Pic-n-Save market, hoping her endangered credit card passed muster as the bagger packed up her modest collection of necessities. Those nights, the continual war between solvency and savings and debt that enveloped and defined her working life chafed her nerves. Not tonight. She glanced at Doyle. He looked good in profile, even with that slight bump in his boxer's nose.

◇◇◇

In its music room/lounge, Tom's Charhouse this week was featuring a guitar player from a Chicago soft rock band that had been briefly famous two decades earlier. Doyle and Cindy stopped to read the poster with the man's name and photo on it. A critical review quoted beneath the picture of the musician stated that his music as a soloist in recent years had become "meditative and earthy, luminous and pensive." Peering into the sparsely populated lounge, they saw an overweight, gray-haired, pony-tailed man bearing not the slightest resemblance to the poster photo from his old band's glory days. He rumbled into the beginning of a Joe Cocker hit that, Doyle immediately decided, he should have left to Joe Cocker.

"Good God," Doyle said. "Let's get a table on the far side of the dining room. Okay?"

The Charhouse host, a harried looking fellow, greeted them at his lectern. Doyle watched as the man carefully scrutinized the night's roster before checking off Doyle's reservation. To Doyle, the host looked a lot like Ralph Nader, but even more humorless. At Doyle's request, and motivated by the double sawbuck Doyle slipped him, the Nader lookalike quickly led them to a table in the rear of the crowded dining room. It was next to a window overlooking the nearby street. Cindy asked their waiter for iced tea, Doyle ordered Bushmills on the rocks. They both opted for steak, the house specialty, a New York strip for Doyle, a twenty-four ounce porterhouse for Cindy. Doyle's surprise was apparent. Cindy said, "No, Jack, I can't polish off a piece of beef that big. But Tyler loves, I mean loves, cold steak. He doesn't get it very often. So, I'll bring him some home." She smiled at him over the rim of her glass. "I'm taking advantage of you here tonight."

"No, the advantage is surely mine."

"What do you mean?"

"I mean I'm here with by far the most attractive woman in the place." He raised his glass. "To you." She clinked her glass carefully against his.

"This is a real treat for me, Jack. I don't often get to go out to places as nice as this."

Over the salad course, Doyle employed what he had discovered years ago was the most effective way to ingratiate himself with women he was dating, or even just dealing with on a business level. He asked Cindy about herself. She responded with a description of her upbringing as a miner's daughter in a small West Virginia town, her marriage and husband's tragic death, the avenue that had delivered her to Heartland Downs for the work, to the trailer park with her mother.

Taking a breath from her narrative, Cindy asked for a glass of merlot. After a couple of bolstering sips, she said, "I'm second generation trailer folk, Jack. Not trash. Just people, most of them hard-trying like mine. Where I grew up was close to a run-down old riding stable, Sheridan Acres, run by a guy named Glen. He was the manager and part owner. He gave me a job after school and on weekends starting when I was fourteen. I loved working with the horses, learning to ride them. I got to be pretty much enamored with Glen. And he knew it." She put the wine glass down and sat back in her chair, arms crossed across her chest, eyes lowered.

"Couple of years after Glen gave me the job, he gave me something else. A baby. I was sixteen, clueless. My Mom convinced me to put the child, a girl, up for adoption. I did. I've regretted it ever since. I've often thought that, years later, when I had Tyler, I was being punished for not keeping that perfectly healthy little girl. But I wouldn't trade my Tyler for anything. There isn't a more innocent, sweeter-natured person in the world."

Tears began to slide down Cindy's face. Doyle handed her a napkin. He didn't know what to say. He was getting more and sadder information than he was used to in such situations.

"Two years later," Cindy continued, " I met Lane Chesney, Tyler's daddy. You probably heard of him, a good jock who died young on the racetrack."

"I have," Doyle said. "That was a very sad thing."

"It was. It was. Anyway, before I met Lane, I met and married another rider, name of Herbie Echols. We were both nineteen. He was a pretty good rider at that time, when he was straight, which lasted about a year into our marriage. Then he got to coking and drinking and running around on me. I divorced him. I didn't even try to get alimony. I was hating him so much I didn't even want money from the little bastard. Herbie moved to California and went downhill in a hurry. Lost his rider's license about three times because he failed drug tests. Last I heard, Herbie was up in northern California trying to be a jock's agent. Hah! The man could hardly sort out the bills in his wallet, much less keep track of a bank account or a condition book."

She picked up her wine glass. "So, Jack, you probably know more than you ever wanted to know about me. I'm sorry I started rambling like that. Sorry for the tears, too."

Patting her hand, Doyle said, "Actually, the comforting of widows has become kind of a specialty of mine." Responding to Cindy's quizzical look, Doyle continued "Oh, there was a lovely woman in New Zealand. Another one I knew, ah, quite well somewhat recently at Monee Park."

Cindy, intrigued, said, "What happened between you and these women?"

"Things just didn't work out," Doyle shrugged. There was a lull in their conversation.

"Is that a pained expression I see on your face?" she said. "You don't look comfortable talking about this. Do you have mixed emotions?"

Doyle paused. "Yes and no," he answered. And they both started laughing.

Their entrees arrived. Cindy's porterhouse extended to the edges of the wide plate. She and Jack both laughed at its size. They laughed again when the waiter presented their baked potatoes, each the size of a large hand grenade. "They give you your money's worth here," Cindy said. She cut into her steak.

On the street outside the restaurant, a horn-blowing wedding party drove raucously past, either away from the reception or toward it. Cindy said, "You should have seen the wedding I was at a month ago."

Where?"

"Back in West Virginia. I flew there for the weekend, left Tyler with Mom. It was a girl I went to school with in Nitro, Mary Anne Bullamore. We were great friends and we've kept in touch and she finally snared a husband."

"Snared?" Doyle asked with a smile.

Cindy said, "Mary Ann weighs about two-fifty. Sweet, sweet girl, but at the bottom of the eligible bachelorettes' list, if you know what I mean. Then, a year or so ago, she wrote me that she'd met this neat truck driver named Marvin Prochnow. Marvin, I found out when I saw him, weighs about one-twenty. Seems to be a nice little guy.

"What can I say? You never know for sure what people will fall in love with what kind of other people. I'll tell you this, though. It was a wedding to remember. And not just because of the differences in the way the bride and groom looked."

Doyle said, "Go on."

Cindy chewed another fork full of porterhouse before replying. "Mary Anne went to university. She got interested in what she called Eastern Studies. I'm pretty sure she majored in it. A lot of Zen stuff. I hardly knew what she was talking about when she'd call me.

"Anyway," Cindy continued, "the wedding ceremony was held at this strange looking little building on the outskirts of town. The front of the building had a Christian cross on it, and a big blue and white Jewish star, and a crescent moon, and some other symbols I didn't recognize. The leader of this church is a man, I am not making this up, who calls himself Swami River. He had on a big flowing white outfit and a long black beard. Below his robe, you could see the Reeboks on his feet. He did the ceremony. It took about ten minutes. There were 'Ommmms' and some deep breathing exercise stuff and about eight minutes of what the Swami called 'meditative contemplation.' You were supposed to keep your eyes closed, but I couldn't help but look at Mary Anne, who was beaming. She was as happy as I'd ever seen her.

"When this was over, the Swami and his helpers passed around little pieces of what he called 'gomunnion'. They were really squares of vegetarian pizza. You were supposed to eat them and then wash them down with wine that was being passed around in goat skin bags by these strange ushers. You should have seen what *they* were dressed in." She paused to put another dollop of sour cream on her diminishing potato.

Doyle had stopped looking on in wonder at the way Cindy was moving happily through her dinner, at the flush in her tanned cheeks as she recounted details of the wedding in Nitro. His meal was good. This narrative he considered better. He waited for more, smiling at this enthusiastic young woman.

Cindy said, "I don't want to bore you with all this wedding stuff, but I've got to tell you about the end, one of the best parts. We left the church to go right next door to Swami River's house. He had cleared all the furniture out of what I guess was the living room. That's where the dancing was. Mary Anne and Marvin stepped out on the floor, they were so happy and cute, I loved it. The music started pretty quick. It was 'Proud Mary.' Remember? John Fogarty, Creedence Clearwater Rival? There was my friend Mary Anne twirling little Marvin around the room. It was great to see. And you know the disc jockey for the night was? Yes. Swami River."

Cindy cut what she said was her final bite of the beef. "This is the best steak I've ever had," she said. "Tyler's going to think so, too."

◇◇◇

The only awkward moment of their night came as they waited for their dessert to be served. Doyle had ordered coffee and a crème brulee, Cindy a small cookie assortment with green tea. Before their orders arrived, Cindy suddenly coughed hard. She leaned forward and Doyle saw and heard something small and hard land in the middle of the plate before her. It appeared to Doyle to be a tooth. It was.

Cindy gasped and covered her mouth with her napkin. There was a moment of very awkward silence before Doyle said, quietly, "I believe you've dropped something."

She looked at him over the top of her napkin. Her shoulders began to shake. Tears emerged, but her eyes were laughing eyes. Doyle stayed quiet. Then he started laughing, too.

"Oh, Jack. That's probably the most embarrassing thing that's ever happened to me." She plucked the false tooth off the plate and, behind the napkin that she held up to her face, carefully inserted it back into the middle of her mouth. Wiping her eyes again with her napkin, she looked at Jack and gave him an intentionally goofy smile. He broke up.

"Sorry about that," she said. "It's never happened to me before, you know?"

Then she began to laugh aloud as he joined in. People at nearby tables turned to look at them. Doyle reached across the table to cover Cindy's hand.

"Care to tell me the story on this?" he said.

She lowered her napkin. "I had my mouth busted open by a two-year-old colt in the starting gate at Heartland Downs two years ago. The trainer, it was Ralph Tenuta by the way, was trying to teach the colt about the gate. I'm the exercise rider that day. First, the colt gnawed on the assistant starter's thumb when they were attempting to lead him in. He was kicking out behind, too, scattering those guys. I'm thinking, 'What am I doing here on this animal? He's nuts.'

"They finally get the s. o. b. into the gate and close the doors. But all of a sudden he rears up and tries to throw himself over backwards. Hit me in the mouth with his neck. I was lucky he didn't crash my head into the top of the gate. One of my front teeth came out. I had to have root canals on a couple of others, right that day, over at the dental clinic. Ralph paid for all of that work. I wound up with this one false tooth, the one that just fell out. Couldn't afford a dental implant, and I had to get something to put in there so I wouldn't look like a cartoon character."

Doyle said, "Hold on a minute. Was that wild two-year-old Editorialist?"

"Sure was. Damn, Jack," she added, "that false tooth has only one other time come loose like that. One day in the spring, I cooked pot roast for Mom and Tyler and me. I marinated it, but I guess not enough. It was like biting into a miner's boot. My false tooth fell out on the table. Mom thought it was hilarious, and Tyler looked scared, and then we all just looked at the tooth. Like you did just now. Once Tyler was over the shock, he started laughing for about ten minutes. He told his special ed class about it for weeks.

"For the most part," Cindy said, "the damn thing stays in place. I don't know why that happened just now." She patted his hand. "I appreciate your, well, your reaction. Or nonreaction. You know?"

Doyle said, "Cindy, you are looking at a man who has starred in far more embarrassing life moments than that." He toasted her with the last of his Bushmills, looking over the top of his glass at this very attractive, healthy, glowing specimen of American womanhood. Missing tooth? So what?

Chapter Sixteen

May 15, 2009

Steve Charous' weekday morning agenda was as routine as a Chicago Cubs late season collapse. Before opening his insurance office in downtown Des Plaines, he breakfasted Monday through Friday at the Golden Greek Grill. Black coffee, small grapefruit juice, one raisin bagel with a schmear of cream cheese. By the time he had speed read the *Chicago Tribune* and *Wall Street Journal*, he'd finished eating and was ready for his business day.

This Thursday morning Ike Pappas, owner and operator for thirty-one years of the Golden Greek Grill, called out, "Steve. Hey, Steve. Got a call for you here on the house phone."

Charous had just drained his juice glass and taken his first sip of coffee and was awaiting the arrival of his bagel. He shrugged, got out of his window chair, and walked to the phone that was next to the restaurant's cash register. "Hello. Hello?" No answer. "Hello, Steve Charous here," he said impatiently. As he did so Iris, his regular waitress, placed the plate with the bagel and cream cheese on Steve's table. It was the last plate she would ever bring him. She returned to the kitchen.

A tall, strong looking man rose rapidly from the table across the aisle from Charous'. He wore a UPS delivery man's uniform, dark sun glasses, carried a clip board in one hand. With one quick motion of his other hand, he dropped a bagel onto Charous' plate, deftly scooping up the one already there. None of his actions were observed by any of the other customers who were subsequently questioned. He walked quickly out the front door. Ike Pappas told investigators later, "No, I never seen that man before. But so what? What the hell happened?"

Charous, back at his regular table, bit into his bagel. He convulsed almost immediately. Horrified diners tried to come to his aid, one retiree applying the Heimlich. It was over quickly.

The subsequent autopsy determined that Charous died of a violently allergic reaction to a peanut-based substance contained in the partially eaten bagel on his plate. "Steve had that allergy condition from childhood," his widow told police. "He wouldn't knowingly go within five miles of a peanut or anything with a peanut in it."

Iris the waitress, distraught, swore she had served "our Steve, that nice man, the same kind of bagel I brought him for ten years."

Ike Pappas produced the receipts from the Brooklyn Bagel Boys Company, supplier to his restaurant. "There ain't a peanut bagel on that list," Pappas fumed. "Jews don't do peanut bagels. I don't know what's going on here."

The day Steve Charous was buried Ike Pappas, for the first time in the history of the Golden Greek Grill, closed the place. He, Iris, and Alex the cook attended the funeral at St. John the Baptist-Greek Orthodox Church in Des Plaines. Also present in the large crowd were the five remaining members of The Significant Seven.

Chapter Seventeen

May 15, 2009

Doyle's hour-long drive to Heartland Downs stretched an extra fifteen irritating minutes, the result of one of Cook County's numerous summer road projects. He tempered the extended time listening to one of his favorite CDs by jazz pianist Keith Jarrett, "You and the Night and the Music," a beautifully contemplative set of songs from that usually volatile keyboard genius. *Jarrett and I must be maturing,* Doyle thought. *A few years ago, this crappy traffic would have had me speeding along the shoulders.*

Finally parked on the south side of the Tenuta Stable barn at Heartland Downs, Doyle locked the Accord. He stretched, then straightened to inhale the early morning backstretch air, a combination of dew, hay, and horses, topped by an aroma of coffee brewing. He unlocked the door to Ralph Tenuta's office and went to work on his laptop computer, continuing, to Tenuta's amazement, to modernize methods that had been in place in racing since the first trainer took a piece of charcoal to a cave wall.

Doyle had managed to convince Tenuta, a staunch Luddite in these matters, that the stable's work routine could be modernized and improved. Instead of having all his Mexican employees come to the office to get their assignments, in rudimentary Spanish from their well intentioned but foreign language-challenged employer, Doyle devised a system that took the mystery out of these morning meetings. He printed out in Spanish what each person was to do that day and handed these papers to them. Every one but old Cesar could read. Emilio read his assignments to him.

At 5:45 a.m., a glum Ralph Tenuta came through the doorway. Doyle, not looking up from the computer screen, said, "Hey, Ralph." When he didn't get an answer, he turned away from the keyboard and watched as Tenuta slumped down in his chair. The trainer said, "I'm having a hard time coming to grips with what's happening with my owners. The Charous wake yesterday? Hell, they just kind of stood around looking at each other. I mean, the five guys that are left."

Doyle said, "Yes, it's hard to figure. I never met Charous, but I know you liked him a lot."

"One of the nicest men you'd ever meet," Tenuta said. "It's a goddam shame."

They sat in silence until there was the sound of running feet outside the door. Doc Jensen poked his head in. "Morning, men," he said. His face was flushed, his eyes alight with excitement. "Come with me," he said, "I'm going to show you one of the damndest things you'll ever see on the racetrack. C'mon."

They hurried across the roadway, turning left at Barn Nineteen, onto the path leading to Barn Seventeen. A large, excited group of backstretch workers had assembled there. Trucks were parked haphazardly. Golf carts used by some of the elderly trainers had been left at odd angles on the strip of worn grass separating the barns. Tenuta, worried, said, "Doc, what's going on? Not more bad news I hope."

"Just something amazing," Doc Jensen said, motioning them forward.

Doyle thought, *I hope one of these good Mexican grooms hasn't spotted an image of Our Lady of Guadalupe in a mound of horse manure.* He was relieved when the veterinarian politely pushed his way through the crowd, saying, "C'mon, people. Let these men have a look."

Jensen positioned Tenuta and Doyle at the door to stall Twenty-Four. "What do you think of that?" he said. Tenuta said, "What the hell?" All Doyle saw was a young filly, back in the corner of the stall, rear end turned to the crowd. Then he noticed motion in the dark corner. He said, "What's that?"

Jensen clapped him on the back. "Believe it or not, that's the little colt that this two-year-old filly foaled about two hours ago. Right here in this stall, with no help from anybody. Not her trainer, or groom, or vet."

"I've never heard of anything like this," Tenuta said. "Neither have I," said a tall, gray-haired, black groom who was standing to Doyle's left. "And I've been on the racetrack since Secretariat broke his maiden."

Doc Jensen motioned toward the rear of the crowd. "Ralph, you know Hank Kasperski, right? I ran into him in the track kitchen a couple of days back. He said, 'Doc, I've got the fattest two-year-old filly you've ever seen. She was vanned up from a southern Illinois farm over the weekend. It's going to take me weeks to trim her down.'

"Kasperski, of course," continued Jensen, "never thought for a minute that an in-foal two-year-old filly would be shipped up to him. Her name is Modern Mimi. Never been to a track before. Anyway, Kasperski's night watchman, Carlos Rentiera, was making his rounds about midnight. He shines his flashlight into Modern Mimi's stall, just after her water bag breaks. Carlos saw her turn around and lie down on her side. He runs back to the office and calls Kasperski, who calls his vet, Margo Sroka, and they both hurry over here to the barn.

"When they arrive, Carlos is in the stall on his knees. He says, 'The feet, they come out, Mr. Kasperski. Here come the nose.' Doc Sroka says, 'This is going fine.'

"The foal emerges, kicks his way out of the sac, and scrambles to his feet. His mama starts licking him clean. The umbilical cord breaks. Doc Sroka tells Kasperski, 'If they all did this so easily nobody would ever have to call us vets out in the middle of the night.'"

Doyle was puzzled. "How could an unraced two-year-old get pregnant? That's not what an owner would have in mind, right?"

Tenuta said, "No, of course not. But these things do happen, although pretty rarely. I guess one night down there in southern Illinois, nine months ago, some stud horse jumped the fence into her pasture and had his way with this little girl." He laughed. "Kasperski must be taking some ragging about this, right, Doc?"

"Believe it," Jensen said. "Poor Kasperski keeps defending himself, telling them, 'I've been in foaling barns. I've seen mares about to produce. I know what they look like. They look slab-sided when the foal moves into position. They start acting different. *None* of this happened with this filly.' He is really embarrassed. Of course they're all over him, anyway. Things like, 'Hank, were you gonna run that filly in the Matron Stakes?'"

"Wait a minute," Doyle said. "How will a two-year-old filly nurse?"

Doc Jensen said, "Modern Mimi won't. They're going to ship her colt to a farm out near Wheaton and put him on a nurse mare."

Doyle said, "Does it work?"

Jensen said, "Most times, yes. Like most things in this racetrack life."

They said goodbye to the veterinarian and began to work their way back through the expanding crowd. A short, middle-aged, red-haired woman plucked at Tenuta's sleeve. He stopped. "Hey, Mary," he said. Motioning over his shoulder, Tenuta added, "Is that something or what?" He turned to Doyle and said, "Jack, meet my old friend Mary Izzerman." Doyle recognized the name of one of Chicago's first female trainers. "Great to meet you," he said to this sixtyish woman with a wide grin on her face.

Izzerman said, "Ralph, I bet you remember that old Western racetrack story about the mare and her foal?"

"Nope," Tenuta said, smiling. "But I bet you're going to tell us."

"This happened at a little track out in the bushes in Colorado," Izzerman said, turning to Doyle. "They had a real fast mare there named Neecee Self. One summer afternoon, she was leading the field around the track, as usual, when she stopped and had a little bay foal that looked just like her."

Izzerman paused letting that line ride out into the morning air. Doyle was into it now, but he waited for Tenuta, who said, "All right, Mary Izzerman, what happened then?"

"Neecee Self, the mare, got on her feet, and caught and passed the field, and finished first by about a length. Her little foal ran second."

Izzerman bent over, hands on her knees, laughing, as Doyle and Tenuta joined in.

Chapter Eighteen

May 15, 2009

Later that morning, Tenuta left the track for an appointment with his dentist, who was located in an office building that Tenuta, an always reluctant patient, referred to as "The House of Pain." Doyle said he would keep an eye out for the blacksmith who was scheduled to replace shoes on four of the Tenuta horses.

Strolling down the dirt corridor to the end of the barn, Doyle spotted a dusty white truck with a horse shoe insignia on the front door. The shoe was pointed up, of course, racing superstition holding that "luck" at that angle would not run down, or out. It was the truck Tenuta had told him to watch for. "The blacksmith's name is Travis Hawkins. Tell him which four horses need shoes. Although he probably knows from his records. He's a sharp guy."

Hawkins was a muscular, brown-skinned African American, maybe early forties. A couple of inches taller than Doyle's five-eleven, broad shoulders and chest, large hands that looked strong enough to squeeze open a coconut. He could have been one of those middleweight boxers that for years emerged from the testing gyms of Philadelphia, eager to inflict hurt. Doyle was glad to find Hawkins to be just as amiable as he was foreboding-looking at first glance. They hit it off within minutes.

"You're Jack Doyle?" Hawkins said. "Heard about you. Been around the racetrack a bit, as I understand it."

"That's right."

Hawkins grinned. "In *various* capacities is what I've heard."

"You could say that," Doyle said, "and you just did. Want to get down to business? We've got four for you to do."

"We?"

Doyle said, "That's right. I'm here helping out Ralph Tenuta for the summer."

"Really?" Hawkins said. He reached into the cab of his truck and took out a worn, heavy leather apron which he strapped on. "Never thought Ralph would need much help."

Doyle briefly thought of confiding in this seemingly trustworthy working man. Telling him what the hell he was doing in Ralph Tenuta's employ while working on behalf of the Federal Bureau of Investigation. He quickly squelched that impulse, remembering that farrier Hawkins, whose work took him all over the Heartland Downs backstretch, was as much a possible sponger as anyone else.

The two men walked down the shed row. Hawkins was wearing a sweat-soaked gray Chicago Bulls tee shirt under his leather apron. His jeans and steel-toed work boots were covered with dust. Doyle asked him if wanted to do Editorialist first.

"I'd rather not deal with that son of a bitch at all," Hawkins said. "I don't much look forward to coming to work when he's due for new shoes."

Doyle said, "Mind if I watch you work? I've never seen this done."

"You're welcome to watch away," Hawkins said.

"How many horses do you shoe on an average day?"

"Depends," Hawkins said, striding forward while effortlessly swinging his heavy tool kit. "Could be anywhere from six to ten. That's four shoes per animal. I can usually finish one in maybe a half-hour, forty-five minutes. Most of them get new shoes every thirty days. Editorialist? With him it could take twenty minutes if he's in the mood, or two hours of wrestling with the big bastard if he isn't. Which he usually isn't."

Hawkins proved to be a model of proficiency. He put racing plates on a couple of Tenuta's three-year-olds in less than fifty minutes total. "That wasn't bad," Doyle said.

"Not bad at all," Hawkins said, placing his hammer and nails back in his wooden work box. "First few years I did this, it was pretty rough. Not too many folks wanted to hire a 'Negro farrier.' But there aren't that many 'smiths around anymore. Most people with good sense won't go into this line of work. You get banged around, bruised, kicked, bitten. It took me awhile to learn how to deal with these racehorses. After a few years, when I showed what I could do, I started picking up more business."

They stopped in front of Editorialist's stall. The horse's head was over the bottom door panel. He had watched them approach. Editorialist uttered a belch-like sound of disapproval and rolled his eyes. "Hello, you son of a gun," Hawkins said. He said to Doyle, "I've been putting plates on this one since he came to the track at age two. You know, most horses don't want to hurt you, but they can do it accidentally. Not this one. There hasn't been a time he hasn't tried to swivel and kick me. But he ain't got me yet, have you big fella?" Hawkins attempted to stroke Editorialist's neck. The horse retreated.

Editorialist's groom, a small Mexican-American woman named Rosario Lopez, appeared from the back of the stall, holding a rub rag and a brush. "Outside now, *Señor?*" she said to Hawkins.

"*Sí,*" Hawkins said.

Doyle stood back, occasionally asking questions as Hawkins worked. Rosario, as determined as she was small, managed to hold the barely cooperative Editorialist's head still. By the time Hawkins had removed Editorialist's four shoes, trimmed the growth around each foot, filed their edges, hammered eight nails into every shoe, both he and Rosario were drenched in sweat. Doyle started to perspire just watching all this.

Finally, Hawkins said, "*Gracias, Señorita.* You did very well." The little groom flashed a big smile, then pulled the big horse around and led him back into his stall, talking to him in Spanish, in a tone that sounded both admonitory and affectionate. Editorialist responded by lashing out with his hind legs. There was no target within his range. He glared back over his shoulder as if to make clear to Hawkins and Doyle, "That's what I could have done before."

When Hawkins had finished with the fourth horse, Doyle said, "How about some coffee?" They rode in the blacksmith's pickup truck to the track kitchen. "It's about lunch time for me," Hawkins said as they joined the cafeteria line of steam tables. When they sat down, Hawkins faced a platter containing eggs, pancakes, fried potatoes, sausages, and a pair of gravy-covered biscuits. With his cup of coffee and doughnut, Doyle watched admiringly as Hawkins rapidly cleaned his plate.

"Guess you fellows work up quite an appetite," Doyle smiled.

Hawkins said, "Oh, yeah, dealing with thousand-pound animals that don't necessarily want to be dealt with, you get a pretty good workout every day."

"How many blacksmiths work here at Heartland Downs?"

"Only about a half-dozen now. The old guys aren't being replaced. Face it, man, it's tough work."

Doyle said, "Of the six farriers here, how many are black?"

"You are one very inquisitive cat," Hawkins smiled, adding, "you are looking at the one and only." He sat back in his chair. "Jack, what brings you back to the racetrack? I heard you had something to do with that old Italian trainer, Angelo Cilio, a few years back. And you helped catch those crooks killing horses for insurance money. Last I heard, you worked in publicity at Monee Park. A woman you worked with there, Shontanette Hunter, is a cousin of my wife's. She used to tell us about you," Hawkins said, smiling, before scraping up the few remaining biscuit bits.

Doyle said, "You seem to know a hell of a lot about me, Travis. You keep your ear to the ground pretty good? Like you say, I've been around in 'various capacities.' I also spent some time working on a Kentucky breeding farm. Then, I decided I'd like to get back to the track. I was lucky enough to get work with Ralph Tenuta."

Hawkins polished off the last of his eggs with three deft scoops before draining his glass of orange juice. "Know something, Jack?"

"What?"

Hawkins said, "I don't buy into the last part of that story. As to why you're here."

For a second or two, Doyle again considered telling this man the truth. Hawkins seemed to be a person who loved his work, and loved horses. Doyle had seen that he was forceful with them, but gentle when applying their expensive aluminum shoes.

Hard for Doyle to imagine Travis Hawkins doing such a cruel thing to horses as sponging them. But, you never know, Doyle reminded himself. He fought down his urge to confide.

Instead, he said to Hawkins, "My Grandfather Doyle, when he wasn't completely sober, which was many a time as I recall, used to recite poems at the family gatherings. He knew dozens by heart. Most of our family ignored him. But when my brother and I were old enough, Grandpa would encourage us to memorize poetry by paying us a dollar a stanza if we could say it for him. One of Gramps' favorites was 'The Village Smithy.' He said he'd learned it in high school. You know it?"

"Before my time," Hawkins said. He buttered another piece of toast. Doyle began to recite.

> *"Under a spreading chestnut tree*
> *The village smithy stands;*
> *The smith, a mighty man is he,*
> *With large and sinewy hands."*

"That's about all I can remember," Doyle said, "except there was something about '*The smithy earns whatever he can, and looks the whole world in the face, for he owes not any man.*' I'm pretty sure that's right."

"That's good, Jack. But I guess that poem doesn't mention the fact that a blacksmith has probably the only job in the world where his head is below his ass most of the day."

Doyle laughed. "No, Travis, I don't believe it does contain that line."

◇◇◇

Hawkins reached the long driveway leading to his rural Lake County home shortly before six o'clock that soft summer evening. As usual, his daughter and son heard his truck coming and left their front porch to greet him in the driveway. Eight-year-old Serena led the way. Brandon, six, trailed by a yard or two in their dash toward Daddy. At their flank was the Hawkins' short-haired German pointer, Andy. The children jumped into their father's brawny arms, their smiles almost as wide as his. Andy got up on his hind legs, pawing his way into the greeting committee, making more noise than the rest combined. Hawkins put the kids down, bent to acknowledge the dog's insistent presence, and said to Serena, "Hey, my girl, how was your day?"

"Great, Daddy. Me and Brandon caught three fish out of the pond."

Hawkins looked at his son. "That true, Brandon?"

"We got three fish, Daddy, and I got two of them."

Hawkins laughed. "Serena, that right? Your little brother outfished you?

Serena scowled for a second, then shrugged. "Well, *today* he did," she admitted.

Hawkins had created the pond the year after he and his family became the first blacks to own property in this otherwise printer-paper-white corner of Lake County. It took him most of their first summer there, digging into the soil on his rented Bobcat, working into the night hours after finishing his farrier stint at Heartland Downs. As a boy in Riverdale, Arkansas, he had spent hundreds, if not thousands, of happy hours in quest of fish. He wanted Brandon and Serena to share his passion for the sport, to learn the patience, calmness, and concentration required of successful fishermen or women. Their progress delighted him.

Hawkins' wife Taliyah was waiting for him inside the screen door. She leaned forward for a brief kiss. "I'll start the grill," she said. "You shower."

"Really? You think I need one?"

"Unless we're all going to sit upwind of you at supper," Taliyah said. "That whiff of horse barn you bring home is strong this evening."

"Glad it is," Hawkins said. "That's the smell of hard work that led to money, honey. Don't forget it." He hugged her. "I had a good, busy day for a change," he said.

"My business is way down. Horse owners are hurting, and so are the rest of us racetrackers. Okay, okay, I'm going."

The children cleared the plates from the outdoor table, Serena directing Brandon how best to scrape them clean before putting them in the dishwasher. Taliyah said, "That girl is getting bossier every day."

Hawkins didn't respond. He was looking out over their back hedge. Taliyah touched his hand. "What're you thinking, Travis? Seems your mind's elsewhere." She covered her mouth with her hand before saying, "You didn't get hurt on the job today, did you? I thought you were kind of limping when you came in from the truck."

Hawkins smiled. He gave her hand a reassuring pat. "Nothing like that. If I'm limping, it's just the same old kick up of the 'thritis in my right knee. No," he continued, "I was thinking about something else. Met a man today at Ralph Tenuta's barn. Name of Jack Doyle. Remember Shontanette talking about him a year or so ago? When they both worked at Monee Park?"

Taliyah said, "Yes, I do. She thought he was a good guy. Kind of different, but okay. As I remember it, they got along good."

Hawkins picked up the pitcher of iced tea. He offered it to Taliyah, who declined. He refilled his glass. "Far as I know," he said, "Doyle has been at least a couple of things around racing in Chicago. What I can't figure out is what he's doing on the backstretch now, working for Ralph Tenuta. It just doesn't seem normal, going from the Monee publicity job to this one. I think there's something else going on with him."

The sun had dropped behind the stand of tall pine trees on the western edge of their property. From in the house Travis could hear his children arguing about which cartoon channel to choose. "Turn that TV off, you two," he said loudly. Silence ensued.

Hawkins got up from his the picnic bench and extended his hand to Taliyah. "It's nothing to get concerned about," he said. "I'm just a little puzzled at Mr. Doyle's new, what do you call it, *presence*, on the backstretch."

Chapter Nineteen

May 25, 2009

Orth had finished his morning exercises, showered, and eaten breakfast and was relaxing on the small porch of his cabin when he heard the first of what he knew would be a day-long succession of firecrackers being shot off, even a few rifle and pistols being aimed skyward. Memorial Day. Early summer madness and excuse for revelry. Just another day of the week to Orth. Restless now, he went inside his cabin, dressed for town, and got into his black Jeep Cherokee.

Boulder Junction was jammed with cars and trucks when Orth parked on the side of the road at the edge of this small town. He had intended to grocery shop and pick up a few items at the town's lone sporting goods store, but decided to delay doing those chores in order to watch some of the parade. It had apparently just begun, its advance guard comprised of small children stomping happily and erratically down Main Sreet, waving small American flags.

People lined both curbs of the four-block long street. They hailed the marchers, some shouting out greetings at the Nelson Lumber Yard parade entry ("Jesus, Swede, pick up those big feet of yours"), or whistling appreciatively at the town's "Holiday Queen," a chubby, deeply tanned girl in tight shorts and a white tee shirt that declared her to be "America's Next Top Model." She waved widely from the back of a recently waxed red Ford pickup.

Main Street here was like the Main Street of many upper Midwest small towns, packed with dark saloons, their walls festooned with deer heads and lengthy stuffed fishes. Wisconsin, home of more than five thousand liquor-license holders, most per capita of any state in the Union, had earned place number one in per-capita binge drinking in a national survey. Badger State residents sported one of the highest incidences of drunken-driving caused deaths in the U. S.

The parade continued with an eleven-piece band from the local high school. A float came by carrying three aged male horn players and a teenaged female cymbal shaker. The sound they produced, Orth thought, was enough to drive all the county's birds southward even this far ahead of migration time.

He was turning away to go to the Pic-and-Save for groceries when he heard the rumble of slow moving motorcycles. Orth looked back. Three cyclists rode in an across-the-street line, two on Harleys, the other on a vehicle emblazoned with the words "Die Hard Chopper." Each bike's handlebars held a small U. S. flag. The riders were all men Orth recognized from high school. They wore black leather jeans and boots, black leather vests cut to reveal their flabby upper arms. All had kerchiefs above the dark sun glasses through which they solemnly gazed at the curbside crowds.

Orth said, "These phony bastards."

A heavy-set woman next to him said, "What was that, mister? What did you say? That's my husband Earl on that Die Hard."

"I know Earl Bardwell," Orth said. "He's never been closer to a war than on his Game Boy. He's full of shit with his flag, his biker patriotism. All Earl's done for this country is take up space. Same with most of this crowd," he added before striding away toward the store.

Thinking of the bikers, Orth recalled the man he briefly bunked with when he worked for Agua Negro in Iraq. Gordie Norquist, from Gilroy, California, the "Garlic Capital of the World," as he often proclaimed. Norquist had captured (or found, Orth suspected) an impressive sword. He dangled it by a thread from the ceiling above the table that held their laptop computer. When Orth first saw this, he said, "What's that for?"

Norquist replied, "It's a weapon of war. It helps me concentrate on my dangerous duties here in Iraq," he added smugly.

A week later, having twice observed Norquist sidestep danger in the dark alleys of Sadr City, Orth returned one night and ripped the sword from the ceiling string.

"All this has made you concentrate on, Norquist," Orth said as he threw the sword into a corner of the room, "is saving your phony ass. I hate guys like you."

Norquist moved out the next day. He must have put out the word on Orth, because Orth roomed alone until Scott Sanderson joined him three weeks later.

Coming out of the store with his bag of groceries, Orth stopped and looked across the street at a raucous group of young men, well into the supply of beer in their white plastic cooler on the curb. They alternately hooted or applauded the parade marchers. They were getting louder by the minute, this group of alcohol and testosterone-spiked youngsters as they tried to impress each other and the coterie of young women standing behind them, who were smoking cigarettes and looking unimpressed.

Orth placed his grocery bag down, leaning it against a parking meter, just as the Local VFW's paltry parade entry approached. Some of the loud punks were deriding the quartet of uniformed oldsters limping down the street, keeping cadence as best they could.

"Pick it up, you geezers," one of the youths brayed repeatedly. Orth sprinted across the street and grabbed the loud mouth by the neck. One of the kid's buddies reached for Orth, who flattened him with a karate chop to the collar bone. "You beer-brained piece of shit," Orth said, his face inches away from the kid's, "you got no right mocking those old men who put on the uniforms of their country." He released the boy with a powerful shove that sent him toppling backward over one of the beer coolers. "Am I clear on that?" The boy, still on his back in the circle created by the young women, mumbled something.

"I said, am I clear on that?" Orth said.

"Yes," the boy managed softly.

Orth shouted, "What?"

"Yes. I said yes. Yes." The boy began to cry. Orth, disgusted both by his attention-drawing actions as much as the young-ster's weakness, slid rapidly through the crowd and back to the street. He ran between the Miss County Snowmobile float and the Seniors Dance Club truck featuring two active couples that any moment threatened to spin their way down onto the street.

"They must be drinking, too," Orth said, shaking his head as he took one last look over his shoulder at the careening, aged dancers. He quickly retrieved his grocery bag.

Still seething when he reached his cabin, Orth got into his running gear and sprinted off into the nearby woods. He ran off most of his anger in the course of the next hour, but not all of it.

"What a fucked-up fucking country," he said loudly as he ran, "full of fucked-up idiots."

Chapter Twenty

June 5, 2009

Doyle picked up Cindy at seven-thirty that Friday night. She came directly out the trailer door as he was parking. Her mother, Wilma, waved at him from the doorway, standing beside Tyler. He waved, too. Doyle had to hustle in order to get out of the car and around to the passenger door so that he could open it for Cindy.

Doyle had called her the previous Wednesday. "Have you ever seen a live boxing card?" When she said no, Doyle said, "Would you like to?" Her answer was in the affirmative. "I've got great seats for the big fight card at the Rosemont Horizon," he said.

"This will be a first for me," Cindy said as she settled into her seat. She wore a gold jersey and black slacks, large silver-colored earrings. For Doyle, who had seen her at work at the track that morning, dressed in dusty jeans and a sweat-stained tee-shirt, she was impressively transformed.

"Boxing," Doyle said, "is one of those things that you like a lot or don't like at all. You can't really tell until you've been there and seen it. But, look, if you find it, well, distasteful, just say so. We can leave and go someplace else."

"I appreciate that," Cindy said. "I heard you were a boxer. Is that right?"

"Yeah, but not at the level you're going to see tonight. These are world-ranked, professional fighters. I was, how can I put this," he said, smiling, "an enthusiastic amateur."

"How long did you box?"

"Junior Boxing Club when I was eight or nine. Golden Gloves five or six years later, AAU bouts when I was in college. By the time I got to the University of Illinois, collegiate boxing had been long banned. That was after a University of Wisconsin kid died as a result of a ring injury."

Cindy said, "You don't look marked up like I thought fighters were."

"I kept my chin down and my hands up," Doyle said. "I still do."

The large Rosemont Horizon parking lot was jammed. Doyle waved a twenty at a valet parker near the main entrance. The man opened their doors and said, "Enjoy."

Doyle picked up their tickets at will-call. He told Cindy, "These are courtesy of a friend of mine, Moe Kellman. He's a big boxing fan. He and I go to a lot of fights together. Moe will be sitting with us tonight. I think you'll like him. He's an interesting guy."

An usher led them to the third row from the ring, which stood on an elevated platform. Two young Latino lightweights were finishing a three-round exercise in glowering and posing. Just before the final bell, the shorter one landed a perfectly placed right uppercut on the chin of his foe, whose pompadour elevated.

Doyle seated Cindy next to him. On her other side, Moe stood up, smiling, the lights glinting off what he referred to as his "Isro" haircut, and also off the three impressive-looking rings he wore. He had on a tan leather jacket, brown trousers, a blue button-down collar shirt. His face crinkled as he reached for Cindy's hand. "Jack wasn't exaggerating when he told me about you," Moe said. He looked over Cindy's head at Doyle. "You brought a knockout to a place where knockouts occur," he said. They all laughed. Once seated, Moe signaled to a short-skirted, cleavage-displaying waitress responsible for serving this part of the VP section. Cindy ordered a Coke, Doyle a beer.

"Nothing for me right now, darling," Moe said.

They chatted between rounds of the next two preliminary bouts, Cindy surveying this new scene. The 10,500 seat auditorium was almost filled. All the prime seats closest to the ring were occupied, the first row by reporters, announcers, and attendants of the fighters. The balcony, she noticed, was populated primarily by Hispanics, almost all men, every one very much riveted to the action below.

Several people came by to say hello to Moe. "Good to see you, Commissioner," Moe said to the head of the Chicago Police Department., introducing the man to Cindy and Doyle. Receiving similarly genial treatment were the manager of one of Chicago's major hotels, the co-owner of a famed Rush Street steak house, and an alderwoman from Chicago's Lawndale neighborhood.

The only visitor not introduced to Cindy and Doyle was an old, stocky man wearing dark sun glasses, a black leather jacket, black tee shirt, dark trousers over black shoes. He was about the same height and age as Kellman. He attempted to embrace the furrier, saying, "You know me, Mosie?" Kellman took the man by his elbow and turned him back into the aisle. They stood there conversing quietly for a several minutes as the ring announcer called up people from Chicago's bottom tier of celebrities: a radio sports talk show host, a cable channel weatherman, an aged newspaper gossip columnist. Kellman and the man shook hands and separated.

Kellman returned to his seat. He said apologetically, "I didn't introduce the last guy to you. You don't need to know him."

Doyle said, "I appreciate that. I know who he is. Mario 'The Clown' Aiello. Just got out of federal prison after spending sixteen years for racketeering. I saw his picture in the paper a couple of days ago."

Moe frowned. "Mario and I grew up together. Like I said, you don't need to know him. You ready for another Coke, Cindy? Jack, a beer?"

Doyle was quiet during the intermission between bouts as Kellman engaged Cindy in conversation. Pretending to peruse the souvenir program, Doyle listened, amused, as the little furrier turned on the charm. When Ms. Cleavage delivered their drinks, Cindy said, "I don't need a glass, thanks." But the waitress ignored her, opening the bottles and pouring Doyle's beer and her soft drink into paper cups.

"Years ago," Kellman informed, "the Horizon management decreed that the beer would be sold only in cups. Before that, they'd had to extend this goofy looking net over the boxing ring."

Cindy said, "A net? What for?"

"So that any angry fans in the balcony, unhappy about a fight decision, couldn't start pelting the ring with beer bottles. The management finally decided to get rid of the net. Actually, it looked like something out of the Coliseum in Rome a thousand years ago back. That's when they changed to beer cups."

The main event was next on the card. It was a heavyweight bout between Rocco Albertani, of Chicago's suburban Elmwood Park, and Luther Rawlings of Miami, FL. Reading from his program Doyle said to Cindy, "Albertani's from near here. Had a good amateur career. When he turned pro, a man named Fifi Bonadio became his manager."

Cindy said, "Where have I heard that name?" Doyle looked to Kellman, who pretended to be studying his own program. Doyle said, "Bonadio runs a big road construction firm, owns some banks, auto dealerships. Lot of things. He's a big sports fan. He had a son who was a very good football player at the University of Wisconsin. The lad is now on the Cook County Board of Supervisors."

Doyle took a swig of his beer. "Some people say Bonadio is the head man of the Chicago Outfit. I wouldn't know about that. All I know is that he's an old friend and current customer, of the man to your immediate left."

Kellman pretended not have heard Doyle's last remark, and Doyle laughed, before saying to Cindy, "Here they come. The guys for the main event."

Rawlings shuffled slowly down the aisle first, wearing a long, tattered white robe, his dark face almost obscured by a hood. His appearance was greeted by a smattering of applause. Three minutes later, the public address system began blasting out the theme from the movie "Rocky." Bouncing down the aisle to a crescendo of cheers and applause was Rocco "The Assassin" Albertani, a ruggedly handsome young man waving his gloved hands above his head to his numerous supporters. "Albertani has won all eleven of his pro fights so far," Moe told Cindy. "His people, some of them I know, think he has a future." Doyle heard that and looked sharply at Kellman, who ignored him.

Cindy said, "Who are you rooting for, Jack?" Doyle watched Rawlings gracefully step between the ring ropes. Rawlings was at least ten years older than the pride of Elmwood Park, who was bouncing around the ring, sweating heavily. Albertani's weight was announced at two-hundred twelve pounds, Rawlings five pounds lighter. Albertani was on edge. Rawlings shrugged off his old robe and strolled around the ring seemingly as unconcerned as if he was in his living room. The small, carefully trimmed soul patch on his dark black face had more than a touch of gray in it. Rawlings did a few deep knee bends, watching Albertani out of the corner of his eye, before going to the center of the ring for the referee's instructions.

Doyle said to Cindy, "I think that, if this is on the up-and-up, Albertani is going to be knocked on his ass. But I would not look for that, to tell you the truth." Kellman, peering at the fighters and smiling, ignored Doyle's comments.

Round one went to Albertani. He moved around energetically, peppering out jabs that Rawlings caught on his gloves. He twice bulled the older man into the ropes, attempting to pound him with kidney shots that Rawlings blocked with his elbows. The popular local lad being obviously the eager aggressor, ringside experts gave him the round.

Rounds two and three were much the same. Albertani did most of the work. Rawlings kept dodging or deflecting punches that became increasingly wild as the Pride of Elmwood Park exhibited his increasing frustration. All of Albertani's previous bouts had ended in first- or second-round knockouts, him doing the knocking out. He was venturing into new territory against Rawlings, a crafty veteran if Doyle had ever seen one.

With a half-minute to go in the fifth round, Rawlings evidently couldn't stand it any more. He easily eluded another of Albertani's wild swings, stepped inside, and chopped a short right to the younger fighter's exposed jaw. Albertani hit the floor like a carton of frozen lasagna.

The referee, whose day job was in the Cook County State's Attorney's office, began counting, slowly, with a lengthy arm gesture, over the dazed Italian-American hope. Albertani managed to sit up with his right leg caught under him. As he tried to clear his head, drops of sweat flew through the air. Then Albertani began to slowly sink back down to the canvas. As the seconds passed, the crowd was in full voice, imploring their hero to arise. The referee hit five on his exceedingly slow way to ten.

Doyle leaned across Cindy to tap Moe on the arm. He said, "This makes the Dempsey-Tunney long count look like it was on speed dial."

"Shh, Jack," Moe said.

Albertani finally struggled to his feet. The bell ending the round immediately rang although Doyle was positive there were at least fifteen seconds left in it. He watched as Rawlings ambled back to his corner. Doyle read the lips of Rawlings' manager, who angrily said to his fighter, "What the fuck did you do in there? Christ!"

The sixth and final round of the fight took thirty-seven seconds. Albertani, breathing heavily and still half-dazed, nevertheless charged off his stool at Rawlings and unleashed a looping right hand. Doyle was positive the blow barely missed Rawlings' chin, but the veteran stumbled backwards and fell on his back to the canvass, arms outstretched, eyes closed. The ref counted him out so rapidly Doyle could hardly get his jacket back on before the fight was declared over. When the ref's count ended, Rawlings bounced right up. Albertani looked as surprised as anyone at this outcome as he wobbled around the ring, arms raised in jubilation.

"Jack, I don't get it. Over so quickly, and Rawlings doesn't even look like he's hurt," Cindy said as the black fighter rapidly departed the ring.

Albertani's Elmwood Park posse charged through the ropes and lifted him to their shoulders. A reprise of the "Rocky" theme song blared.

"Well, I enjoyed that Mr. Kellman; I mean, Moe," Cindy smiled as they walked to the Horizon exit. "I've never seen anything like that before."

Kellman reached forward for a hug, eagerly provided, then said, "Jack, what did you think?"

"Don't buy any shares in Albertani's contract."

Kellman said, "You're right. I don't know, some of these old dagoes, they get excited when they discover a young stud. Fifi said to me last week, 'The kid reminds me of Rocky Marciano. Tough, strong, determined.'"

Doyle said, "Hah! This kid's more like Maraschino, the cherry."

They all waved goodbye.

Chapter Twenty-one

June 11, 2009

Doyle was watching replays of the previous day's races on Tenuta's television in the office when the trainer came bustling through the door. "Jack, listen to this," he said, waving a copy of *Racing Daily* before him. "There's another kind of hustle going on. It's un-damn-believable," he fumed. Tenuta's face was the color of a hydroponic tomato. Doyle took Tenuta by the arm. "For Chrissakes, Ralph, calm down. What's going on?"

Tenuta opened the newspaper to page three. "It's this story here. There are trainers now using shock wave therapy on their horses. *Shock wave therapy*. This happened in Australia, where they suspended a couple of those guys."

Doyle reached for the paper. It was turned to a piece by *Racing Daily's* senior columnist, Jeff Hovey, who described a veterinary procedure administered to a major race winner Down Under named Rick's the Man. He read, "The horse received a session of extracorporeal shock wave therapy (ESWT) five days before the race. This is a procedure most commonly used on humans to pulverize kidney stones without invasive surgery. Used on horses, it is believed to have a perhaps healing and pain-killing effect. The treatment works to hyperstimulate nerves so that they no longer transfer pain."

"Ralph," Doyle said, "you ever hear of this before?"

Tenuta walked over the office coffee maker, poured himself a cup. Composed now, he sat down in his chair. He shook his head. "When I came up in racing, the rule was feed your horses only oats, hay, and water. That was all. Sure, there were some guys hopping horses back then, taking an edge, but most of them were caught. There were others who'd do something along the same lines as this wave therapy. They'd have their vet cut the nerves above an injured horse's bad ankle or foot. Then the poor animal couldn't feel the pain. It was called 'nerving.' That, thank God, got banned a long time ago.

"But damn, Jack, things are moving so fast in this business. There are what they call 'designer drugs,' which are undetectable for awhile. Once they're detected, some chemist will come up with a new version designed to make horses run faster. We went through all the 'milk shaking' years," he said. Tenuta was referring to the practice of loading bicarbonates into a horse's stomach through a rubber tube. The purpose was to lower lactic acid in their muscles and the bloodstream, thus supposedly preventing them from tiring. This illegal scam was eventually discovered by racing authorities and banned. Violaters were severely punished. "Now, shock waves!" Tenuta said. "Enough to make you weep."

Doyle looked across the desk at this distraught, honest little man. An upright, rule-following advocate of "what's best for the horse" from the get-go. "Ralph, I'm sure the local authorities are on to this. I know they've developed tests for blood-doping, the kind used by those Tour de France cycling marvels."

Doyle, knowing what the answer would be, but wanting to ask the question anyway, said, "Honest to God, Ralph, are you ever tempted to try some of these new methods on your horses?"

"Get serious," Tenuta replied. "When I lead one of my horses over to the paddock to run, I know that horse is drug-free." He paused. "The only thing I do that doesn't come from the old days is sometimes I hire a massage therapist to work on my stock. You get a horse that's real tightened up, his muscles bunched, I call this woman. Name of Ingrid Rosengren. She comes and gives the horse a forty-five minute treatment. Man, it really works.

Massage and acupuncture. Not on *every* horse, but definitely on some of them. The horses love what she does. She charges sixty bucks an hour. But to see the way my horses respond, Jack, it's worth every penny.

"A lot of the vets around here won't give her the time of day. She's probably cutting into their business.But I'll tell you, she's on to something. Ingrid says when one thing is out of balance on a horse, things start to snowball. She's a big believer in preventative treatment. Doc Jensen, my regular vet, has started to use her a lot. He's become a believer in what Ingrid can do."

Doyle said, "Are you talking about that tall, statuesque Swedish-looking lady that I've seen in the track kitchen. Very pretty blond woman?"

Tenuta looked down. He said, "Well, yes. That's probably her."

Doyle said, "Ralph, am I perhaps seeing you blush at the very mention of her name?"

"Don't give me any of your *perhapses*," Tenuta barked. Doyle was getting a kick out of this, never having seen the trainer flustered. Answering Doyle's question, Tenuta said, "Yeah, that's probably Ingrid. I mean Ms. Rosengren. Very nice woman, everybody likes her."

Doyle said, "I can certainly understand why."

Tenuta glared at him. "I've been married to my first and only wife Rosa for almost thirty years. I don't fool around, Jack, or have eyes for other ladies. That's not what I do. *Capice?*"

Doyle, grinning, got to his feet. "I happen to know another Italian-American paragon of marital virtue named Tirabassi. FBI guy. Far as I know, Tirabassi is as faithful as Old Faithful. You two guys," Doyle said, moving to the door and shaking his head,"are kind of tarnishing my image of the Italian, what do you call them, Lotharios? Casanovas? Sinatras? They marry young, quickly father children, then move on to explore other, um, romantic interests. I thought it was in the blood."

Seeing how he'd gotten his friend riled up, Doyle could not resist. "Doesn't what's her name, Ingrid the massage lady, kind of remind you of that Swedish beauty in one of the old James Bond movies? Ursula Andress? The one who came out of the sea wearing not much more than an appealing look?"

Tenuta swiveled his squeaky chair around, turning his back to his stable agent.

"Get the hell out of here, Jack."

Chapter Twenty-two

June 15, 2009

It had been a long, demanding day for Chris Carson. A breakfast meeting address to a group of newly minted CPAs. Lunch with one of his major clients, an electronics magnate who paid Carson an annual retainer larger than Carson's father earned in ten years as a printing plant foreman. Finally, a well advertised and received speech, delivered *pro bono*, to a group of Milwaukee County high school seniors who had expressed interest in becoming certified public accountants. Carson thought that "exhausting but rewarding" would be the way he would describe his day to his wife Portia when he finally got home.

Home for the Carsons was a restored farm house on a small country road north and west of Chris' Milwaukee office. The commute usually took at least forty-five minutes, fairly long for Wisconsin but, in Carson's view, well worth it. He and Portia loved the privacy and serenity of the place, formerly home of a wealthy dairy farmer.

Carson turned his dark blue BMW coupe off the highway onto County Road W. It was a dark but well-paved stretch of minor highway, running parallel to a line of bluffs on the left side. A deep ravine bordered it for a half-mile on the right. Carson knew the road well and was familiar with its users, neighbors for the most part, who rarely drove this stretch after dark. So he was surprised to see pair of bright headlights advancing rapidly toward him. Not relaxed now, Carson tightened his hand on the steering wheel. He punched the radio button into silence. "Who the hell is flying along here at this hour?"

The approaching vehicle, a black SUV, sped closer. When it was a hundred yards away from Carson's car, its bright lights went off, then back on. Carson quickly flashed his own brights on and off, trying to signal for relief. The SUV's brights came back on. The oncoming vehicle picked up more speed. When it was some fifty yards away, it suddenly veered out of its lane and headed directly at Carson.

"God almighty," Carson shouted. "What is this guy doing?" Instinctively attempting to avert a head-on collision, Carson pulled hard on his steering wheel. To the right. Onto the narrow gravel shoulder. There, now out of his control, his car slammed through the old wooden guard rail and sailed through the air into the dark maw of the ravine.

The blue BMW bounced high off a jutting boulder before it plummeted onto larger rocks and turned over three times, coming to an explosive halt at the ravine's bottom.

The SUV's driver braked sharply a couple of hundred yards down the otherwise deserted road. He quickly U-turned and drove back to the gaping hole in the guard rail. He didn't have to leave his seat in order to see the flames shooting up from Carson's car. With his window down, all he heard was grackles' excited calls from the ravine's trees. He was too far away to hear the crackle of flames.

Orth put black his black Jeep Cherokee back into drive. "That, dude," he said, "is what we call a game of Ultimate Chicken.

"You lost."

Two mornings later, Doyle bought a copy of *Racing Daily* in the Heartland Downs track kitchen. Carrying it and a cup of coffee on his way back to Ralph Tenuta's barn, he abruptly stopped when he glanced at the front page and saw a story written by Ira Kaplan.

MILWAUKEE, WI—Milwaukee County officials yesterday reported the death of Chris Carson, prominent in horse racing circles as one of "The Significant Seven," owners of the outstanding runner and sire The Badger Express. Carson's auto was spotted by an early morning motorist at the bottom of a ravine off of County Road W outside of Milwaukee. The motorist called the county sheriff's office immediately.

Carson's car was hundreds of feet off the road, and the motorist made no attempt to climb down the steep ravine to the vehicle that had evidently been burning for some time.

Carson's wife had earlier reported him missing.

County Coronor Paul Lendeman, in a preliminary report issued late yesterday, said he would not speculate as to whether Carson died of injuries from the crash or from the resultant blaze.

County Sheriff Ed Kaminski said it appeared Carson had veered off the road and through the wooden barrier. "I can't figure out why," Kaminski said. "There are no skid marks on the pavement.

"I knew Mr. Carson very well, from our Elks Lodge," Kaminski continued. "He had a very successful business. He never drank alcohol to my knowledge. I'm sure he was not a drug user, although the autopsy will determine that, of course. My heart goes out to his family."

Carson, 53, owned a prominent accounting firm in Milwaukee. A long-time racing fan, he and six of his friends from their student days at the University of Wisconsin-Madison came to national attention when they won a record Pick Six bet at Saratoga Race Course in New York seven years ago. The Significant Seven, as they were known, proceeded to build upon that success by purchasing and racing the major stakes winner The Badger Express.

Carson is the third member of The Significant Seven to die this year. Judge Henry Toomey drowned in Wisconsin's Lake Geneva after suffering an apparent heart attack while swimming. Steve Charous, an insurance executive in Illinois, died suddenly as the apparent result of a violent allergic reaction in a Des Plaines, IL, restaurant.

Carson is survived by his wife Portia; sons Chris Jr. and Tim; and a grandson.

Funeral services are pending.

Chapter Twenty-three

June 18, 2009

"I know you aren't wondering why I asked for this meet," Doyle said. He was seated in the back of Damon Tirabassi's drab government issued green Ford Taurus. He had entered it moments before when Tirabassi and agent Karen Engel pulled up to the curb in front of Doyle's condo.

Tirabassi drove carefully north on Halsted, then east toward the Outer Drive.

Karen said, "What's going on, Jack?"

Doyle said, "Hold it until we park at the golf course."

"If that's how you want it," she said.

Doyle, seething, tapped his fingers impatiently on the worn plastic seat. The sun continued its slide up the east side of Lake Michigan, spreading a deep orange blush across the horizon. It was a Thursday, just after daybreak, in the second month of Doyle's employment by Ralph Tenuta and the U. S. government, Tenuta being the lone paying entity for Doyle in this arrangement thus far.

Tirabassi pulled into the parking lot of the Judge George Lincoln Marovitz public golf course. Even at this hour, it already held several cars. Doyle could see golf nuts of all ages hauling bags and carts out of their cars, ready to duff their way through the morning dew. Thousands of Chicagoans played here every week, many of them first thing in the morning or, after work, in the shroud of dusk.

Tirabassi said, "Let's use that picnic table over there away from the clubhouse."

Doyle followed the agents to the table, which was moist. The agents were dressed for work in their downtown Chicago office in dark suits, shades. Karen carried a McDonald's bag. She took out a handful of napkins and wiped the bench seat on their side of the table. Doyle waved off her offer of the sodden wad when she'd finished. "I'll stand."

Karen said, "Jack, an Egg McMuffin? Or several? I bought a bunch of them. I remember your appetite and cholesterol-defying eating habits."

"Any coffee in that bag?" Doyle growled. "I'll start with that."

"So, Jack," Tirabassi said, "tell us what's happening. You sounded a little, maybe overwrought, when you left us your message last night. Or, maybe, half-smashed." He bit a chunk out of his sausage biscuit.

Doyle ripped the top off of his coffee container before answering. "Why wouldn't I be, Damon? Why wouldn't I be?" He rummaged in the carry out bag until he located a small container of half and half. The agents waited patiently.

"Coming up on ten weeks now," Doyle began, "me going faithfully to work at Heartland Downs, seven days a week. Nosing around. Eyes wide open. Ears to the ground. Senses attuned. Have I found the sponger, or the sponging team? No. Do I feel as if I'm making progress? No. Do I think it's time for me to turn in my junior G-Man badge this morning and resume my regular life? You bet I do."

Karen said, "Jack, there hasn't been one sponging incident since Princess Croft. Maybe these crooks know what you're there for and are backing off. Who knows? Maybe your presence has served as a deterrent. Maybe the spongings are over. That's a kind of progress, isn't it?"

"A mighty slight sort," Doyle said. "Even if there is actually a non-coincidental connection between my presence there and the reduction in spongings. Which I am by no means convinced of."

Tirabassi put down his half-eaten sausage biscuit. He looked tired, frustrated, defeated. Doyle felt a pang or two of pity for this boring little civil servant with whom he had so frequently crossed swords.

Tirabassi sighed. "Jack, you're all we've got working for us on this case. The few informants we pay so far have been worthless. The fact that there have been no recent spongings is great. But we still need to arrest the person or persons who carried out the previous spongings. That's what we are charged with. We've advertised a reward, gone on radio and television pleading for any useful information. You have any idea how frustrating this is for us?

"But Jack," Tirabassi continued, "we, or you I mean, can't give up now. Just say you'll stay on the job for another nine or ten weeks. By then, the Heartland Downs racing meeting will be over. If we haven't found the sponger by then, you're done. We wouldn't ask anything more of you. If this were not such a major case for Karen and me, believe me, I wouldn't have asked you to get involved at all."

Doyle finished his coffee and paused with the empty cup in his hand. He crushed it. Walking to a nearby metal waste basket, he slammed it in. He turned his back to where the agents sat and looked out over Lake Michigan. The sun was now climbing in full force above the dark waters.

"Ten more weeks," Doyle said. "Until the track closes. I'll go along. Then I've got to get on with my life. Such as it is," he muttered.

Tirabassi said, "Thanks, Jack. I mean it." He extended his hand across the table.

Karen said, "Goes for me, too, Jack." She stood up and tossed the McDonald's bag into the metal basket with the practiced ease of the athlete she'd always been. She was frowning, though, when she came back around to Doyle's side of the table.

"Jack," she said, "have you ever considered taking a course in, well, controlling your angry impulses? I'm serious. We've known each other for a few years now. You always seem to have a lava load of anger buried just beneath your surface. Have you always been that way? Don't you feel it's hard to live like that?"

"Karen, darling," Doyle was grinning at her now, "it's in my genes, my heritage, my DNA, my psyche. Built in. I've tried to change routes several times in my life. I always get back to riding down life's third rail, if you know what I mean. It's just me, babe. But thanks for asking."

She wasn't finished. "Have you ever read one of the instructive books about controlling anger? I've had friends who found them very helpful." She paused before adding, "My ex-husband might have benefited from one of them."

"Actually," Doyle said, "my second and last wife gave me a couple of books by one of those so-called anger management experts years ago. Paid a lot of money for them. Had me watch one of his videos, too."

"Did you read them?" Karen said.

"Read the first one, skimmed the second," Doyle said. "They really pissed me off. The video, too."

Chapter Twenty-four

June 21, 2009

Doyle slept fitfully for a couple of hours, got up, started his CD player just after two. He lay on his couch and listened to the new Karynn Allison, an old Anita O'Day, an even older Al Hibbler with the Ellington band. Music he loved.

But he couldn't lose himself in these ordinarily intriguing sounds. The Question kept reoccurring. Why were these horse owners dying, long before their time? Were the deaths really accidental? Did they have anything to do with the sponging? Three out of seven, gone in less than two months, what the hell is that? Should he raise this with Tirabassi and Engel?

At dawn, he got into his jogging clothes and started for the lakefront. By eight, showered and with his first cup of coffee in hand, he was ready to call Moe Kellman in the furrier's Hancock Building suite of offices.

Kellman picked up on the first ring. "Jack, I'm late today, but I'm about to head for the club. You want to work out?"

"No, I had a run already. You'll have to go to Fit City by yourself. But I need to talk. Help is needed."

Kellman said, "My least favorite words. Second only to 'We Ship' when Leah and I are in Europe."

"Moe, I'm serious. How about lunch, or dinner?"

"Cannot do, Jack. I'm tied up for lunch. And I'm not going out for dinner tonight. I've got another engagement. Hold on, Jack," Kellman said, placing Doyle on hold.

A minute later, Kellman came back on the phone. "Listen, I've got to be at this thing tonight. How about you come along with me? I'm going to a bridal shower. We can talk then."

Silence until Doyle said, "Are you into the Negronis over there at this early hour? Did you say a bridal shower?"

"It's for Fifi Bonadio's only granddaughter. Angela. Love of his life." Moe paused to drain his second cup of herbal tea.

"I've got to be there, Jack, and I've got a full-up day. Why don't you come along? You might get a kick out of it."

Doyle thought, *My life seems to get nuttier by the month. But, what the hell.* Of all the things that Moe and his life associations added up to none, as far as Doyle knew, was ever boring. He said, "Okay. I'm game."

"I'll have Pete pick you up at six. And wear a suit."

Doyle could not resist. "To a shower?"

Moe hung up.

◇◇◇

Dunleavy that evening drove them north and west from the center of the city to a wedding hall in Elmwood Park. It was a large, one-story brick building with an impressive faux Roman portico and a huge parking lot that was nearly filled with expensive automobiles. Dunleavy pulled up next to the front entrance. An attendant quickly opened the rear passenger door. Kellman said, "This'll take a couple of hours, Pete. You want to go somewhere, I'll call you on your cell phone."

"Thanks, Mr. Kellman. There's a real good Italian restaurant not far from here."

"At least a half-dozen of them in this town," Kellman said. "Try Panino's. You can't go wrong there. Get the osso bucco."

Kellman and Doyle were greeted inside the door by the proud grandfather of the bride-to-be. Fifi Bonadio kissed Kellman on both cheeks before giving Doyle a brief nod. Bonadio's thick head of hair was as white as Kellman's, but that was the extent of their physical similarities. The top of Kellman's head came up to Bonadio's chin. Bonadio was about Doyle's height, dressed in a beautifully tailored dark blue suit, blue tie on a shirt so white it reflected ceiling light. Bonadio's long face, with its thin lips and strong chin, was deeply tanned. Had it not been for his prominent Roman nose, he would have qualified as superbly handsome. The package presented, Doyle thought, was formidable.

Bonadio and Kellman had been friends since their boyhood days on Chicago's near West Side, Kellman being one of the few Jewish kids in the small, insulated, Italian-dominated neighborhood. Their friendship extended more than sixty years.

Their host led them down a flower-bedecked corridor into a vast room that was overhung with garish, gold-colored chandeliers. Looking neither left nor right, Bonadio walked them past dozens of tables and several hundred people already seated to the front of an eight-chair table centered in front of the stage. The atmosphere in the room was a combination of enticing cooking odors from the kitchen, strong and expensive perfume on well-dressed women, powerful after shave on some of their male companions, and the palpable sense of expectations for the program ahead.

There was one table in the front row slightly set apart. It held a small, operating, electric fan. Its occupants, five extremely aged Italian men, in black suits and tie-less white shirts,were drinking Chianti from straw-encased bottles, smoking the acrid little dry-cured cigars popular long ago in their Sicilian youth. "There's no smoking allowed in here," Bonadio said. "My granddaughter Angela is death on smoking. In the middle of the table, that's my papa and his *goombahs*. Angela gave Papa and his old friends special permission."

A waiter approached just as the three men sat down at their table. Bonadio said, "Bruno, two Negronis. Doyle?"

"Bushmills on the rocks."

Bonadio waved Moe to a seat, then positioned himself in the center facing the stage. He motioned to Doyle to sit next to Moe. Almost immediately two very large men arrived. They nodded respectfully to Bonadio and settled into chairs on the other side of the table, their broad backs to the stage, eyes on the room.

Doyle looked at the large man on his left. "I know you," he said. "You were with the Bears, right?"

Bonadio said, "Meet Rick Fasulo. Yeah, he used to play for the Bears. He works for me now. That's Frank Andreoli next to him." Both men nodded at Doyle. Andreoli was not as large as the former NFL linebacker, but physically imposing in his own right, wearing a sport coat Doyle estimated to be about a size fifty long. "They're in charge of crowd control," Bonadio said.

Their drinks were delivered. So was an antipasto tray big enough to accommodate a Bears practice squad. "*Buon appetito*, Mr. Bonadio," the waiter said, bowing. Bonadio placed a century bill in the waiter's hand. "*Grazie*, Bruno," he said.

Moe and Bonadio clinked their glasses, Moe then touching his to Doyle's. They drank deeply. Bonadio said, "Gentlemen, excuse me for a few minutes. I have to greet the parents of my future son-in-law." He moved briskly toward the room's entrance, extending his hand toward that of a well-dressed, solidly built, blond-haired man whose diminutive wife clung to his left arm as if to a life preserver in an ocean gale. After the handshake, Bonadio reached for the little woman's hand and kissed it. She blushed.

"Is your pal Bonadio always so courtly?" Doyle said to Moe.

Moe said, "Ah, no. We've known each other since first grade. He's always been a pretty serious person." He took a sip of his drink before adding, "But Feef has a lighter side."

Doyle said, "A lighter side? Like Pol Pot had a lighter side?"

Moe said, "Just cool it, Jack. Enjoy the scene."

"It's big enough."

Kellman surveyed the room, a look of pride and satisfaction on his face. "If this were winter, Jack, 90 percent of the women here tonight would have checked their Kellman the Furrier coats on the way in. Or kept the best ones on the backs of their chairs to impress the neighboring tables."

After signaling Bruno for a refill, Moe said, "You call this 'big,' Jack? *Feh*. The wedding reception will have three times as many people. These youngsters will be married in Holy Name Cathedral downtown. The reception will be at the Dayton Hotel on the river. All class, and very, very pricey." He sat back in his chair. "When I was a kid on the West Side," Kellman said, "one of our favorite things was night wedding receptions in the summer. My pals, the Italians, their families knew how to do it right."

Doyle said, "What was so special?"

"When we were thirteen, fourteen, special was putting on your only sport coat if you owned one. Otherwise you borrowed from a brother. You waited near the basement door of the school gym. The wedding reception would be upstairs. They'd serve dinner, then people would get up from their tables and take to the dance floor. That's when we would slide through the basement door. Me, Feef, Mario, Augie, Tommy, a bunch of us punks. Acting like we belonged once we got upstairs, pretending to be wedding guests. We'd go up to the bartender and he'd draw a seven-ounce glass of tap beer for everyone of us. Whoof! That was exciting."

"But the best part came about ten-thirty those nights. The wedding dinner's long over. The guests have all had wedding cake, their anisettes, grappas, coffee, whatever. The band takes a break. And up from the basement kitchen come women carrying laundry baskets full of Italian beef sandwiches wrapped in wax paper, best sandwiches I ever ate. People just reached in and picked up their sandwich. A lady named Marie DiCastri was the chief cook for the whole deal. She was a legend on Taylor Street."

Moe drained his Negroni glass. He signaled the waiter for another as Bonadio rejoined them. "Things all right?" He included Doyle in his look of inquiry.

"Beautiful, Feef," Keelman said. "Relax. Enjoy."

As the dinner continued, Doyle noticed a stocky, black-haired, middle-aged man making his rounds of the tables. He wore an expensive-looking suit, and his designer haircut swept his long, lightly graying hair back across his handsome head. He shook hands with the men, bestowed kisses on the cheeks of the delighted women. The old men at the lone smoking table all got to their feet and bowed when he reached them.

Doyle nudged Moe's elbow. "Who the hell's that? The Papal Emissary?"

"Jack, show some class. Remember where you are."

"I am. My question remains."

Moe, seeing Bonadio in conversation with one of the several priests in attendance, leaned closer to Doyle. "The guy you're asking about is Dominic Romano. You never heard of him?"

Doyle said, "Does he have a Chicago newspaper name? Like Dominic (Greasy Thumb) Romano? Dominic (Little Tuna) Romano? Golf Bag Dominic Romano? I thought this neighborhood was the home of colorful Outfit nicknames."

Moe turned away. Doyle said, "Aw, c'mon, Moe, I'm just jiving."

"Then keep your Irish Bushmills voice down, okay?"

"Okay. What about this Romano?"

Moe leaned closer. "That man is Elmwood Park's contribution to the Illinois State Senate. Dominic has, well, an interesting background for a now prominent legislator. As a youngster, he worked as a burglar, but he was terrible at it. Later, his Uncle Feef put him in the restaurant business. Another disaster." Moe smiled. "Success finally came to Dominic at O'Hare Airport, while he continued with his Outfit apprenticeship."

Doyle said, "At O'Hare? Doing what?"

"This was during the summers, when Dominic was off from college. He and a couple of his buddies worked the long-term parking lot at O'Hare. Feef got them the jobs, I am sure. Dominic worked there for two summers and made a hell of a lot of money for all concerned."

"How?"

"Say a guy parked his car long-term and told the attendant what day he'd be back. If he'd be gone two weeks, say, Dominic and his buddies rented out the guy's car for a few days. To people they knew, or who heard about them from people they knew. People who didn't want to fuck with Hertz or National. They charged half price of what the rental companies did.

"Word got around. They developed a nice list of clients, many through referrals. Men and women flying into Chicago, needing a car short-term for business, bringing it back and paying cash for what was them a bargain fee. But a nice fee for Dominic and Company. All cash, all off the books."

Doyle said, "Wait. Wouldn't the car owner suspect his car had been used?"

"Jack, Jack," Moe smiled. "You don't think Dominic's crew had keys to fit these cars and knew how to adjust odometers?"

"What if the renter, getting this bargain deal, gets the car dinged up? How does that look to the owners when he comes back to retrieve his car?"

"Dominic would tell the guy that some bad driver, unbeknownst to him, must have clipped the guy's car while it was parked in the lot. They'd tell the owner, 'Call your insurance company.'"

"One time," Moe said, "one of their renters got sideswiped on the Kennedy. The car, a BMW I think it was, got bashed in pretty good. The renter called Dominic in a panic. Dominic had a tow-truck there in a half-hour. They haul the BMW back to O'Hare. Two days later, the BMW's owner gets off his plane and take the bus to long-term. When he sees his car, he goes nuts. Dom tells him there was some reckless guy leaving the parking lot in a hurry who hit his BMW. Couldn't get the guy's license plate, he says. Tells him how sorry he is. The guy, still pissed, says, 'Aren't you responsible for what goes on here?'

"Dominic's assistants join the conversation, big, mean-looking Dagoes. Dominic tells the BMW owner, 'Go ahead, file a complaint if you want to. You're Mr. So-and-So and you live at such and such.' They've already identified this guy, figuring there might be trouble. 'And you've got three young kids', and, so on and so on. The guy gets the message. That was the end of that problem."

Doyle, thinking about perhaps parking his Accord some time in long term at O'Hare, asked, "Moe, is this scam still going on?"

"No, no, Jack. Dominic and his buddies were the last of that. Dominic got his degree, did some lawyering for a few years, got on the state ballot, got a nice big push from the boys downtown, and has stayed in the legislature and kept his nose clean."

"I'll bet," Doyle muttered.

"Well, mostly," Moe said.

The stage curtains opened, revealing an eight-piece band and its singer-leader wearing a Tony Bennett-type tuxedo and hair style. He launched into an enthusiastic rendition of "*That's Amore*," a song Doyle well remembered his parents playing years ago on a record, the Dean Martin version.

Two more numbers followed. Then the singer-leader introduced himself "to this wonderful group of friends of Mr. Bonadio and his wonderful family" as Tony Molinaro. He went on to inform them that "the bride-to-be, Miss Angela Bonadio, and her lucky, lucky, I mean lucky, husband-to-be, Carson Briggs, will now join us."

From the left of the stage emerged a couple of twenty-somethings. The girl was stylish in a black cocktail dress, her companion in a suit similar to Fifi Bonadio's. She was beautiful, slim, dark-complexioned, long legged, a bountiful bust above her small waist. "She looks a lot like her late grandmother. Feef's late wife was a dazzler," Moe whispered to Doyle. Angela waved to the crowd. Briggs stood next to her in the spotlight, gripping her left hand like a watchful attendant. He was a sturdy lad, blond hair close-cropped, a confident look on his handsome face. Doyle was reminded of some of the college jocks he had known, wrestlers mainly.

All the people in the room were now on their feet. Bonadio stopped his loud applauding to say to Moe, "This kid Briggs, he's a good kid. Not one of us, but a good kid. I vetted him out real good. Angela's crazy about him. They'll do fine. Briggs will take over that bank of ours down in Park Forest, I'll start him there. Angela still wants to keep teaching at Parker School, so they're going to live in the Lincoln Park condo I bought them."

Moe raised his Negroni. "*Salud*, Feef." They bumped glasses. Doyle sat down. He said to the solicitous waiter, Bruno, "Another Bushmills."

Tony Molinaro asked the crowd to be seated. Into the microphone he shouted, "Let the gifts begin."

In the next half-hour, Doyle looked on in amazement. Backstage workers began by wheeling out a fifty- inch flat screen TV, then a CD player and Bose speakers, compliments, Tony Molinaro said, "of our friend Peter Salerno, the asphalt king."

Next came a set of expensive-looking living room furniture, "compliments of Chicago's prince of produce, Joe Pomponi." Cartons of crockery and china and cutlery followed, the contributor of each loudly identified and applauded. As the bedroom set was trundled forth, emcee Molinaro had in his mind a risqué cheer of his own. But when he peered through the spotlight at Bonadio, he changed his mind. A hulking refrigerator, two smaller television sets, an antique dining room table "from nearly the time of the Borgias," Molinaro joked, were placed on the crowded stage. At the arrival of each present, Angela and Carson hugged and clapped and waved their thanks.

Midway through this parade of houseware and appliances, Doyle signaled Bruno for a refill. He tried to compose himself. He knew the look on his face must be an alcohol-driven one of mirth and amazement at this exhibition of extravagance. He ignored what he knew to be Moe's occasional warning looks. Bonadio's eyes remained riveted on Angela.

The band struck an attention-getting chord that ended in a flourish. The lights dimmed. It took four attendants to push into the stage spotlight the blue and white Mini Cooper convertible that, Molinaro shouted, was a "special gift to Angela from her proud grandpa, our host tonight, Mr. Fifi Bonadio." The room erupted in applause. Angela hugged Carson before running down the stairs from the stage to embrace Bonadio. The band played on.

Doyle excused himself and went to the washroom. Rick Fasulo got up from their table and walked beside him. "Amazing stuff," Doyle said to the big ex-Bear. "Oh, yeah," Fasulo grunted. Andreoli walked on Fasulo's other side, equally large and noncommital.

Dinner was served family style. On their table, Doyle watched as Bruno the head waiter supervised his helpers in the positioning of three bowls of different pasta, two large platters of chicken Vesuvio, platters of meatballs and sausages in red sauce, salad bowls, bread baskets, butter trays. Doyle dug in. "Great food," he said to Bonadio. Moe nodded in agreement, the little man having already rapidly polished off his first full plate.

Several bottles of Chianti were disposed of in the next hour. After dinner drinks and desserts followed. Undoubtedly emboldened by the alcohol irrigating his brain cells, Doyle asked Moe if he had heard anything from Arnie Rison in the wake of the recent deaths of his three Significant Seven partners.

"No," was the answer.

"Damn amazing," Doyle said, "three of the lucky friends getting fatally unlucky in such a short span of time. Wouldn't you agree, Feef?" he added, jabbing his host on the arm. Across the table, Rick Fasulo let out a low growl.

Bonadio removed Doyle's hand from his sleeve. He sat back in his chair, smiling. "What are you, fishing for information, Doyle?" Bonadio said. "Strange deaths occur, and you figure I might know something about them?" He leaned across the table and said to Fasulo and Andreoli, "*Questo Irisher deve pensare che sappiamo qualcosa di tutti le morti sospettose, l'eh?*" The three laughed uproariously.

Doyle, his face red, said, "I thought I heard my name in there in the midst of all your Italian. What a beautiful sounding language. Want to tell me what the fuck you're saying about me?"

Fasulo started to get to his feet, but Bonadio motioned him to sit down. "All right, all right," Bonadio said, "that was not polite on my part. I apologize. But my point, Doyle, is that if there's money and death involved, my people are not necessarily involved every time. *Capice*? There's been so much *merde* coming out of that TV show, *Sopranos*, it makes me sick. You know? Small timers on that show. The way they operate, they wouldn't last two weeks around here." The bodyguards laughed. Bonadio smiled before finishing his glass of grappa. He said, "But the horse guys you mention, their deaths? I got no idea."

Chapter Twenty-five

June 22, 2009

Doyle dialed Damon Tirabassi's cell phone number early the next morning. "Bad news, Damon. The goddam sponger got another one. I just talked to the security people, and the horse's owner, and the state vet."

Tirabassi said, "How about that? Only a few hours after your big night at the Bonadio bash, you've bounced back pretty good."

Doyle said, "What is this bullshit? You mean your people are following me?"

"Don't flatter yourself," Tirabassi replied. "We've got an agent in place, close to the Bonadio family, all the time. Hoping for one of them to screw up. Our man saw you there at the bridal shower in Elmwood Park last night."

"There was a sleepy looking schlub over in the far corner," Doyle snarled. "I should have recognized him as one of your operatives."

Tirabassi barked back, "Jack, drop it. I'll pick up Karen and we'll come out to Heartland. Where do you want to meet?"

"At Tenuta's barn. The stable gate officer can give you directions. Flash your Feeb badges. You know, Damon, between another sponging and you receiving reports about my social whereabouts, I'm starting to get really ticked off."

"Glad to hear it, Jack. That's when you do your best work." Doyle could hear what might have been Tirabassi chortling before the connection ended.

◇◇◇

An hour later, the agents joined Doyle in Tenuta's office, where Tirabassi introduced Doyle to "Special Agent in Charge of the Chicago office, David Goodman." A tall, dark-haired, thin, bespectacled man in his late thirties, Goodman was trying to pace the floor, but the room was so small he quickly gave up. He was excited, speaking rapidly in his partly muffled cell phone conversation. "If I'm ever going to witness anybody wringing their hands, this will be the guy," Doyle whispered to Karen Engel.

She said, "Keep it down, Jack. Goodman is heavy duty."

"No wonder I've never envied you your occupation," Doyle said.

Goodman clicked off his phone and cleared his throat. "Okay, folks, listen up. That man at the doorway"—everyone turned around and saw a heavy-set, middle-aged man holding a brief case at his side—"is Dr. Harold Brockhouse. He's the veterinarian for Homestead Gal, the latest horse to get the sponge treatment here. I want him to tell us how this criminal act was discovered. Go ahead, doctor."

Doyle raised his hand. "Yo, Agent Goodman, I have a question. If the good doctor is going to describe to us what we should be on the watch for, why are we keeping his knowledge in this little room. Why not have him talk to a meeting of the horsemen?"

Goodman sighed so forcefully and with such disdain he nearly ruffled the papers on Ralph Tenuta's desk. "Do you think, Mr. Doyle, we haven't thought of that? That's in the future. In the very present here today is knowledge I want Dr. Brockhouse to share with those of us, I mean agents Tirabassi and Engel, even you, Doyle, most closely involved in this ongoing investigation." Goodman perched one of his skinny haunches on the edge of the desk. "Go on, Doctor."

Dr. Brockhouse cleared his throat. Attention was paid. "Good morning," he said. "Some of you may remember an allowance race here at Heartland Downs a week ago. The heavy favorite was Homestead Gal. She ran well for the first half-mile. Then she stopped badly and finished eighth in the nine-horse field. I'm told there was loud booing of her jockey by fans at the rail after the race was over."

The vet paused to glance at his notes. "The filly's trainer, Logan Bailey, was mystified. The horse had been training very well. She'd run second in a Grade Two stakes race in her previous start at Belmont Park. On paper, she appeared to tower over her field in the Heartland race.

"Logan Bailey called me the day after the race. He said Homestead Gal had a bad nasal discharge. She was also very dull looking, but restless in her stall. I said we'd put her on antibiotics for a couple of days. We did, but it didn't help. There were still large amounts of mucus draining from the nostril. I said bring her to my clinic.

"Bailey vanned her over the next morning. We looked in there through a scope and saw this blue-green object in the filly's nasal passage. At first I thought it was a tumor, a nasty one. It wasn't. It was a sponge."

Tenuta said, "Damn! Is she going to be all right?"

"Yes," the vet said, "physically she'll get over it. But it is a very traumatic experience. I hope it doesn't ruin her."

Doyle leaned forward. "Let me ask you something, Doc. Do you know if there was any security at Bailey's barn before that race."

Goodman got off the desk to answer. "Yes, there was. Bailey employs a night watchman. But that doesn't mean the watchman was standing in front of that horse's stall all night. Bailey has twenty horses here, at the end of Barn Thirteen. Half are on one side, the other ten around the corner on the other side. Bailey says Homestead Gal is a nervous, sensitive sort that doesn't like to be handled. So, it appears that whoever was able to insert that sponge in her was a practiced, accomplished horse person.

"This is the fourth sponging incident at Heartland Downs this summer. Bettors have been cheated out of hundreds of thousands of dollars because of these favorites being prevented from winning. It's an embarrassment."

Doyle said, "Agent Goodman, have you again examined the betting patterns of these fixed races? Do they tell you anything about who is benefiting? Where they might be?"

"Well, of course we have, Doyle. We've worked with the Racetrack Security Bureau. We've had computer experts on this for weeks. Whoever is doing this, making the bets knowing that the favorite will be out of the money, has left no trail. Some of the big exotic bet payoffs came here at Heartland. Others were at tracks around the country through the simulcast betting network. Other bets were made over the Internet in states where that is legal.

"None of the bets at any one place were so large as to attract attention. That's why this ring must operate out of several different locations. They're damn smart. There is no way," Goodman continued, "that the trainer of every favorite in every race here can afford to pay for twenty-four hour security. But we had better urge them to try. That's why we've planned a general horsemen's meeting for tomorrow after the races. It will be in the clubhouse dining room. Hope to see you there." Goodman collected his papers, nodded at them, and hurried out the door.

When Dr. Brockhouse and the other agents had left, Tenuta said, "How the hell can people do it, Jack? Mistreat horses like that? I've been around the racetrack since I was a kid. Most of the racetrackers I've known love horses, are proud of them. They work to protect them, not harm them. I just don't get it."

Doyle said, "Ralph, when I was boxing in AAU tournaments as a kid, my best friend, Lonnie Beard, was in the same weight class with me. Our trainer tried to keep us apart, entering us in different tournaments, but we met in the finals of the same tournament twice. Each time my buddy, Lonnie, an altar boy, Eagle Scout, super student, class officer, all around paragon of American youth, tried to thumb me in the eye.

"He'd come in and feint a left hook to the belly. Then he'd shoot out his right hand at me, thumb of his glove extended, trying to gouge my left eye. The first time he did it, in the second round of the first fight, I ducked and he just scraped my eyebrow. I knew it was no accident. I complained to the ref and so did my corner. What Lonnie did was intentional, Mr. Perfect, the son of a bitch. But all he got was a warning.

"The next time we fought, Lonnie comes out in the first round and tries to thumb me again. Unbelievable! My buddy. Grade school on up. Until then."

Tenuta said, "Who won the fights?"

"I flattened the bastard in the third and final round of each one. After the second bout, Lonnie quit boxing. He never spoke to me again. I used to think about that a lot, what our friendship had been, asking myself how Lonnie could bring himself to rough me up like that. I guess he wanted to win so bad, he'd try anything. That," Doyle said, "must be like what's going on with whoever's hurting these horses. They want to win bets so bad they'll do anything."

Doyle stood up. "Ralph, how about an early lunch? I'll buy. We'll go to Frankie's for Italian beefs, okay?"

In Doyle's car, Tenuta said, "Whatever happened to this Lonnie, your former buddy?"

Doyle reversed out of his parking place before answering. "Lonnie's a lawyer. He's running for State Supreme Court next year. As my old man used to say, 'How do you like them apples?'"

After the ninth and final race the next afternoon, Doyle and Tenuta trooped into the Heartland Downs clubhouse along with more than one-hundred other horse people. Most were trainers, but there were some concerned horse owners and jockeys on hand. Tenuta knew all of the trainers. "Hey, Jumbo" he said to one little man who was on his way to a seat. The man smiled back over his shoulder, his Chicago White Sox ball cap snugged down on his wrinkled forehead.

"Jumbo?" Doyle said. "That little old guy?"

Tenuta said, "That's Jim Gural. His nickname is Jumbo. Because he's got a terrific memory, like an elephant. Been around here years. Great little guy."

"Why Jumbo? He isn't much bigger than the jockey sitting next to him."

"There was an old Disney movie I think, or maybe a book, about some elephant that had a great memory. Jumbo. So does my friend Gural. Got it?"

Tenuta sat back in his chair, smiling. "When I came on the racetrack," he said, "there were all kinds of people with nicknames. All kinds."

"Like what?"

"Well," Tenuta said, "there was Duckbutter, Hambone, Cadillac Jack, Daddy Rabbit, Yum Yum, Two Shoe Nick." He paused, revving up his memory. "And Harry the Hat. Earl the Squirrel. Bundle Boy, Maestro, Place and Show Joe. Hell, there were more than that, Jack. It was a different time. Lot of real characters."

Doyle said, "I've seen quite a few characters around here lately." He patted Tenuta's arm. "Including you."

The room became silent when Dr. Brockhouse went to the podium, tested the microphone, and began his report.

Thirty-five minutes later, it was a glum crowd that filed out the Heartland Downs clubhouse.

Chapter Twenty-six

June 30, 2009

Doyle looked up from the computer on Tenuta's desk when he heard a familiar voice at the doorway saying, "Hellooooo, Jack." The morning sun was behind the small man standing there, making him difficult for Doyle to see. But he didn't have to see him to know him. He knew that voice. "Morty Dubinski," Jack said. He smiled as he went around the desk to the door. They shook hands. Jack stood back and looked the little man over. "Long time no see, Morty. You're looking good."

Dubinski laughed. "Don't kid me, Jack. I've never looked good. I'm still trying to upgrade myself to 'more presentable.' Can I sit down?"

Motioning Dubinski to a chair, Doyle said, "Last time I saw you, Morty, was at Bob Zaslow's funeral. When you were still bruised and battered from those Canaryville goons. You look a hell of a lot better today."

Morty said, "Bettor today is what I'm here to talk to you about."

"Better/bettor with an 'e' or an 'o'?"

"Both. That's what I came to talk to you about. Better betting."

"Ah, Morty," Doyle groaned. "Let's go get some coffee."

As they walked to the track kitchen, Doyle glanced at the short, sixtyish man beside him. Morty hadn't changed. His long white hair was still combed straight back on one of the longest heads Doyle had ever seen, an elongated skull that caused Morty to be known in racetrack circles as "Melon Head." Morty's old brown-framed glasses still perched on his glistening reddish nose. Morty wore one of his two light blue sport coats, his one dark blue bow tie. The only difference Doyle could discern from a year or so ago was that Dubinski had finally discarded one of his threadbare, formerly white dress shirts. This morning he was wearing a glistening new number, the cardboard crease marks still evident across his chest.

The track kitchen, a large restaurant and cafeteria, was filled with trainers, grooms, exercise riders, hot walkers, a few horse owners. The air was permeated with the odors of hot grease and cigarette smoke. Doyle and Morty snagged a small table in the back of the large, noisy room. Doyle said, "Morty, what can I get you?"

"Coffee, cream. Prune Danish. Make it two."

"You got it."

After Morty rapidly downed the two sizeable pastries, he wiped his mouth with his napkin. "So, when are you going to say it?" he said.

"Say what?"

"Say that you're wondering why I showed up here this morning, out of the blue."

"Morty," Doyle said, "what could I possibly be doing except wondering?"

The little man said, "I was always wondering about something, too, Jack. Not about why you left Monee Park and helped me to take over your publicity job. What I've been wondering, and I'm not the only one, is why you never came back to visit Monee.

"You were a big hero there after saving lives and killing that creep that tried to kill us. But we never saw you again, never heard anything from you. People still ask me about that, and about you."

Doyle said, "I'm getting another coffee. You want one?" Morty said no.

Waiting in the coffee line, Doyle briefly considered asking Morty about Celia McCann, his employer at Monee Park. One of the most attractive women he'd ever known. One of the most intelligent, and interesting, and…He gave himself a mental slap upside the head. "I am *not* going there again," he muttered, his reluctance to do so based on layers of regret.

"What's that, Jack?" The question came from Miss Ruth, order taker in perpetuity in the Heartland track kitchen.

Doyle said, "Sorry, Miss Ruth. Another large coffee, black, please."

Morty looked up anxiously when Doyle again sat down across from him. "Talk to me Morty."

"Jack, I need just a small, short-term loan from you. A thousand. I'm going to be in the Super Handicapper Contest in Las Vegas next week. I qualified in one of their satellite contests. But the entry fee is ten grand. I've got nine. I would have had the ten, easy, if I had perfected my new system a few days earlier than I did. But I didn't. That's why I came to see you today." Morty, relieved that his pitch was delivered, sat back.

Doyle looked across the table at the man known at Monee Park as a "Jonah," the embodiment of a wagon load of bad luck, a train car full of futility, a loser of such disconcerting magnitude that Biblical analogies had to be applied to him.

"You have got to be kidding," Doyle said. "The longest winning streak I ever saw you on lasted about a race and half. Remember that horse you touted me on at Monee? Your quote, mortal lock of mortal locks, unquote? Comet Colin, the horse that led all the way around the track into the stretch and then jumped the fence and ran into the infield lake and drowned?"

"C'mon, Jack," Morty said, his head down, "how could I forget?"

Doyle said, "What would make you think you should enter a Las Vegas handicapping contest? Sharp shooters from all over the country will be there. And you, with your history of terrible luck? Morty, you're a smart guy, and you know horses, but this plan has disaster emblazoned on it."

"Jack, I can't argue, my horse playing history is not good. But," Morty said, "all that is in the past." He leaned forward. "I've got a new system for betting horses. Took me years to develop it," he said softly. "But, Jack, it *works*. Like you'd never believe possible."

"A system. God help us," Doyle sighed. "Damon Runyon said all horseplayers die broke. Which I don't believe, because I know some that do make a good living at it. But somebody besides Runyon added, 'System players die earliest.' From what I've seen, I tend to believe that."

"Not *my* system," Morty said emphatically. "Jack, it is honest to God amazing. After all my years in the game," he said, looking around the room before continuing in a whisper, "I have found the treasure of Sierra Madre. The Yukon gold strike. What's that other big thing? The Rosie Stone? Like what the great trainer Charlie Whittingham called 'Where Molly hid the peaches.' I have found the truth." He was as earnest as a dog at dinner time.

Doyle had always liked this little lifelong bachelor, resident of his aged mother's Berwyn, Illinois basement apartment, industrious but paint-by-the-numbers racetrack publicist. To observe the glow of conviction emanating from his former Monee Park assistant gladdened Doyle. But giving him a grand to test the deep waters of the Vegas contest? Could this be termed enabling? "What's the deadline for this thing?"

"Tomorrow," Morty said. "I've got to wire them the entry fee by noon. Jack, if you can loan me the grand, I'll double it for you in three days. Swear to God."

Doyle was not sold, and Morty knew it. He took a thick envelope from his sport coat pocket and extracted five sheets of paper. They were covered with names and numbers describing horses and their odds, their finishes, the amount and kind of bets made on them, an ROI (return on investment) column. He said, "Please, just look this over. I'll go get us some more coffee. Want a Danish?"

"Just coffee."

Ten minutes later, when Doyle returned the papers to him, Morty said, "What do you think?"

Doyle said, "I've got to admit, I'm impressed. Besides astounded. You, with a terrific return on investment. But this is just three weeks of system results here. How can you be sure you can keep winning at this rate over the long run?"

Morty scooped up the papers and stuffed them back into the envelope. "Because I *know*, Jack. Because I know. This system is super legit. I swear it. Have I ever lied to you about anything?"

Doyle finished his coffee. He said, "No, my friend, you never have. Come on. We'll go to an ATM machine in the grandstand. You've got the grand."

"Aw, Jack, I knew I could count on you," Morty beamed. He reached across the table and heartily shook Doyle's hand. "You will not regret this, I guarantee."

"Words that have brought down major civilizations," Doyle almost said, but held back. He thought of Sinatra's famous version of "My Way," its reference to "regrets? I've had a few," and laughed.

"Of all the regrets I've had, Morty, no matter how you do in Vegas, this loan will not be in my top ten. Great luck to you, my friend."

During their short drive to the Heartland Downs grandstand, Morty said, "Jack, would you think about coming out to Vegas during the contest? You could stay with me. Give me, you know, moral support. I've never been in a big contest like this," he admitted. " I might need a little boost from a friend."

"Let's just get you your money today, Morty. Me joining you in Vegas? I'll think about it."

Chapter Twenty-seven

June 28, 2009

Orth emerged from the cool lake after his early morning swim and found a message on his cellphone. "Call."

Showered and breakfasted, he drove to the Qwik Stop outside of Boulder Junction and used the land line. Sanderson picked up on the first ring. "Need a meet. Can you be in St. Louis by tomorrow night?"

"Affirmative."

"See you at the Airport Marriott," Sanderson said.

Orth drove to Madison the next morning and paid cash for an afternoon flight to St. Louis. He cabbed to the motel, registered as Edward Walsh, and was napping when he heard two taps on his door. They were light taps, but Orth's trained response to anything aural within yards of him brought him off the bed and to the door in seconds. He looked through the eye hole before unlocking.

After greeting each other, Sanderson ordered from room service, identifying himself as "Mr. Walsh in 318." Neither he nor Orth ever used their real names when they met. Sanderson intended to catch a night flight back to Dallas-Fort Worth, a flight which like all other domestic air travel was dinner-free. He stayed out of sight as Orth accepted the tray and paid the bill in cash with a good tip.

Sanderson eagerly dug into his shrimp salad, a turkey club sandwich with French fries, apple pie *ala* mode. Orth watched impassively. As long as Orth had known him, Sanderson always had an appetite that verged on gluttony. Yet, the sinewy bastard never seemed to put on a pound. "A man who has three growing kids and a wife that loves to spend money," Sanderson had once explained, "your metabolism kicks into overdrive."

Sanderson finally put down the only remaining remnants of his meal, one of the cellophane decorated toothpicks from the sandwich. He reached into his shirt pocket, looked at a small piece of paper, and smiled.

"We've got three targets left," Sanderson said. "The reason I wanted to see you was that I understand the remaining targets are getting kind of nervous. Apprehensive. Cautious."

"Hard to blame them."

"Yeah," Sanderson said, "and we're going to have to be very, very careful dealing with the next three. They're all bound to be on the lookout, maybe even have hired security. I'll find out about that part in a day or two."

"Is the money still solid?"

Sanderson smiled. "Oh, yeah. Five hundred grand total for us, plus expenses."

"I can count on you to pad the shit out of those, right?"

"You got it, bro."

The next hour was devoted to planning. Sanderson kept looking at his watch until he saw Orth tightening his jaw, heard him say, "Forget the fucking time, you'll make your flight. I want this figured out right. It's my ass on the line out there."

"Sorry, bro. You're right," Sanderson said.

Orth said, "If you'll get me just a few important pieces of information, I'll take care of these last three." He described what he wanted. "I'll take care of it," Sanderson said.

When it was time for Sanderson to leave for the airport, Orth got up, stretched, walked over to the wide window overlooking the parking lot. His back turned to Sanderson, he said, "One thing before you go. I never asked you before during the other deals we've done. Never wanted to know. But I'd like to know now about this, our biggest project. Who are we working for? Who is paying?"

Sanderson said, "Damn it, man, we've been super careful to create as many cut outs as we could. Right from the start. That's how you said you wanted it, and that's what I've done. I think we should keep it that way."

"I know you do," Orth said. "But I don't, not this time. I want you tell me, right here and now, who's paying us all this money for this project."

Sanderson briefly thought of continuing the argument. But then he saw the look on Orth's face. Sanderson spoke softly for less than a minute. When he was finished, the normally imperturbable Orth shook his head at what he had just heard. "I'll be god damned."

Chapter Twenty-eight

July 3, 2009

The races were over. The Tenuta stable had enjoyed a very productive afternoon: three starters, one maiden winner, one second, one fourth. The grooms sat around the barn, relaxing on bales of hay and drinking beers that Tenuta had brought in a cooler, anticipating this morale-boosting and successful pre-holiday afternoon.

Doyle nudged Tenuta's arm, almost spilling the trainer's iced can of Old Style. They were standing outside of Tenuta's office, enjoying the early evening air. Doyle said, "Ralph, who's that?" He pointed across the stable yard to a short, young, Latino man who was leaning back in a camp chair, leisurely smoking a cigarette. "I thought nobody was supposed to smoke back here. Too dangerous, right? Some of these old wooden barns. All this hay and straw."

"That's the rule, Jack, but that punk over there doesn't pay much attention to rules. Name is Junior Garza. There must have been a senior, but I never met him. One of these Garzas is enough. Junior works now for trainer Marty Alpert, who is stabled right over there. I sure as hell don't know why," Tenuta said disgustedly.

"What do you mean?"

"Junior is trouble," Tenuta said. "He came around a few years back, said he wanted to be a jockey. Didn't work out. He got hurt pretty bad in his first and only year of riding. Broke a collarbone, wrist, ankle. Never rode in a race again. After he healed, he came back and started working as an exercise rider. He's good at it. But I'd never use him on one of my horses."

"Why's that?"

"Don't trust the little bastard, that's why. Seems like wherever he works, things go missing. You know? Saddes, bridles, blankets. He's never been caught, but most people think he's the one doing the thieving. Alpert, well, Marty's got a big heart. He says he wants to 'give the kid another chance.' We'll see how that works out. How come you're asking about him, Jack?"

"I saw him here in your shed row last week, late in the afternoon. It was the day before Editorialist's last race. I was waiting for your night watchman to come back from the wash room when I saw this kid near Editorialist's stall. I hollered at him, 'What're you doing,' something like that. He just looked at me, real insolent, and walked off without answering. I'm sure it was him, Junior over there."

"Glad you chased him off," Tenuta said. "I don't want him anywhere around my stable. Kid's a thief, maybe worse. Everybody knows it, but nobody has nailed him yet. I don't know why people keep hiring him."

Chapter Twenty-nine

July 9, 2009

At the end of that week—one in which Doyle had again handled the stable entries, arranged for the services of the jockeys Tenuta wanted to use on them, paid some stable bills, placed feed and vitamin orders, and answered numerous phone calls in his role as stable agent—the little trainer invited him to his home for dinner. "I'll call my wife, Rosa, and let her know you're coming. Okay, Jack?"

"Fine with me," Doyle said. "I don't get many home cooked meals, especially Italian, and I'm big on Italian food." Tenuta gave him an odd look but didn't say anything. They walked to their cars, Tenuta saying, "Just follow me. It's about three miles. Five-eleven South Belmont in Arlington Heights in case we get separated."

Ten minutes later, Tenuta pulled his maroon Buick Regal into the driveway of a red brick ranch house, motioning Doyle to park behind him. The lawn and shrubbery, Doyle could see, were as well maintained as Tenuta's racetrack barn. He was not surprised.

The front door opened as they approached. Out stepped a short, dark-haired woman wearing a floral apron over a red blouse and black skirt. "Jack Doyle," she said, extending her hand, "welcome to our home. I've been looking forward to meeting you."

She smiled warmly as Doyle said, "Thanks for having me." Rosa then turned to her husband and offered her cheek, which he kissed briefly, giving her shoulder a hug at the same time.

Jack and Ralph sat on the back deck of the house for a few minutes, drinking beer. From under a picnic bench limped an obviously very old dog. "That's Sammy," the trainer said. "C'mere, c'mere, you mutt," he said fondly. He scratched the aged canine's back for a couple of minutes until Rosa called them in, reminding Ralph to "wash your hands." Sammy followed Doyle to the dinner table and slowly positioned himself beneath its center. Doyle made sure his feet were not a bother to the dog.

Their first course was a salad that Doyle did not recognize. Rosa, digging into her plate, said, "This is a grapefruit display with French dressing, mushroom croutons, cream cheese balls, on top of red leaf lettuce."

Tenuta forced down a couple of forkfuls, groaning quietly. Doyle, whose ingestion credo had always been extremely liberal, cleaned his salad plate. Rosa beamed at him. "I'll bet you've always been a good eater, Jack."

"I certainly have, Rosa."

Rosa took the salad plates into the kitchen. Ralph leaned across the table. "Jack," he said softly out of the side of his mouth, "this meal tonight, most of my meals now, come out of a Kentucky cookbook that a friend of ours at Keeneland racetrack sent to Rosa early in the summer. These meals have been going on for over a month, because she's really into it now. On Sundays, she relents, and we have my pasta, red sauce, veal meatballs. Rest of the week? All these Kentucky adventures. This, from a woman who could cater to angels using her old recipes. But I can't talk her off it. Whoops! Here she comes."

Doyle looked on with some trepidation as the next course was set before him.

"Have you ever had a genuine Kentucky Hot Brown?" Rosa said brightly. "It's a Kentucky tradition, an open-faced turkey sandwich on white toast with bacon strips and a whitish Mornay sauce. There's Parmesan cheese in the sauce and also a sprinkle as a topping."

"Well, it must be good, because it's got good things in it," Doyle said bravely. "Actually, I have had a Hot Brown. During the time I worked in Kentucky a few years back." He began to cut the mound of food on his plate into bite sizes. Thinking about his previous culinary experiences in the Blue Grass State, he recalled his first breakfast at Louisville's famed Brown Hotel, where the Kentucky Hot Brown had been created. He had ordered ham and scrambled eggs that morning and the waitress said, "Hon, you want country ham?"

"What's country ham?"

The waitress drawled, "Well, it's cured, and salty, and kind of tough, but tasty. We don't serve them until they're a year or more old."

Doyle had smiled up at this nice lady. "I believe I'll go with the city ham," he said.

Tenuta broke into Doyle's reverie to say, "When you were in Kentucky, that was when you were helping catch that horse killer, right?"

Doyle nodded. Rosa looked from her husband to her guest. "Do I know this story?" she said.

Between scoops of the Hot Brown, Doyle provided an abbreviated summary of his past while he was working on behalf of the FBI. "Is the guy still in jail?" Ralph asked.

"Yeah. Federal prison. Many years to go."

Rosa said, "There are some real cuckoos in the racing business."

"I've trained for my share of them," Ralph sighed, "though not crooks like that." He reached for his wine glass. Glancing at his wife he added, "Including Salvatore 'Slow Pay Sal' Rizzo, Rosa's cousin."

"Distant cousin," Rosa huffed.

"Not distant enough," Ralph fired back. "He was a real pain in the you know what."

Rosa said, "Well, yes, Sal could be. Tell Jack about the dogs and Salvatore."

"I trained for Sal a little more than three years," Ralph said. "Every year, his horses made money. Not a lot, but more than enough to cover his owner's expenses. Which he hated paying. The guy was always two, three months behind in his training bills. If Sal wasn't related to Rosa, no matter how 'distantly,' I would have given him the boot."

Rosa ignored that jibe. She said, "Ralph, get to the dogs." Then she paused. "Wait," she said, "let me get dessert. Just take a minute."

Doyle and Tenuta didn't make any small talk in the short interim. Doyle concentrated on his friend's apprehensive expression. Rosa quickly returned and laid the dessert dishes before the men, saying, "This is a mocha-macaroon freeze with lemon curd topping." She smiled as she took her first bite. Her husband muttered, "Whatever happened to homemade cannolis?" But he dutifully dug in, as did Doyle, who thought this was pretty good stuff. "Go on, Ralph," Rosa urged, "tell Jack about the dogs."

"Sal and his wife Myrna bred champion hunting dogs that were used in competive field trials," Ralph said. "They had this one outstanding dam…"

"Bitch," Rosa corrected.

Ralph said, "You talking about Myrna? Oh, you mean the mother dog."

"Very funny. Go on Ralph."

"Okay, Sal and Myrna breed one litter from this female champ every year. Her name is something like Champion Mannheim Mitzi of Blue Island, some damn thing like that. They called her Mitzi. She'd produce anywhere from five to eight pups each litter. These are German short-haired pointers. And the Rizzos sell them all at big prices. Except this one year."

Tenuta was smiling, relishing his remembrance. "Five years ago, there was one pup that was a real runt. About half the size of his brothers and sisters. The Rizzos don't try to sell him, don't even want dog people to see him, because he could hurt Mitzi's big reputation. Sal comes to me at the barn one day and says, 'Ralph, I know I'm behind on my bills to you, sorry, I'll catch up, blah blah blah. Just to show you my good faith, I am going to give you one of champion Mitzi's pups.'

"I tell him, 'Sal, Rosa and I already have a dog. It's an old lab-terrier mutt we've had for years. He's so smart, I taught him how to find the TV remote control when I can't. My car keys, too. Our Sammy, he's all the dog we need.'

"Rosa, this is getting to be long. You want to start coffee?" She gave him a look. "Okay," Ralph continued, "Sal goes on to say that if we don't take this puny pup, they'll have to put him down. He shows me a photo of the little fellow, who is plenty cute, but obviously very small against what Sal called the 'standard of the breed.'"

Doyle said, "Why would they destroy a well-bred dog like that?"

"In the dog world," Ralph said, "you got to have pedigree and conformation. A breeder doesn't want to reveal to the dog world that he's got some inferior product like this pup. Now, I'm thinking, our Sammy is getting up there in years. I don't want to see this young little guy go under. I talked to Rosa, and she said, 'Yes, take the pup. Give that cheap cousin of mine a month off his training bills.' And we did."

Doyle could feel old Sammy under the table shifting his weight onto Doyle's feet as Ralph continued. "It took us about four months to figure out that Sammy and the pup were not having happy lives together. The pup was active all day, the old guy wanted his rest. It wasn't working out. I'm thinking, 'I've made a mistake. I can't let the pup ruin Sammy's golden years.'

"There was a guy stabled near me at Heartland Downs that year named Jimmy Binnard. Nice guy. He owned field trial dogs. He'd race his horses in Chicago six months, then go hunting or trialing or whatever they call it for a couple of months down south each fall. I told him my situation. Jimmy agreed to take our pup that we'd named Shorty. He said, 'Ralph, I've got give you something for him. This is a real well-bred pup. He's grow-ing pretty good. He's got a nice look about him, too.'

"'Yeah,' I said, 'but he's just a little guy. His big-time breeder didn't want to keep him.' Jimmy, God bless him, would not let it go that way. He said, 'Ralph, if I do any good with this pup, you get half.' I just laughed. I said, 'Jimmy, half of what?' Jimmy said, 'He looks smart. He could grow more. You never know, he might turn out to be a good hunting dog. If he does, in a year or so I'll take him with my other dogs to a couple of field trials in South Carolina where they compete for money. Okay?'

"I said, 'Sure, Jimmy. Just take care of this little guy.' So I said goodbye to Shorty."

Rosa had slipped away from the table, gotten the coffee pot, and come back to pour. She was smiling. She nudged Doyle with her elbow as she set his cup down. "This is the beauty part," she said.

"Over the next year, Jimmy Binnard trains Shorty for the field trials," Ralph said. "This little guy develops, grows big, turns out to be a multichampion down there in the Carolinas. His second year there, he wins $28,000 in prize money. Jimmy sends me my half! After Shorty had won his first two or three trials, who shows up at the barn one morning but Cousin Slow Pay Sal. He must have heard about how good Shorty was doing. Sal makes some small talk, gives me a check for about half of what he owes me in current training bills. Then Sal says, this is the kind brass balls he's got, 'And Ralph, how's *our* pup doing?' I said, 'You mean the little runt you were going to kill? He's doing fine. Now get the hell out of here.'"

Doyle said, "I love it. What a jerk, Slow Play Sal."

Ralph said, "They were different, Sal and Myrna. The three years I trained for them, they would tell me when they were having Champion Mitzie Schmitzie or whatever her name was bred. They would observe the breeding. Then, and I am not making this up, they would breed themselves."

Rosa, blushing, said "Ralph, you don't have to tell that," and retreated to the kitchen carrying the dessert plates.

Doyle said, "Come again?"

"I am saying that every year for three years when the Rizzos bred their champion dam, bitch I mean, they would be active along those lines themselves. Myrna had a baby a year three years in a row."

"The dog breeders breeding after breeding their dog?" Doyle said, laughing louder than perhaps he should have.

Rosa came back to the table. "That's enough, Ralph," she said. "Jack, how about some more dessert?"

"Don't mind if I do. Thanks."

She said, "Would you like a little grappa to go with it?"

"I would," Ralph said.

Rosa said, "I'm not asking you, hon. I know what it does to you."

"I know what it does to me, too," Doyle said. "I gave up grappa a couple of years back. Used to drink it with my friend Moe Kellman until I had hangovers that made me seriously consider suicide. Wonderful stuff while it's happening, brutal stuff the next day."

"I'll just get you men coffee, then."

Chapter Thirty

July 11, 2009

Joe Zabrauskis drove the 323 miles from his Northbrook, Illinois, home to his northern Wisconsin property in six and a half hours, including his stop for lunch in Green Bay at Brett Favre's Steak House. He loved the place. A life-long Chicago Bears fan, Joe liked nothing better than entering enemy territory and finding Packer backers to josh with. They were almost always good-humored and disrespectful to people they referred to as FIBs, "Fucking Illinois Bastards," providing great fun for Joe, an Illinois native with longtime ties to the Badger State.

Zabrauskis began to anticipate his departure days in advance. Rising early as he always did before going to the main office of his extensive beer distributorship, he drank coffee in the early morning mist on the back patio of his house, imagining that he was already smelling the northern pines, hearing the sounds of gently lapping lake water that awaited him.

The solitude he enjoyed this one summer week each year served to invigorate him, restore his spirits for the other fifty-one. For many previous years, Joe had joined male relatives in Wisconsin during fall deer season. Then had come a marked increase in hunting accidents involving both livestock and humans. Each autumn, some cows would be fatally misidentified as deer by hung-over, once-a-year hunters. Some large dogs, too. Five years before, a man had somehow mistaken his next-door neighbor for a doe and shot her dead from a distance of two-hundred feet. After that, Joe acceded to his wife's pleas to give up these autumn adventures. He told her he would confine himself to his summer getaways.

Joe arrived at the cabin that had been in his family for half a century in late afternoon. By the time dusk dropped onto Lake Cedar, he had caught a walleyed pike legal sized enough to be his dinner, plus several less sizeable bass that he returned to the cold, dark water.

The cabin was isolated on a two-acre stretch of lakefront property, blocks from the nearest home. Across the lake there were hundreds of acres of state-owned land that could not be privately developed, thus promising protection from boating crazies and Jet Ski enthusiasts from the cities.

As was his custom on these trips, Joe erected a small tent in the clearing north of the old cabin. He kept his beer and perishables inside the building in the refrigerator, an appliance still referred to by his mother as "the icebox." When he was a boy, there was nothing he enjoyed more than sleeping outside at night, hearing the wind riffling the nearby pines, loon calls resonant across the water. The week after Christmas, when Zabrauskis brought his family north for a vacation of cross-country skiing, ice fishing, snow mobiles and watching college football bowl games, the seven-room cabin was put to full use. But not when he was alone on the property in the summer, his favorite time.

Even though he was sleeping outside, Zabrauskis spent much of his first night airing out the musty cabin, sweeping up mouse droppings, washing the windows. He hated to think of this cherished place being anything but in great shape.

Joe's practice was to rise very early each day, make a fire in the outdoor pit, and cook a big breakfast of bacon, eggs, and brew coffee improved by a shot of Christian Brothers brandy, a staple of many northern Wisconsin diets. After scouring Lake Cedar for fish from his small motor boat until late morning, he'd go into nearby Antigo for a couple of glasses of beer and a sandwich at Weasel and Betty's tavern. Everyone there knew him,

Big Joe from Chicago. Early in the afternoon, he returned to the cabin for a nap. His favorite time of the day was late afternoon, when he went out again to fish, this time from a canoe in the pools of water beneath a stretch of overhanging pines on the west end of the lake.

After spending most of the day replacing some rotted portions of his pier, Orth was relaxing inside his cabin, watching a DVD of Ultimate Fighting Championship highlighted bouts. He looked on appreciatively, gripping his bottle of Leinie, as that brutal sport's current heavyweight champion, a big, blond man from nearby northern Minnesota, dismantled his opponent. Orth's cell phone went off just as the bout concluded in a cascade of loser's blood.

"Yeah."

Sanderson said, "He's there, Number Four."

"Got you."

Two hours later, Orth followed Sanderson's directions to Zabrauskis' remote cabin. He parked two miles down the road in a stand of trees just off an old logging road. Put on his camouflage outfit, blackened his face, and began almost two days of boring, scrupulous observation of his target, equipped with binoculars, a sleeping bag, dried food, and a vault of patience. The second night, he used his cell phone to call Sanderson. As usual, they kept it short. "Things okay?" Sanderson said.

"He's in my sights. I've got it figured. I'll be done by dawn." Orth buried the phone under a tall pile of brush.

Observing Zabrauskis for those two days, Orth had come to admire the man's discipline, sense of order, qualities that Orth respected. Joe Z followed the same routine each night. He set the outdoor fire that he would light the next morning, prepared the battered iron coffee pot to be set upon the grate over the flames. "This guy is as regular as a master sergeant," Orth whispered to himself the second night. "All the better."

Zabrauskis that evening had caught a bunch of pan fish. He cleaned them and fried them in the black iron skillet he always used for his meals here. After dinner, the big man sat in a camp chair next to the fire pit, watching the night advance, completely content in his northern retreat. He stomped the glimmering fire out at just before eleven. Orth watched as Zabrauskis stripped to his shorts and duck walked through the flaps of the canvas tent, just as he had the previous two nights at about this time.

Orth waited until half past midnight. He slipped on his night vision goggles and stepped out of the nearby woods on his way to the tent. A cloud mass briefly obscured the bright moon, and Orth dropped to his belly and crept forward. He heard snoring as he neared the tent entrance. Carefully parting the tent's opening, he saw Joe Z deeply asleep on his side. Orth crawled forward. He stopped when he was next to the big man. Orth reached over his shoulder and took from his back pack the weapon he'd brought. He had thoroughly tested it during his two days and nights of waiting and observing. It did, indeed, transmit a powerful electrical pulse affecting the nervous system. Orth was convinced that this was the real deal, what police officers all over the country were now grateful to have in their hands. The recipient of voltage like this was immediately rendered incapacitated.

Zabrauskis stirred, sensing something. He had been sleeping on his left side. He turned his head and saw the night-goggled, black-faced figure crouched beside him to the right. For an instant, Joe Z imagined he was in the midst of a science fiction-driven dream. He shook his head to clear it. He felt a pressure on his back as he attempted to turn over.

Orth was quick. He jammed the Taser X21 into the middle of Joe Z's back and pulled the trigger. Zabrauskis shuddered as he was hit by the electrical charge, then lay still.

Orth turned the Zabrauskis onto his back. He straddled his torso. Zabrauskis was stunned and helpless. Orth grabbed the small pillow that had lain under the big man's head and clamped it down over his face. For a second or two, the powerful old lineman instinctively attempted to fight his way out of this death trap. No go. Orth pressed down and took Joe Z's breath away.

As he'd predicted to Sanderson, Orth was out of the woods well before dawn. He drove the speed limit south, not to his cabin, but to Wittenburg, where he pulled into a highway rest stop and went to sleep. When he awoke, he had breakfast at popular local diner. Before leaving Wittenburg, he bought ten pounds of the famous smoked bacon sold at the Neuschke's outlet. It was a breakfast treat once described by the late *New York Times* critic R. W. Apple as the "beluga of bacon." Orth never read what he knew to be the leftist *Times*, but he enjoyed this smoked meat. He'd seen the quote from Apple in the meat company's promotional material. Orth found it humorous that he was for the first and only time in his life in agreement with the fucking liberal media, at least on this subject.

At the end of the week, when Joe Z's frantic family asked local authorities to locate him, animals had gnawed Joe Z to little but bones. The report was "dead for two or three days, cause unknown."

Chapter Thirty-one

July 17, 2009

Most of the way on their trip to downtown Chicago was taken up with talk about Joe Zabrauskis' sad fate, reported in that morning's newspapers. Jack drove as Cindy speculated about the "chances that four guys, four friends, of about the same age, could pass away in such a short period of time. I don't get it."

"Neither can I," Doyle said. Earlier in the week, Doyle had persuaded Cindy to take a weekend off from her rigorous, punishing schedule. "We'll go to Grant Park to the Chicago Jazz Fest, then have dinner in the Loop. What do you say?"

She said yes, after her mother agreed to give up church bingo to stay home with Tyler; after Doc Jensen told her, "Enjoy yourself. You work too hard."

Her decision delighted Doyle. Glancing sideways at Cindy, Doyle thought, *She looks so good this afternoon, I wish I had a convertible to show her off in.* Cindy was dressed casually in a short-sleeved, light blue dress, light brown sandals. Her hair was tied in the pony tail she used when working horses in the dawn racetrack hours.

He parked in the huge underground garage off Michigan Avenue. Cindy was excited. She hadn't been to this part of the city for several years and had not seen the Grant Park additions, including the famous "Cloud Gate," or "the Bean" as it was called, the massive glimmering sculpture where delighted visitors waved at their distorted reflections.

"These other two pavilions are new this year," Jack pointed out. "They're temporary. Commissioned to commemorate the 1909 Plan of Chicago laid out by Burnham."

"Who was Burnham?" she asked, putting her arm through his as they strolled.

"Daniel Burnham was a famous urban planner early in the twentieth century here. He designed the chain of parks that run along Lake Michigan. Big public works program. Burnham said, 'Make no little plans.' He sure didn't. Chicago has benefited ever since. There's no American city, maybe none in the world, that has as much open lakefront acreage running for miles and miles."

"I want to go back to the Bean," she said. "I should have brought my camera." She waved at herself in the reflection, then clapped her hands in delight. Dozens of other visitors were doing the same.

Doyle said, "Wait here." He trotted west across Michigan to a Walgreen's. He was back within minutes with a throwaway Kodak camera and had no trouble persuading a Japanese gentleman to take their picture. "This is great," Cindy said. "I've got to get out more. When I can afford it," she added, so softly Doyle did not hear her.

The main stage Jazz Fest music began at five o'clock. Doyle had scored some good seats from the woman in charge, an old friend, Penny Tyler. He and Cindy were three rows from the front, center aisle. The Kelly Brand Sextet kicked things off in rousing fashion, followed by the trio of the amazing Chicago pianist Willie Pickens. Then came one of Doyle's favorites, Eric Schneider and his quintet, Schneider being one of the latest in the long line of tremendous Chicago saxophone players.

At intermission, Cindy's head was on Jack's shoulder. When the crowd rose to move about, she shook herself awake. "Hey, I'm sorry," she said. "I loved the music. But that's what happens when you're used to getting up at four in the morning, getting to sleep early at night. Who plays next?"

"It's one of those Free Jazz groups that the *Trib's* critic keeps promoting. Not for me. Sound to me like lost souls screeching. Shall we go? Maybe we can get to dinner a little earlier than the reservation."

"I'm ready if you are."

They worked their way through the large crowd. Minutes later, they were at their table in Trattoria 10 on Wabash Avenue. "I've been here," Doyle said. "You won't go wrong, whatever you order. They have terrific ravioli dishes here. I wish," he smiled, "I could have brought Ralph Tenuta here with us."

Cindy said, "Why?"

Doyle went on to detail the unusual, Kentucky-cookbook dominated menu schedule in the Tenuta home. Cindy laughed as she listened. "He misses his Italian dishes, but he won't revolt?"

"That's right. Our good friend, trainer Tenuta, goes along with his Rosa."

Cindy said, "Ralph is such a nice man."

"Here's to him," Doyle said, touching his wine glass to Cindy's in a toast to Tenuta.

They exited Trattoria 10 at nearly nine. In the Accord, driving north on the Outer Drive, past Navy Pier and its giant, revolving Ferris wheel, Doyle said, "Let me ask you something. How about you staying in the city at my place tonight? You don't have to exercise horses tomorrow morning. Why not just take it easy?"

Cindy looked out her window at the rippling white waves of Lake Michigan. She went into her purse for her cell phone. "Mom," she said, "I'll be staying in the city tonight. Where? At Jack's place."

Doyle could hear Wilma's cackling on the other end of the phone. He looked over at Cindy. She was blushing right through her tan. "Ma, stop it. Tyler's asleep? Good. See you in the morning." She put the phone back in her purse. She said, "I didn't bring an overnight bag, you know."

"There's a 7-11 on my corner. You can get a toothbrush there."

Cindy grinned. "I don't imagine they sell night gowns there, right?"

"Why would you need one?"

"Why, indeed?" Cindy said.

Chapter Thirty-two

July 19, 2009

Arnie Rison, Mike Barnhill, and Marty Higgins were met in the foyer of the White Eagle by the widow. This traditional gathering place for members of Chicago's large Polish-American community hosted banquets, wedding receptions, business meetings and, today, post-funeral gatherings for the family and mourners. Little Louise Zabrauskis, about half the size of her recently deceased husband, hugged each of the three men. "Thanks again for being pall bearers. And thank you, Arnie, for what you said about my Joe." Arnie put his arm around the widow. "I meant every word," he said.

Joe Z's funeral at St. Stanislaus Kostka Catholic Church on Chicago's near west side had been a sellout. Zabrauskis' five children, seven grandchildren, six sisters, a brother, and his parents sat with Louise in the front pews of the old church, centerpiece of the first Polish parish established in Chicago, a building designed by an Irish-born architect from Brooklyn who was also responsible for the city's famed Holy Name Cathedral.

They heard Father Joe Bigalski say the memorial Mass. Listened as two of the Zabrauskis children, Jim and Jack, remembered their father. Heard Arnie describe the lengthy friendship he had enjoyed with the former UW lineman who had been found dead in the northern Wisconsin woods.

Arnie recounted their first meeting in Madison as freshmen in the same dorm. The autumn afternoons Arnie watched his buddy mow down Big Ten running backs attempting to run off tackle. Their many days of horse playing, and the later Saratoga bonanza, and The Badger Express. "Joe took everything in stride and in good humor and, for such a big man, with great gentleness," Rison said. "He was as good a friend, as good a man, as anyone could ever know."

The oldest eulogist was Gene Rafferty, Joe Z's line coach at UW. "Joey was one of the strongest, toughest, smartest, and nicest football player I ever coached," Rafferty said. "We kept in touch over the years. This," the old coach said, gesturing at the coffin, "leaves a hole in my heart."

On his way out of the church, Arnie was clapped on the back by five of Joe Z's former Wisconsin teammates. Three of them limped down the aisle as honorary pallbearers behind the coffin being carried by Arnie, Mike, and Marty on one side. Three of Joe Z's tall, sturdy sons were on the other side. When they left the foyer of the air-conditioned church, the late summer heat slapped them.

Burial was in All Saints Polish National Catholic Cemetery on West Higgins Road in northwest Chicago. When the last goodbye had been uttered, most of the numerous mourners entered their cars and followed funeral director Stanley Pocius and his assistants down North Milwaukee Avenue to the White Eagle.

The Zabrauskis family, Father Bigalski, and the pall bearers were ushered to the head of the long buffet line. Rison said to Barnhill, "Wouldn't our man loved to have had a shot at all this?"

Louise Zabrauskis heard him. She turned around, smiling. "You know Joe's favorite saying when we'd come here? *Jedzcie, pijcie, i popuszczajcie pasa.* Eat, drink, and loosen your belts." Arnie patted her on the shoulder as she turned to stand beside her daughter Sophia.

The Zabrauskis family paid just polite attention to the lavish buffet spread of hunter's stew, three kinds of salads, potato and cheese *pierogies,* stuffed cabbage, *kielbasa*, poppy cake and cheese cake. So did the three remaining members of The Significant Seven. They put small portions on their plates and walked away from the buffet line. Rison said, "Let's go down that hall. There's a room we can sit in in private."

"I need a drink," Barnhill said. "Arnie, take my plate. What do you guys want? I'll bring them back." Rison and Higgins both said "The usual." Barnhill returned to the main room and headed for one of the large, busy bars.

Higgins and Rison sat in silence, their food plates put aside. When Barnhill came back with the drinks, he handed them out. Raising his Manhattan, he said, "Here's to our Joe. May he rest in peace." All three touched glasses.

Rison walked to the window overlooking the crowded White Eagle parking lot. Not turning around, he said, "What do you two think?"

"About what, Arnie?" Higgins answered.

"About the fact that the three of us are sitting here after the fourth funeral of best friends of ours that we've gone to in the last couple of months. I lie awake at night thinking about this. Henry, Steve, Chris, and now Joey, all gone. Like that. Henry drowns. Steve collapses in a restaurant having eaten a goddam bagel he was allergic to. Chris drives off his road going home? Chris, the accountant, one of the most cautious little men you'd ever meet? And Joey, Joe the Bear, eaten by one?"

Rison thumped his empty tumbler down on the window sill. "There's some shit going on here, my friends. I don't know what the hell it is. But we better find out. Soon."

Barnhill jumped up, almost dropping his drink. "Damn right we better find out. There's no odds that say this could be happening to the partnership, guys in their fifties dying off like this. But who would want to kill us?" He spilled some of his Manhattan. "Christ, I haven't spilled a drink since high school. This is all really getting to me," said the old fullback.

They looked up when there was a knock on the door. Barnhill opened it. "Hey, Paulie, come on in," he said to the oldest of Joe Zabrauskis' large sons. Barnhill put his arm around Paul's broad shoulders as he walked him into the room. The young man's face was flushed. He had a can of Old Style in his big right hand."I've got to talk to you guys." Rison motioned him to sit down on the couch next to him.

Paul Zabrauskis pulled out a handkerchief and wiped his forehead. "Paulie, what's up?" Rison said.

"I've just gotten a going-over out there from the other widows of the partnership. Not my Mom. She's still pretty zoned out over this funeral deal. I'm talking the wives—no, the widows—of Judge Toomey, Mr. Charous, Mr. Carson. They got my brothers and me in a corner. Asking us, what the hell's going on here?' Four deaths of old friends in, what, three months? Your wife, Mike," he said, looking at Barnhill, "she says what's happened is 'against all odds.' How could I not agree with her?"

Paulie drained the last of his beer. He crumpled the can like it was a piece of cellophane. "What do you guys think?" he said. "What's going on here?"

Rison reached into this pocket for a Marlboro, lit it quickly, and inhaled, setting off a series of violent coughs. "Damn, Arnie," Higgins said, "when are you going to give up those things? You're the only guy I know our age who still smokes."

With his cough finally under control, Rison said to Paulie, "If The Significant Seven is being eliminated, what's the reason? It can't be women, or jealousy, or revenge. Not that I can think of, anyway. Even if some nut was angry enough to bump one of us off, where do the others figure in?" He reached in his pocket for another cigarette, but when he saw the looks on their faces, he stopped. "What do you guys think?"

"You hear about stuff like this," Higgins answered. "Sometimes in the papers, sometimes on television. Whenever there is a question of 'why', the answer most of the time is money. Or maybe it's some crackpot who envies or resents our success. Face it, we were about the luckiest horse players in the world. It could be some jealous nut. Who knows? The extent of human lunacy, who could tell?"

Rison said, "How could it possibly be money in our case? Sure, the recession has hit hard. Hell, I could hardly give away cars off my lots these last few months. But we've made hundreds of thousands with our Pick Six that led to The Badger Express. The contract is intact."

"You mean the last survivor part?" Higgins said.

"Yes. The last surviving member of the seven turns The Badger Express' profits into a foundation that saves and cares for retired, discarded thoroughbreds. It's there in black and white, just as we agreed years ago. If Marty and I die before you, Mike, you're in charge of the money. And vice versa. I guess twice vice versa."

They sat in silence for a few minutes.

"Look," Rison said, "with just three of us left, am I the only one thinking that maybe one of us could be causing these deaths? Yeah, yeah, it sounds nuts. The way we've been friends for more than thirty years. The way the contract is set up. But I can't be the only one who's thinking crazy thoughts like that." He finished off his Manhattan, not looking at the other two. Paulie Zabrauskis looked at Rison in amazement.

Higgins shook his head. Barnhill said, "You aren't the only one that's thought about that, Arnie. But I don't believe that possibility for a fucking minute."

"Neither do I," Rison said. "We've been great friends for more than thirty years. I can't imagine one of us moving against the others."

"Neither can I, Arnie," Barnhill said. "Me, either," added Higgins.

The partners stood up and huddled in the middle of the room in a clumsy three-man embrace. Paul Zabrauskis got to his feet and watched them.

"We'd better go and spend some time with Louise and the rest of your family, Paulie," Rison said.

Chapter Thirty-three

July 23, 2009

Doyle parked his car next to Tenuta's barn shortly after seven. The area was bustling. Grooms and hot walkers were leading horses onto two large vans. There were some two dozen runners involved. The air was filled with horse sounds, conversations and orders in both English and Spanish from the men and women carrying out an apparently hurried evacuation.

Tenuta came out of his office and said good morning to Doyle, who asked, "What's going on, Ralph? Aren't those all Paul Barry's horses?"

"They were. They aren't anymore." Tenuta shook his head in disgust. "Some of these guys never learn, damn them."

Paul Barry, Doyle knew, currently ranked among the leading trainers at Heartland Downs. He was a veteran horseman who had escaped the ranks of professional mediocrity for the first time just this season with an explosion of winners. For the first time in Barry's long career, horses he trained starting finishing first at a remarkable rate, not just for Barry, but for any trainer. Their improvement was so dramatic it was bound to attract scrutiny. Evidently, the scrutiny had proved disastrous for the middle-aged bachelor from Minnesota.

"Barry is out of business," Tenuta explained. "The stewards have suspended him 'indefinitely.' His owners, mad as hell, decided to move their stock elsewhere. Half of those horses are going to Oklahoma, the rest to Louisiana."

Doyle said, "I haven't heard anything about this. What's the story, Ralph?"

"It'll be in tomorrow's *Racing Daily*, I guarantee you. When Barry all of a sudden started winning races in bunches, like he never had before, a lot of guys got suspicious. Still, all his winners passed their post-race drug tests. Time after time, winner after winner. The racing commission chemists never reported a positive finding on one of them!

"Then, Ed Arenas, the state steward here, ordered a surprise search of Barry's barn office. The security people swarmed over it yesterday afternoon. Know what they found? You won't believe it," Tenuta said.

"So tell me."

Tenuta said, "They found several containers of cobra venom."

"Cobra venom? What's that for?" Doyle was not taking this seriously. "You use it when you're shooting craps trying to get somebody to roll snake eyes?"

"Jack, this isn't anything to laugh about. Cobra venom. I talked to two veterinarians this morning, asking them the same question. 'What for?' Both told me it was, I'm trying to remember this, 'an unregulated neurotoxin.' It works as a powerful pain killer. The damn stuff never shows up in the tests they're using now. But it is very much an illegal medication under all horse racing laws in the world."

Doyle thought about this. "I get it. It can make a sore horse run better." He paused. "Can it mask other drugs as well?"

"I've got no idea about that. Could be. One way or the other, they're going to nail Paul Barry for possession of that stuff. Cobra venom! Who could make it up?"

They walked into Tenuta's office. The trainer turned on the coffee pot. His dejection was obvious. "This Barry thing is going to be a big story, in the papers, on TV. It's going to hurt all of racing. Makes me sick, Jack."

Doyle said, "Ralph, this Barry isn't the first guy caught with illegal drugs."

"Of course not. There will always be some smart asses looking for an edge, an angle, some drug that can't be detected. They almost *always* get caught. But the damage they do is to the reputations of all the rest of us, the guys who've always played by the rules, and never tried juicing their horses, guys like me, who still get branded when the Paul Barry stories hit. The papers will say 'horse racing scandal.' Hell, there's more damn larceny in the banking business than there has ever been in horse racing. But people who don't know us don't know that. It's a damn shame, Jack."

Four hours later all of the Tenuta stable's morning work had been done. Horses worked, horses cooled out, watered, fed. Doyle and Ralph were in Tenuta's office, working on the entry schedule for the weekend, when Travis Hawkins poked his head in.

"I've got two on my schedule for you tomorrow, right, men?"

Tenuta said, "Right, Travis."

Hawkins said, "Are you both coming to my party tomorrow night?"

"Bet your life, Travis," Tenuta said, "Rosa and I will both be there. Looking forward to it."

Hawkins looked at Doyle. "Jack?"

Doyle said, "Travis, I don't know anything about your party. This is the first I've heard of it. Thanks for the invite."

Hawkins smiled. "Ralph, tell your man here what it's all about. I'll see you fellows there." He waved goodbye.

"You're in for a good feed, Jack, I'll tell you that," Tenuta said. "Travis makes the best barbequed ribs you'll ever taste. His wife Taliyah produces side dishes to remember. Corn on the cob in the husk, a killer potato salad, tomatoes she grows on their property, an amazing sweet potato pie. I'm getting hungry as I think about it."

Doyle said, "How do I get to Hawkins' home?"

Tenuta gave him directions. "Things get going early in the evening. Are you going to bring Cindy with you?"

"Nope. We were supposed to go to a movie, but she promised Tyler she'd take him to Six Flags Great America. Her mother's going, too. Then they're going to hit the Gurnee Mills shopping center before heading home. I'll happily miss that scene."

Tenuta said, "All right. See you at Travis'."

Chapter Thirty-four

July 24, 2009

Doyle bought a case of Heineken before starting his long drive to Travis Hawkins' Lake County home. He never showed up at social events new to him empty handed. He even pulled into a roadside vegetable and flower stand on Highway 12 and bought an expensive plant for Mrs. Hawkins. It was a lovely summer afternoon. He thought of Cindy, Tyler, and Wilma at the undoubtedly crowded Great America amusement park and smiled at his good luck.

The driveway was already almost filled with vehicles when Doyle turned in. He saw Doc Jensen's truck, a bunch of cars with Heartland Downs parking stickers affixed to them. He could smell the enticing aroma of burning meat, hear a stereo system from which came Cannonball Adderly's classic song "Mercy."

"All *right*," Doyle said, walking up the driveway, "I think I'm going to enjoy this scene."

When Hawkins spotted Doyle lugging the case of beer with the potted plant on top, he grinned and hurried out from behind the two massive black cookers he was monitoring, steel half-barrels designed for barbequing. "Jack, you didn't have to," he said, picking up the plant.

"Enjoy it, Travis," Doyle kidded back.

Hawkins took Doyle around the yard to meet Taliyah. She gratefully accepted the plant. "Thank you, Jack. It's great to meet you. You probably know most of the people here." Doyle smiled at Ralph and Rosa Tenuta, Doc Jensen, a bunch of younger men from the Heartland Downs racing office who were clustered around the two half-barrels of beer. "I know a lot of them," he said. He waved across the yard at horse owner Steve Holland, whom he had gotten to know during his stint at Monee Park.

The next hour was spent socializing and playing. Doyle pitched horse shoes against Hawkins, and got drubbed. "I should have known you'd be good at this," he told the farrier. The Hawkins children invited him to play bean bag. They were as good at that as their father was in tossing the elements of his trade. When Shontanette Hunter, his former colleague at Monee Park, arrived, he went to greet her and her husband, Cecil Tate, a Chicago attorney.

Doyle shook hands with Cecil, then hugged Shontanette. "You look good, Jack," she said. "I hear you're working up at Heartland Downs. Do you like it?"

"I do. I'm working for a great guy, Ralph Tenuta." He paused. "How are things at Monee?"

Shontanette gave him a sharp look. "Things are fine, Jack. The video slots have saved the track. Business is great. So is Celia," she added.

"I'm glad to hear that, Shontanette," he said, referring to the widowed co-owner and operator of Monee Park, perhaps the loveliest lady he'd ever known. "Very glad," he added.

Doyle sat down for dinner with the Tenutas at one of the numerous tables Travis had positioned around his property. The sun had dwindled and the air changed, a cool breeze now in gentle motion. "These ribs are fantastic," Doyle said.

"Every year," Tenuta answered. "Travis uses his secret formula rub on them, then sauces them after they've cooked. The son of a gun won't tell me what the rub recipe is." He broke off abruptly. "Oh, Jesus," he said, "there's Ollie."

"Who?"

Rosa scowled. "The poor man's Hugh Hefner," she said. "Look at those bimbos with him."

Doyle saw a bespectacled middle-aged man wearing a straw boater, blue seersucker sport coat, khaki shorts not quite covering his knobby white knees, walking arm in arm with two much younger women, both in skimpy shorts and tee shirts, great looking items. "He calls his girl friends his 'nieces,'" Rosa said. "There are new ones every couple of months."

"Ralph," Doyle said, "who is this guy?"

Tenuta cleaned the meat off another rib bone before answering. "I trained for Ollie O'Keefe for almost three years. He has a lot of money. I mean, a *lot* of money. His old man, now dead, founded a very successful Chicago insurance company that insured, at very low rates, thousands of black people on the South Side. The old man never had anything to do with horses. But Ollie, the heir, loves racing. And I had horses for him. For awhile."

He took a sip of iced tea. "Ollie was a crazy man. Fun, very generous, the biggest spender I've ever known. Whenever we won a race, Ollie would run down the clubhouse steps from our box shouting to people in their seats, 'C'mon, get your picture taken with the winner. Everybody's welcome!' And he meant it. He'd invite fans, complete strangers, to come into the winner's circle with him. This went on for most of one summer, and we won a bunch of races. Finally, Bob Benoit, the track photographer, came to me. He said, 'Ralph, I can't deal with that man anymore. It's dangerous for me and the winning horse to have all these people crowded in there. It's a mob scene. A lot of them order copies of the photo I take with them in it, but hardly any of them pay for what they ordered.'

"Ollie, when he heard this, offered to Benoit to make up the difference between those who paid and didn't. He was like that. I mean, Ollie was as generous a guy as you would ever meet. But Benoit said, 'No thanks. I can't keep track of all these people, and I don't want to hire a bookkeeper.'"

Doyle said to Rosa, "What was so bad about this guy? He paid his bills. Had fun. Tried to share the fun. What was the problem?"

"You tell him, Ralph," Rosa said.

Tenuta said, "Jack, he almost killed me with his life style. His fun wore me out. The man is a boozer like I've never seen. You remember how in some of those old movies, men wore what they called smoking jackets?"

"You're dating yourself, Ralph," Doyle said. "But I think I know what you're talking about."

Tenuta said, "Ollie O'Keefe didn't have a smoking jacket, he had drinking jackets. He's probably got one on now."

The trainer stood up to demonstrate and opened his sport coat. He pointed to the lining on the left side. "Here, in Ollie's specially tailored coats, are twelve little slots, or small pockets. On the right side, another twelve. Two rows of six on each interior lining.

"What were they for? They were for holding those little miniature bottles of booze, like they have on airplanes. Ollie kept what he called his 'brown beauties' on the left side, mostly bourbon, some brandies and scotch, and his 'silver sisters' on the right side. Vodkas, gin, always at least one sambuca. He drank out of that jacket from morning to night. Never got drunk. Kept fresh supplies in his car. Well, it wasn't just a car, it was a Lincoln Town Car driven by his chauffeur, bodyguard, attendant, named, I am not kidding, Igor. I never knew Igor's last name. Never wanted to. He was this big Russian hulk. Scary as hell."

Doyle said, "Okay. But what are you saying, Ollie affecting your marriage, that stuff? What was that all about?" He looked at Rosa. She looked away. "Let him tell."

"My wife is a very tolerant woman," Tenuta said. "And I am not much of a drinker. But Ollie would insist that he and I go out after the races. Drinks, dinner. More drinks. Maybe some Rush Street action. Ollie paid for everything. He told jokes, he sang Irish songs, he knew everybody, everybody knew him at the late night piano bars, oh, Jack. I felt like I had to go along with him at the time. I was training just twenty horses, and fifteen of them were Ollie's. I was getting home just in time to get up and go to work. Man was wearing me out.

"One night—no, morning—Igor drops me at my house. I'd been dozing in the back of the Lincoln. Igor dropped off Ollie and his girl friends at Ollie's house in Wilmette before that. I get to my door and Rosa yanks it open before I can even fumble with the key. She's in her housecoat. I thought she'd be steaming. And I wouldn't have blamed her. But all she says, in a real quiet voice, is 'You should have been to the barn by now. Your horses are waiting.' She turns around and slams the door. Who could blame her? I got into my car and drove to the track. I felt like crap. In a number of ways." He stopped to put his hand on Rosa's.

"Next day, when Ollie and a couple of his 'nieces' show up about noon, I tell him, 'Ollie, you're a great guy, great owner, a generous man, but I can't keep up with you. I'll help you find a new trainer. I want all of your horses out my barn by the end of next week.'

"The funny thing was, it was almost like Ollie saw this coming. He just smiled at me. He wasn't mad. He reached into this jacket and took an entry from the 'silver side' and polished it off. He said to me, 'Ralphie, okay. We've done very well together. But I respect your decision. No hard feelings.' That's the last I saw of him until this afternoon. But he sent me what he called a severance check—for ten thousand! Unbelievable guy."

Rosa said, "That was his one saving quality as far as I'm concerned. I hated the way he made fun of his ex-wives."

Ralph grinned until Rosa shot him a look. He said, "Ollie was mostly Irish, but he claimed he had some Cherokee in him on his mother's side. So he'd come up with what he called his 'Injun names' for women he'd divorced, or who'd divorced him. There were three. He called one Princess Spreading Butt, another Princess Wampum Spender, the third Princess Flapping Jaws."

Doyle said, "Does he still own horses?"

"Yeah," Tenuta said. "When we parted ways, Ollie was out of racing for three or four years. He financed and produced two movie bombs in Hollywood. When his old man died, he inherited another pile of money."

"Not a pile," Rosa interjected, "a big mound of money."

"To answer your question, Jack, yes, Ollie's got a small stable at Heartland Downs. Buck Norman just started training for him. Buck's already starting to look the worse for wear dealing with Ollie's life style."

Doyle saw O'Keefe's small entourage expand by two more young women as it moved toward the stretch limo where the stolid Igor awaited. Ollie turned and doffed his skimmer to Travis, who waved goodbye. Then he got into the back seat with all the women.

Rosa said, "I want to go and say hello to Travis and Taliyah. I'll be back in few minutes. Then we better go home, Ralph."

Tenuta was thoughtful for a few moments before he said to Doyle, "You know what? The hardest thing about the training business isn't training the horses, it's training the people that own them. Now, I'm not talking about Ollie here. He paid his bills on time, which made him one of the exceptions, and he never questioned what races I put his horses in.

"But over the years, I've had owners who would call me in the middle of the night with suggestions, or just to complain. Guys, like Slow Pay Sal, who always were late with the money. I wish I would have known some of the current economic double-talk years ago. I could have said to an owner whose beloved horse stunk, 'You, madam, are facing a period of illiquidity because your horse is as slow to run as you are to pay.'"

Doyle laughed. "Illiquidity, yeah. Don't you love it? When the stock market fell down the shaft, my broker would tell me, 'The sell-off continues.' Hello. The sell-off? Do you mean the evaporation of my money?"

Ralph got up from the table when he saw Rosa waving to him. "You going to stick around, Jack?"

"Naw, I'll thank my host and hostess and see you in the a.m., boss," Doyle said. "This was a good time."

Chapter Thirty-five

July 24, 2009

Returned from the Hawkins picnic, Doyle found a message on his home phone machine. He heard Damon Tirabassi's voice. "Jack, we need to talk soon. Karen and I will meet you at that Greek joint near you at six tomorrow morning, so you won't be too late getting to the track after that. She and I have a meeting with Special Agent Goodman at ten o'clock. We need to know where we are with the sponging case. This is important. Don't let us down, Jack."

Petros' Restaurant was bustling even at five to six in the morning. Doyle arrived first, greeting Petros' wife with his usual kiss on the cheek, signaling waitress Darla to start his breakfast regimen. Doyle had eaten here at least three times a week for a few years, but his current racetrack assignment had cut back on his patronage of Petros'. The owner noticed. Peering out from the kitchen, Petros, who considered himself a dead ringer for Telly Savalas, shouted, "People, get ready, the big shot famous Jack Doyle is here."

"Stay back there with the grease, El Greco," Doyle shot back. They were both practiced in this kind of affectionately insulting exchanges.

The FBI agents walked in a few minutes later. Karen ordered coffee, grapefruit juice, and a toasted bagel with chive cream cheese. Doyle nodded approvingly. He said to the waitress, "My usual, Darla my dear."

"And you, young man," Darla said to Tirabassi.

"An egg, basted, one slice of dry wheat toast. Just a glass of water with that. I'm watching my weight."

Eyebrows up, Darla murmured, "I've been here eighteen years and never written an order that skimpy." She flounced toward the kitchen order window.

Tirbassi said, "We haven't heard anything from you, Jack. We check phone messages and e-mails twice a day. Nothing. That's why we asked to meet you this morning. What is going on? Have you found out anything about the spongings? We're under a lot of pressure to move this along."

Doyle waited as Darla returned to fill their coffee cups. "Let's eat, then we'll talk," Doyle said. Their plates were soon set before them. Tirabassi looked at Doyle's meal with a mixture of envy and amazement. It was a thick cheese and ham omelet, four pieces of crisp bacon positioned next to a two-layer stack of syrup-covered French toast. Darla set his side order of hash browns to the left of Doyle's full plate. "Everything, okay, folks?"

Karen spread cream cheese on her bagel. Doyle looked appreciatively at her. "You look nice and tanned, Karen. You still in that volleyball league?"

"Yes. We're in first place, as a matter of fact. Undefeated. I'm playing doubles with Holly Stanton. We were on the team at Wisconsin. She's good."

"Folks," Tirabassi said, "could we get down to business here?"

"What the hell is our business?" Doyle shot back. "Me flapping around at the racetrack in futility? I haven't gotten a sniff of the sponger." He finished the omelet and began working on the French toast. "I've gotten nowhere."

Karen said, "Can you think of anything else we might do? I know the horsemen's association has offered the $50,000 reward for information regarding the spongings. But that hasn't produced any response yet. Do have any ideas, Jack?"

"No, Karen, I don't. I also can't quite figure out why these Significant Seven guys keep dying. Four so far. All under weird circumstances. How can this be coincidence? Doesn't seem possible."

Tirabassi said, "I know about those men dying, but none of the authorities where they died have come to us. There's no indication of murder. We don't have connection to those matters. The deaths all appear to be accidental or natural."

"Four friends gone in a few months?" Doyle said. "From the same group of famous horse owners? That doesn't raise your suspicions?"

Tirabassi said, "Suspicions are the lifeblood of the tabloids. Not us."

Darla brought the check to the table. Doyle picked it up. "Damon," he said, "the only time I've seen you pick up a check was to slide it across the table to me. This time I'll save you the trouble. You get the tip. Karen," he added with a smile. "Why is it I take such pleasure in ribbing your partner?"

"Only you can answer that, Jack."

Looking at the two hard-working, dedicated agents, Doyle thought again what an unusual combination they made. Pretty Karen from Kenosha, business-like but friendly, not averse to even laughing some times at Doyle's jibes. Usually dour Damon, soccer dad and coach, driven crime buster from when he grew up in an Outfit-controlled Chicago neighborhood.

Doyle put his wallet back in his pocket. "Seriously," he said, "how long do you expect me to keep under cover at the racetrack, getting nowhere? What should I do?"

The three sat silently for nearly a minute. Karen said, "Years ago, an uncle of mine told me a story about horses. He was my mother's brother, a real Virginia gentleman, a champion equestrian rider, Randolph Bayliss. During World War Two, he enlisted in the Army. Because of his background with jumping horses and show horses, Uncle Randy was assigned to the U.S. Cavalry. Even though the Army was mechanized by then, they still had a small cavalry division based in Kansas, I think. Maybe Nebraska. It upheld the long tradition of Army cavalry, I guess.

"Anyway, Uncle Randy was made an officer and put in charge of this little base. When he got there, he was horrified. He sent a telegram to his commanding officer, saying, 'I've got one hundred wild horses here who have never seen a man. And I've got a hundred draftees from New York City who have never seen a horse. Please advise.'

"The answer," Karen continued, "came back almost at once. One word. 'Proceed.'"

Doyle and Tirabassi laughed along with her. "And that's what Uncle Randy did, Jack, and that's all we can suggest you do. Proceed."

Chapter Thirty-six

July 26, 2009

Doyle and Tenuta stood near the Heartland Downs starting gate, watching a two-year-old filly named Lucy of Artois getting an education. It was a cool morning, dawn only an hour back. The odors of mown grass, sweaty horses, and cigar smoke from the veteran head starter, Willard Dodge, mingled in the sunny air. Besides Tenuta's trainee, which he referred to as "Our Lucy," finding the French word Artois too much for him to pronounce, three other young horses were there being taught how to enter the large green starting gate, referred to as "the Iron Monster," and then wait patiently before quickly emerging from their stalls when the bell clanged and the front doors opened. Young horses, finding themselves enclosed in stalls with only two inches of space on each side of them, a rider on their backs, an assistant starter balanced on a thin ledge next to them, frequently freaked out. That's why morning lessons were necessary. "It takes most horses about a month of preparation to get them ready to come out of there and run their races," Tenuta said.

"Where do they get the guys to do this work?" Doyle asked, as he watched a half-dozen very fit-looking men working with these excitable creatures. "It's not easy work."

"Not easy?" Tenuta snorted. "That's an understatement. These men school horses every morning for a couple of hours, then come back in the afternoon to start the nine races. Most of these guys are former exercise riders, or ex-trainers. All are experienced horsemen. And they've got the scars to show it."

"What do you mean?"

Tenuta said, "I know all these guys pretty well, and if there's even one of them that hasn't been taken from the racetrack to the hospital emergency room at least once, I never heard of him. They get bruised and battered. Pulled muscles, dislocated hips, smashed fingers, broken collarbones, broken backs. It's very physical, very dangerous work. I'm always amazed they can get people to do it. Wait, I think they're getting her ready."

"Who owns Our Lucy?" Doyle said.

"Nice guy named Kirk Borland. He bred her and looks forward to seeing her make her first start. He calls me about Lucy every day."

"Is this your Lucy's first time in the gate?"

"Here," Tenuta said. "She had some pretty good gate training down on the farm in Florida where she was raised and broken. That's real important as a beginning. Because how horses break from the gate can determine whether they win or lose. If they don't settle in there, and react to the bell, and jump out at least when all the others do, they've dug themselves a big hole. Especially horses just beginning their careers."

Led forward by one of the assistant starters who'd grabbed her bridle, a young man referred to as Muzzy by starter Dodge, as in "Muzzy, go in with her," Lucy of Artois calmly approached the gate and entered stall two. "She's doing fine so far," Tenuta enthused.

"That she is," Doyle answered. He looked at his employer, who was standing with his arms folded across what Doyle noticed, for the first time, a considerably reduced paunch. Doyle frowned. "Ralph, are you losing weight?"

"Quiet, Jack. I'm concentrating on the filly."

The other three assistant starters carefully walked their two-year-olds up to the back of the gate. They led them in, then let each horse back out, stand, examine this situation which was seemingly disturbing to at least two of them, who skittered and balked before re-entering. Lucy of Artois, meanwhile, was quiet and alert in her stall.

Doyle and Tenuta looked on as a big bay colt reared up backwards, almost hauling his handler off the ground, then came down and planted his feet and lashed out with the rear ones, narrowly missing head starter Dodge, who unleashed a string of curses that sizzled through the Heartland Downs air. "Put that crazy bastard on the list," Dodge yelled to an assistant who was carrying a writing pad.

Doyle said, "What list?"

"His. Willard Dodge's. He won't let the owner of that colt enter him in a race until he's better-mannered at the gate. The trainer, Buck Norman I think, will have to keep bringing him here for schooling until Dodge okays him to race."

All four horses were finally in the gate. Dodge waited to let them get their feet and heads settled before pressing the button. The doors flew open. One of the four stepped toward the back door of his stall. Another walked out the front. Lucy of Artois and another filly shot out of the gate like old pros.

"All *right*, Jack," Tenuta said happily, slapping Doyle on the back. "See how she came out of there?" He excitedly clapped Doyle on the back again. "C'mon," he said, "I'll buy you coffee." Tenuta gave a thumbs-up to 'Our Lucy's' groom, saying, "I'll see you back at the barn, Emilio."

Walking across the infield toward the barn area and its track kitchen, Tenuta said, "What did you ask me before? I know you asked me something."

"I asked whether you were losing weight. I just noticed this morning what appears to be a weight loss on your part. Am I right?"

They dodged a tractor pulling a harrow down the main dirt track. Doyle could hear Tenuta's sigh even in the wake of the noisy maintenance machinery. "I'm still under attack at home. In the kitchen. It's that damn Kentucky cookbook Rosa's got."

Doyle said, "Aw, c'mon, Ralph, how bad could it be? You always say Rosa's a terrific cook. The meal I had at your place, it was great. Remember the Kentucky Hot Browns? I thought they were good."

Tenuta groaned at the memory. "Rosa used to be a great cook. I don't think I told you, but before we were married, I had Rosa kind of go into training with my mother. At my suggestion, if you know what I mean. Learning exactly how to do it right. How to make homemade pasta the right way, the way veal should be done. Meat and spinach ravioli, a great red sauce made with pork neck bones. Cannolini, lasagna, oh, Jack, what that woman could do in the kitchen! My Mama was a good teacher. Rosa was a good student. But now, she's into this new stuff. I've lost fifteen pounds since she started this."

Doyle turned his head so Tenuta could not see him trying to stifle his laughter. "You're not taking this seriously, are you?" the trainer said. "Let me tell you last night's fiasco. Rosa started us off with something called apple carrot soup. The vegetable was a quote broccoli ring unquote. It looked like some kind of jello mold that had sat too long. Tasted like it, too. Then she came out with the doves."

"I beg your pardon," Doyle said. "Doves?"

"Doves. Damn right. I asked her where she got them. Her friend at Keeneland, Frances, the lady who sent her the damn cookbook, knows some hunter down there who reached into his freezer and Fed-Exed the birds to us. I guess hunting doves is legal in Kentucky. Or somewhere down south. Anyway, they wound up on my dinner table," he said glumly.

They crossed the racing strip and started heading for track kitchen. Tenuta said, "Are you Catholic, Jack?"

Doyle stopped walking and looked at Tenuta. He hadn't been asked that question in years. "Raised Catholic."

"Me too," Tenuta answered. "A long time ago. The Holy Ghost is a dove, am I right? Isn't there a peace symbol dove, or something? How can people shoot and eat birds like that?"

Doyle had to turn his face away again before saying, "Ralph, what kind of a dove dish was it? Or dove recipe? You know what I mean."

"Don't make fun of this, Jack," Tenuta barked. "The little birds came in a mushroom soup casserole with cheddar cheese on top. Along with what Rosa said was sweet potato hash browns. Something called apricot horseradish sauce on the side."

Doyle was tempted to say "That's probably the best way for the little things to be presented," but he held his tongue. They walked on in silence.

Chapter Thirty-seven

July 28, 2009

Doyle flew Southwest Airlines from Midway Airport to America's capital of gambling, sin, and family-friendly resort hotels. After listening to Morty Dubinski describe on the phone his "tremendous progress" during the first two days of the current Super Handicappers Challenge, Doyle decided to visit his money, and his friend, in Las Vegas. He told Ralph Tenuta he needed "a couple of days off. My first of the meeting." Tenuta agreed. Doyle did not bother to inform Agents Engel and Tirabassi of his impending absence. Having made absolutely no progress in uncovering the Heartland Downs sponger thus far, Doyle figured a day or two away couldn't hurt.

He took a cab from McCarron Airport to the Delano Towers Hotel, site of the handicapping contest. When he hit the sidewalk, the midday heat hit him. "Jesus," Doyle said to the doorman, "what's the temperature?"

"Here?"

"Hey, wiseass, you don't look to me to be an expert on heat indices in Budapest. Yeah, here."

The doorman grinned. "One-ten in the shade. And there isn't any. Want me to take your bag?"

"No, thanks," Doyle said, handing the young man a five. "I can manage getting that far by myself."

At the registration desk, Doyle told the clerk he was a "guest of Mr. Dubinski." Morty, as a paid contestant, had been given a suite with two bedrooms on the hotel's tenth floor. "Very comfortable," Doyle said to himself as he unpacked. Then he went downstairs to find the little handicapper.

Doyle was directed to the large room devoted to horse playing. He stood in the doorway until he spotted Morty's large white head bent over a pile of papers at one the many wooden carrels, second row from the front of the room with its lectern and microphone for the contest supervisor. Each of these small, comfortable spaces contained a desk, two chairs, and a small television set, even though the room's wide walls featured enormous flat screens showing racing action from around the country. Morty, like all the rest of his rivals, was busily changing channels on the television set from racetrack to racetrack, glancing up at the wall screens, down at the papers with their trip notes, sheet numbers, and the *Racing Daily* past performance pages containing lettering, underlining, and symbols known only to themselves. With their equations and notations, some of these mounds of research materials looked like prep sheets at Las Alamos in the early stages of the development of the "Big One."

Next to Morty's carrel sat a gray-haired gent wearing a tee-shirt with "Grandpa-Pittsburgh" on its back. To the right of his television set was a framed color photo of a dozen or so young children. A string of black rosary beads hung from Grandpa Pittsburgh's neck.

Immediately to Grandpa Pittsburgh's right was a studious-looking young Chinese-American woman. Long black pigtails sprouted from under her backwards ball cap that proclaimed her to be "Pearl of the Orient." On Morty's left was a middle-aged white woman wearing a multicolored mumu large enough to protect the Wrigley Field pitcher's mound during a rain delay. She was happily conversing with the older man to her left who, Doyle thought, bore an amazing resemblance to the Grateful Dead's late Jerry Garcia.

"How I love this stuff," Doyle said. It crossed his mind, not for the first time, that the entire sport/business of horse racing was balanced on the bankrolls of folks just like this. The nation's breeding farms, lavish or modest; jockey fees, trainers' incomes, feed suppliers, manual laborers at the tracks, mutuel clerks and janitors and bartenders, all supported by a percentage of the dollars provided each day by bettors like these from Seattle to Miami and all the way in between.

Morty jumped up, smiling, when Doyle tapped him on the shoulder. "Jack, Jack, great to see you! Really great! Thanks for coming." He pumped Doyle's hand. "Did you find our room okay? I mean our suite?"

"Sure did. Very impressive, Morty." Doyle pulled a chair out from the desk. "How goes it?"

The little man beamed. "Jack, listen to this. I'm in a good position to win this whole thing. Look at the leader board up there on the front wall."

Morty, Doyle saw, was in second place in the standings. Each contestant was obligated to make fifteen mythical $2 win and place wagers each day of the three-day tournament. They could make these bets on races at any track around the nation. Morty had "started kind of slow the first day," he said. "Then I caught fire yesterday and moved into the top ten. Jack, I was so pumped I could hardly sleep last night. I just stayed up, going over and over my system figures for today. It paid off."

With only one race remaining on this, the final day of the contest, Morty trailed the leader, Mike Conway, also from Illinois, by only $10. Conway's total was $282. With two hundred fifty men and woman competing, Morty was a cinch to earn prize money.

Doyle said, "Who are you betting next, Morty?"

"A horse from Heartland Downs back home," Morty replied. "Seventh race. I like that turf filly, Tuck's Tweedie, trained by Mark Gordon. She showed speed last time out going a mile and a sixteenth. She's only going five and a half furlongs today. I like it when they drop back in distance like that. Tuck's Tweedie looks solid to me. She fits all my new system guidelines."

Doyle reviewed Tuck's Tweedie's past performances in *Racing Daily*. Her speed figures indicated she was a standout in this comparatively weak eight-horse field. "I heard Conway made his last bet of the day and got nothing," Morty whispered. "Jack, I'm in the driver's seat here."

They watched on the massive screen on the right wall as Tuck's Tweedie approached the Heartland Downs starting gate. Doyle frowned. "She's not exactly on her toes, is she?" he said. Morty's eyes were riveted on the screen. With considerable urging, Tuck's Tweedie entered her stall in the gate. The race began at once.

Sixty-five seconds later, Tuck's Tweedie struggled across the finish line in last place. There was booing from the Heartland Downs crowd. The upset winner of the race, Brody Be Good, paid $24.20, thus vaulting the woman previously in fifth place, the mumu lady next to Morty, to the contest victory. Her celebration rocked the area. With favored Tuck's Tweedie out of the money, the trifecta paid $7,898.

Morty continued to gaze up at the TV screen, as if he had just seen a re-run of another dismal portion of his betting life. Doyle kept his eye on the television as Tuck's Tweedie, her head down, body language dismal, was led away by her groom. Disgusted, Doyle got to his feet and heard the bewildered Morty say "Jack, I don't get it. My horse was a super standout in my new system. But she stopped like a bad check. And I lose the contest to my neighbor here, this hair dresser from Topeka. Nice lady, but… Is there no justice, Jack? How do you figure it?"

"I've got a good idea about what happened to your horse, Morty. And Tuck's Tweedie is stabled right next to Ralph Tenuta's horses. *Damn.*"

Tuck's Tweedie's loss dropped the anguished Morty back to fifth place in the final standings of the contest. Still, his reward of $20,000 was, as he said, "The biggest payoff of my life. Thanks, Jack, for loaning me the grand to get me here."

Doyle was happy for his friend. He didn't mention that, had Tuck's Tweedie won, Morty would have taken down the first prize of $150,000. Doyle knew Morty knew that.

The ride to Chicago, nearly from the time the plane crossed the Mississippi until it reached western Cook County, was a nightmare. The craft was buffeted by winds that caused it to bob up and down in a violent rhythm. The seatbelt sign was on. The interior lights suddenly went off. Doyle, trying to devise some kind of plan that would thwart the increasingly effective horse sponger, had his thought train thoroughly derailed over Springfield. That was when the plane stopped bouncing up and down and began going side to side like dice in a desperate crap-shooter's hand. The youngest stewardess shrieked and lurched toward a perch in the back. Just as she strapped herself in, the galley's refrigerator doors burst open, scattering bottles of wine and beer and cans of soda and juices forward down the aisle as the planed dipped downward again. The crew made no attempt to retrieve these items. People screamed with fright.

Doyle glanced at his seatmate, a young woman who had been listening to earphones and working on a spread sheet in her computer. Her pretty face was tinged with terror. She grabbed Doyle's wrist. He laid his hand across hers'. To Doyle's right, a dark complected young man was rocking back and forth in his seat, possibly in prayer or abject fear. Children began howling. Some adults, too.

Seven and one-half terrifying minutes elapsed before, with a wonderful suddenness, the plane steadied and resumed a normal trajectory. The young woman let go of Doyle's wrist. She said, "I'm Tracy Hartenstein. And I was scared shitless. Hope you didn't mind me grabbing on to you."

"No problem. I'm Jack Doyle. I was starting to say a rosary for the first time in many years when you latched on to me. It made me pray faster."

They smiled at each other as their pilot, Captain Brett Steele, came on the intercom. To Doyle, the pilot's name had a reassuring ring to it when announced following takeoff from Las Vegas.

Now, Captain Steele, after fumbling momentarily with his sound system, intoned very calmly that "That little patch of weather is all behind us, folks. Sit back and enjoy the rest of your flight."

"Thank you, Lord," Doyle said. Tracy Hartenstein took Doyle's hand again, this time in a gentler grip. "Thank Him for me, too," she said.

Twenty-four hours later the Illinois state veterinarian Mary Holliday confirmed that Tuck's Tweedie had been found to have had a sponge clogging her air passage during the previous day's race.

Chapter Thirty-eight

August 2, 2009

"Jack, this is Renee Rison. Do you have a minute?"

Doyle was driving back to Chicago after the day's races. Traffic on Willow Road was moving right along for a change. "Sure, Renee."

"I need to talk to you face to face. I have a business proposition I'd like to discuss with you. I thought maybe we could meet this week. I know you're a jazz fan." There was a pause before she said, "Would you be interested in going to Ravinia tomorrow night to hear the Lincoln Center Jazz Orchestra? Unless, of course, you're doing something with your friend Cindy."

"Actually," Doyle said, "I had already planned to be at Ravinia tomorrow night. It's a great band and leader Wynton Marsalis is a big favorite of mine." Doyle angled onto the southbound Edens Expressway before adding, "Cindy's in Kentucky this week, working horses before the Fasig-Tipton sale." He jerked his steering wheel to the side to avoid being rammed into by a small woman driving a red Cadillac Escalante, cell phone in one hand, cigarette in the other, precariously balanced on top of her steering wheel. He swore.

"What?" Renee said.

"Nothing, nothing. That was just a short comment on the driving habits of some of our fellow citizens."

She laughed. "Sounded obscene to me."

"So are the habits of many American motorists. Anyway, let's do it. I usually don't like to discuss business in a social setting. But for you and Wynton, I'll make an exception. What time should I pick you up?"

Renee said, "No, I'll meet you there. I'll ride out with some friends, but they will not join us. I guess you'll be coming from the track?"

"Right."

"Okay. I'll leave work early and pick up a picnic dinner for us. Is that okay?"

"Sounds good to me," Doyle said. "How about I bring some wine?"

"Veuve Clicquot would be nice."

Doyle winced, well aware of the cost of that famous French champagne. On the other hand, tomorrow could be a great summer night at one of his favorite Chicago area music venues. And in the company of someone who, if she had a job proposal in mind, might become his only current paying employer. "You've got it," Doyle said. "Where shall I meet you?"

"You know that staircase to the Martin Theater right behind the main entrance? I'll look for you about six. Thanks for doing this, Jack."

Doyle paid the $10 lawn admission and walked through the gate of this Chicago area treasure, Ravinia Park, now more than a century old. The thirty-six acre venue hosted nearly one-hundred and fifty events each summer. This was where George Gershwin played "Rhapsody in Blue" in 1936. So many people attended, Doyle had read, that hundreds boosted themselves up and listened while seated on the limbs of trees that surrounded the pavilion and lawn.

On the Martin Theater stairs, little Renee sat behind a large picnic basket placed on the step in front of her. She was wearing a long-sleeved white and black shirt that had The Badger Express' photo on the front, sandals, black jeans. A black sweater was tied around her neck. She was paying no attention to a much older man, sitting to her right, who was apparently trying to engage her in unwanted conversation. Above his north suburban standard-issue whale pants, a dark blue shirt bulged at waist level.

Renee stood up and gave Jack a chance to peck her cheek before she looked down at the pest next to her. "This is my bodyguard, the ex-boxer," she said. "Would you like to meet him?" The heavy set, middle-aged man hefted himself to his feet. Eyes averted, he pulled his straw hat farther down on his face. "Nice to meet you," he mumbled before sidling off.

"What was that about?" Doyle said.

"Not much. A lonely lecher with booze on his bad breath bothering me when I told him I didn't want to be bothered."

"Oh."

Renee handed Doyle the picnic basket. Lifting it, Doyle said, "Are you planning to feed the multitudes. What the hell's in here?"

She smiled. "Never mind, Jack. Just follow me."

He did, admiring the swing of her curvaceous little butt, as were men to both his right and left and a woman or two as well. Renee veered off the walkway, motioning him forward, until they reached the blanket that she had earlier spread beneath a tall oak tree. "I ran over and took this spot when I got here," she said. "Okay with you?"

"Looks fine." He helped her straighten the blanket and unpack the basket. She'd brought a couple of small salads, some deviled eggs, chips and salsa, a roast chicken, other small plastic containers. She lit a small insect-repelling candle before setting out the napkins, plates and plastic utensils. He unveiled the portable wine cooler he'd brought containing its bottle of Veuve Clicquot, the $39.99 price tag still affixed. He quickly scraped it off.

"Where did you get all this?" Doyle said admiringly.

"There's a deli in my neighborhood that does this kind of thing very well."

"What's the neighborhood?"

"Lincoln Park. I have a condo there." Renee pried open one of the plastic containers and opened a small package of water crackers. "Would you like some of this caviar and cream cheese spread, Jack? It's delicious. Even if I didn't make it myself."

"How could I refuse?"

They nibbled. On soft summer nights such as these, Doyle couldn't think of too many other places he'd rather be. It was the setting, not necessarily all those populating it, that so appealed to him. Ravinia had perhaps the best sound system of any outdoor music venue in the U.S. And the crowd, which for Chicago Symphony Orchestra performances was generally whiter than the Arctic rim, tonight was liberally laced with people of color along with the usual majority of whities. A party of suburban-ites passed pâté portions across their nearby portable, candle-lit table, the men careful not to drop canapés on their laps as they shared stock market news, their wives chatting about children, careful not to disturb the silver wine buckets sweating at hand. Next to that group, two African-American couples were lined up side by side in folding chairs facing the pavilion, the men good-naturedly arguing Cubs vs. White Sox. The two women were reading paperback books. They appeared to be sisters. The one seated next to the man who apparently was her husband would occasionally reach over with her hand on his arm and shush him down without looking up from her book.

"Should we talk now?" Renee said. "Before we eat, and the music starts?"

"Sure. Would you like some champagne now?"

"Absolutely."

Doyle said, "*Mea culpa*, but I forgot to bring cups. I'll get some from the concession stand. I'll be right back."

He picked his way over the blanket- and chair-covered green lawn that was now dappled by the retreating evening sun. Thousands of people were spread out across the park. Many more would arrive later from nearby restaurants and take seats in the large pavilion before the eight o'clock performance start. In the interim, jazz music floated from the numerous speakers barely visible in the trees. He dodged a couple of casually but expensively dressed youngsters who skipped past carrying Dove bars. Doyle thought of the two little black boys he'd seen early that morning as he waited in his Accord for the light at Diversey and Ashland. Sleep in their eyes, hope in their hearts as they offered for sale packages of M&M's for, "Hey, mista, just a dolla." He bought two.

There was a long line at the outdoor bar. When Doyle finally faced the bartender, he said, "I'd like two large plastic cups. Put three ice cubes and enough Bushmills to top the halfway mark in one cup. Then add a splash of water. Nothing in the other cup."

The maroon-vested bartender, who didn't look to Doyle to be old enough to even be in the presence of liquor bottles, filled the order with alacrity. Doyle paid and left a $5 tip. The young man's face lit up as he said, "Thank you, sir."

Picking his way back through the increasingly large crowd, Doyle had to step carefully to avoid bumping into a well dressed young man who was evidently trying to put a move on one of the park's few female security officers. She was smiling back at him. Doyle thought of his college pal Mickey Linn, who had such a thing for women in uniform it had gotten him lucky once, nearly jailed on several other embarrassing occasions. Doyle remembered Mickey announcing, "I don't know why, these women can be as plain as vanilla yogurt, but damn, they turn me on with those outfits."

Renee was lying on her back, eyes closed, when Doyle returned. She quickly sat up, accepted the plastic cup, and said, "Aren't you drinking champagne, Jack?"

"Never liked it. I'll open the bottle for you. I'm sticking with Irish whiskey and water." He filled her cup. "*Sláinte,*" he said. "*Sláinte,*" Renee responded, "and, in honor of 'The Widow,' *tchin, tchin, à votre santé.*" They touched cups.

Doyle put some of the caviar spread on two crackers, offering her one. He said, "So, what is this all about?"

Renee vamped her reply, saying, "Are you asking why I lured you here tonight, *monsieur*?" Then the half-smile left her face.

"I can't even pretend to be light-hearted about this, because I'm not close to being that. I'm worried to death about my father. I need your help."

Doyle set his drink down. "Go on."

Renee said, "I'm sure you heard about what happened last week to Mr. Zabrauskis. He was the fourth of Dad's friends, and partners, to die in the last few months. Dad said to me the other day, 'I've never gone to so many funerals in one year in my life. I loved those guys. This is killing me.'"

Renee paused and sipped her champagne. She shook her head. "Unfortunately, that's not all that's killing him." She took a deep breath before adding, "My Dad has lung cancer. In a very advanced stage. He only has a few months to live." She lowered her head.

Doyle could see her long eye lashes moist with tears. "Jeez, I'm sorry to hear that, Renee. Very sorry." He reached to pat her hand before realizing the ineffectiveness of that gesture. "When did Arnie find out about the cancer?"

"He started feeling not well about five months ago. He was coughing a lot, he'd lost energy. But he's had that damn smoker's cough for years," she said bitterly, "and I never thought much about it. I don't think he did, either. My mother died of breast cancer eleven years ago, so the thought of cancer is never far from my mind. But Dad kept going. To work at the car dealerships, to work out at the gym three times a week. Then he started coming home very tired, not like him at all. I finally convinced him to see his doctor. Tests were taken, CT scans and MRIs and PET scans. We got three opinions, but they were all the same. Lung cancer in an advanced stage. I've taken him to the Mayo Clinic, Kettering in New York, Kellogg Cancer Center in Evanston. They all came to that same conclusion. He has an inoperable tumor that has metastasized."

Doyle looked away from her pained expression, momentarily watching the parade of music lovers heading toward their seats in the Pavilion. Renee said, "It's unreal, Jack. Dad and his buddies were going great after their big winning bet at Saratoga,

The Badger Express, all that. These were all healthy men in their fifties." She wiped her eyes again. "One of Dad's sayings over the years, I can almost hear his voice now, was 'Dying is for other people. I just don't have time for it.'"

"If only that's how life worked," Doyle said softly. Renee extended her cup and Doyle filled it. Dusk was advancing and some of the lights in the Ravinia trees began to glow softly. Doyle remembered a statement once made by one of his favorite authors, William Saroyan. "Everybody has to die, but I was under the assumption I'd been granted an exemption." Doyle decided not to share this recollection.

Renee shifted to sit cross-legged at the edge of the blanket. She looked devastated. "I wanted to take Dad to Mexico. There are supposedly a number of cancer-fighting specialists there. I went on the Internet. There are new treatments. Holistic, otherwise. They all claim to be successful. But Dad refuses to try anything like that. He tells me, 'That's what I get for forty years of smoking. I've got nobody to blame but myself. And I plan to die right here in these United States.' He can be a very stubborn man."

Doyle set his drink down on the blanket. "Obviously, you love your father very much, Renee. This must be brutal for you."

She looked away for a moment, shaking her head from side to side. She wiped her eyes again and brushed a swirl of black hair from her forehead. When she turned to Doyle, it was with a rueful smile. "Know what Dad said to me after we left Kettering? He put his arm around me as we were standing there on the curb in the rain, waiting for a cab. He said, 'Mayo Clinic put the over-and-under on me at three months. I've already gone four. I'm going to get a few more, Renee. I promise you.'"

Doyle smiled. "Your father is a strong man with a sense of humor and a sense of reality." He uncrossed his legs and leaned forward on the blanket. "Do you have siblings, Renee?"

"No. I had a brother, Cal, five years older than me. There were just the two of us kids. A great guy, a great brother. We were very close. After college he became a Navy SEAL." She paused and held out her cup. Doyle filled it with champagne.

"Cal was killed in the early stages of the Iraq War. Right after 'Mission Accomplished,' she said bitterly. "'Gung ho from the get-go,' Dad used to say about Cal. We were proud when he went into the service after college. Until…" She stopped and dried her eyes again. Doyle noticed the couple on the blanket next to them watching with concern.

Doyle waited for her to compose herself. She said, "You must be wondering why I am telling you all this. Here's why, Jack. My father is quite, no, *extremely* suspicious about the deaths of his four friends. He told me he thinks there is some kind of terrible plot being carried out, a conspiracy against The Significant Seven. He has no idea why. But Dad is convinced it's happening."

Renee leaned forward. "I know it sounds crazy. You might think Dad's theory is a product of the stress he's under with his illness, his car business suffering along with the rest of the American economy. But, whatever it is, delusion or unwarranted fears, it is very real to him. And I don't want my father to be worried about his safety at this…" She hesitated before saying "This late stage of his life."

"Well," Doyle shrugged," I don't like to point this out. But if your father is, as you say, a guaranteed goner because of lung cancer, where does the other concern for his safety come into it? I mean, as I remember it, one of the Seven had a heart attack and drowned. Another died in a road accident of some sort. There was the poor guy who mistakenly got the bagel with peanuts in it. And the last one, Zabrauskis, died while camping out. This is wild stuff odds-wise, I grant you. So many deaths in such a short span of time among one close-knit group of humans. But, when it comes to your father, can you imagine him being the target of any serial killer zeroed in on The Significant Seven? If, and it's a big one, such a killer exists? I mean, considering your father's medical condition, what would be the point? Your father, unfortunately, is on his way out, on his own."

Renee glared at Doyle. "The point? The point? The point is my father wants to die in his own home. He's already arranged hospice care. He's planned his funeral and the wake and the burial. He does not want to join the list of weird deaths among his friends. He wants to die on his own terms. And I want to make sure that he can."

Doyle swirled the Bushmills in his cup before placing the cup down on the blanket. "All right. I can understand that, Renee. But where do I come into this?"

"I want to hire some absolutely topnotch security people to guard my father. I don't want to be calling these rent-a-cop firms full of minimum wage ex-cons or cons-to-be. I know you have connections to the FBI. I remember the insurance fraud case that you helped them with. You must know people who could recommend quality guards I could hire. Or, if you don't know, you should be able to find out."

The Lincoln Center Jazz Orchestra started warming up. Their sound erupted from the nearby speakers. Renee said, "I take Dad to chemo a couple of times a week. These are last-ditch attempts to fight off the inevitable. I spend most of my time with him now. So I don't have time to vet this area's security firms. I'm asking you if you could help me out by doing that. That's all, Jack. We'd pay you well for your time."

Doyle hesitated. "I can't imagine there's a serial killer of horse owners at work here. What would be the point?" He stopped himself then, reflecting on this situation. Here he was, sitting across from this very attractive young woman, not showing any eagerness to accept money from her. *What has happened to all my basic instincts?* he thought. "All right, Renee, I'll do it." They bumped cups.

"I'm going to tell you something that has to remain between us," Renee said earnestly. "Do you have a problem with that?"

"Not yet."

Renee said, "The partnership agreement that my father and the rest of The Significant Seven entered into, when The Badger Express was about to go to stud, was very carefully constructed. At Moe Kellman's suggestion, my father hired a Chicago attorney named Frank Cohan. Supposedly the city's top contract lawyer. Cohan drew it up. The contract specifies that 'Any profits from the stallion career of The Badger Express be equally divided among the partners. When a partner dies, whatever succeeding profits do *not* go to his heirs, but are to be divided among the remaining partners. This continues until the last partner dies, at which time that partner's designated heir, or executor, shall devote the profits to a reputable organization that cares for retired racehorses.' These men, my father and these friends of his, they loved racing and racehorses. They wanted to give something back."

Doyle said, "I'm impressed. You remember all that legalese?"

"I have a good memory," Renee said.

"Okay, Renee. I'll ask around and find the best security people that I can. It might be expensive to hire the best," he warned.

"Money's not an issue. Preserving my father's peace of mind is."

On the Ravinia stage, the great jazz orchestra finished tuning up. It was almost eight. Doyle drained his drink. He offered to pour Renee more champagne, but she declined. They both stretched out on the blanket now, Doyle with his windbreaker bunched under his head, looking up at the star-filled summer sky.

In one of his first meetings with FBI agent Karen Engel a couple years back, at the start of the horse-killing case, the normally calm Engel had lashed out at what she considered to be Doyle's obstinacy. "You're colder than a bail bondsman's heart," she said.

Ah, but not anymore, Doyle thought. *I'm beginning to lurch toward generous gestures, again.*

He listened with his eyes closed as Wynton Marsalis' golden trumpet soared above the dense, rolling sound of his band mates who were putting their all into Duke Ellington's "Take the A-Train."

He glanced at Renee. Eyes closed, she was smiling, too.

Chapter Thirty-nine

August 4, 2009

They'd agreed to meet at Fit City at seven a.m. Doyle was there on the dot. Kellman, as usual, had arrived earlier than agreed and begun working up a sweat going through his fifty sit-ups and one hundred fifty push-ups before he attacked the treadmill. He waited to start jumping rope until Doyle was there. Doyle took one look at the little furrier as he increased his tempo and started criss-crossing. "Stop fucking trying to impress me," Doyle said. "I'm already impressed. Besides, I could probably enlist a couple of young black girls from the projects who would you make you look ordinary."

Kellman smiled but did not stop. He said, "I saw Sonny Liston jump rope when he was in training for his first fight against Floyd Patterson in Chicago back in the sixties. Liston trained up at a place near Lake Geneva, right over the state line. He was one of the scariest-looking men I'd ever seen. Liston used to just abuse all his sparring partners, then jump rope. They played the record of 'Night Train' while he was doing it. You remember that song? A big R&B hit. No, you're too young. Anyway, his trainer kept it going on a record player set up next to the ring. Which was already splattered with some sparring partners' blood. Over and over with the song. Liston was amazing. Glowering, sweating, moving his feet like he could do it forever. A frightening sight."

Doyle said, "I heard he fell down for Clay, or Ali, in their second bout. The so-called phantom punch. Years later Liston died in Vegas, supposedly of a drug overdose. But everybody who knew him said Sonny was scared to death of needles, this big guy, they made him tremble. That he never touched drugs."

"I wouldn't know about any of that," Kellman said.

Doyle took off his sweat shirt and started to shadow box around the room, moving in the direction of the light bag for some energetic, rhythmic tattooing. "I'm starting slow. I had a late night."

"Hah," came the derisive answer from the amazingly fit septuagenarian. Kellman, a grateful survivor of what he termed the "Fucking Korean Conflict that those of us caught in it called a war," had been a workout fanatic for half a century. His level of fitness never seemed to vary. Kellman ascribed much of his age-defying endurance to an extraordinary diet of Italian food, many vegetables, garlic prominent among them, and the occasional treasured introduction of a "big Jewish hot dog or a fatty pastrami on onion roll." Doyle often detected the odor of garlic in the film of sweat emanating from Kellman during these workouts.

Doyle, warmed up now, feeling better already as he let loose on the light bag, laughed as he asked, "Is *Hah?* a kind of probing question? A declaration of doubt? Believe me, I had a late night." He sent the speed bag spinning with a final two-handed flurry.

"How late was your night at Ravinia? With Ms. Rison? Two nights back?" Kellman stopped jumping and hung the rope on a wall hook before reaching for a towel.

"How'd you know about that?"

Kellman said, "Guy I know happened to see you there. Happened to mention it to me."

Doyle sighed. "Have you ever thought about offering your services to our government? You know, to find Osama bin Laden? Jesus!"

"Jack, don't get riled. It was a coincidence that my friend spotted you. What's the big deal? So you're still working for the Feebs trying to catch whoever is sponging horses. And now you're maybe going to provide protection for Arnie Rison's very, very attractive daughter?"

Doyle gave the speed bag another furious rap. He said, "It just seems that sometimes, Moe, you seem to know more about where I'm going than I do."

Doyle walked over to the heavy bag. "Hold this for me?" Kellman complied, steadying the one-hundred-fifty-pound canvas bag hanging from its ceiling chain. Doyle let go with a series of combinations that dented the bag and caused Kellman to set his feet as he tried to keep the bag straight. Doyle shifted his stance and changed the angle of his punches, increasing their intensity, as he worked through what he estimated to be a three-minute round. Then he stepped back, sweating, grinning.

"Did you see my left?" he said to Kellman.

"Not bad, kid. A veritable blur."

Doyle said, "Not *bad*? Like a goddam piston. Of course," he grinned, "it's a lot easier to do to a bag that doesn't hit back."

Showered and dressed, they went to the Fit City juice bar. Kellman quickly downed two twelve-ounce glasses of pomegranate-cranberry juice. Doyle asked for water.

"You want anything to eat, Jack? I'm buying. I'll wait and have breakfast at my office."

"Naw, Moe. Thanks. If I feel up to it, I'll stop at Petros' on my way to the track. Get a load of restorative grease before I go to work. I don't have much appetite this morning."

Kellman said, "What's got you so down this morning?"

Doyle fiddled with his napkin before saying, "A couple of things. I'm not making any progress finding the horse sponger. And these guys that keep dying, Ralph Tenuta's clients in The Significant Seven, that's fucking depressing. I feel sorry for Arnie Rison. He's a done deal with that lung cancer. I feel sorry for Renee, worrying about her father's current safety. His short future. A load of woe, Moe," Doyle said softly.

They sat in silence. Then Kellman said, "Let me tell you a story. But first I got to ask you, you know that book by a writer named Mark Harris? About baseball players? Called *Bang the Drum Slowly?*

"I haven't read the book, but I saw the movie years ago on television. Robert De Niro, Michael Moriarity. One of their team's coaches was that comedian Phil Foster?"

"Right."

Doyle said, "I loved the movie, even though De Niro, batting, looked about as authentic as, well, little broads with big silicone boobs."

"There's a line in the book," Kellman said, "that I'll never forget. One of the coaches is talking about the De Niro character's impending death. This revelation, he says, is 'Sad. It makes you wish to cry.' But another coach comes back with, 'It is sad. It makes you wish to laugh.'"

"I remember that in the movie."

Moe said, "What I'm getting at is this. I'm in Miami one winter, doing some business. Yes, in case you're wondering, people buy furs in Miami."

"I wasn't wondering. Go on."

"One of my oldest friends has come with me, so we could play a little golf, take in some night life. Jerry Greenberg, from the old West Side. We grew up together. Very funny man, always with the dead pan humor. Could have been a comic, but went into the clothing business and made a fortune instead.

"Meanwhile, back in Chicago, is another very good friend of both of ours. Al Goldstein. Another kid from the west side. Diagnosed with leukemia months before, treated, didn't work, forget it. Great guy."

Kellman paused to order another glass of juices. "So," he said, "Jerry and I are sitting at the bar at Joe's Stone Crab in south Miami Beach, waiting for our dinner call. Bartender says to me, 'Mr. Kellman, there's a call for you. It's your wife. She says it's urgent. You can take in that corridor around the corner of the bar.'

"'Leah,' I say, 'what's the matter?'

"She says, 'Al's gone. Can you come home tomorrow? They'll be sitting shiva at their house.' I tell her yes, of course, and put the phone down."

He drank more juice as Doyle checked his watch, knowing that there was no hurrying his friend on a memory like this.

"I never cry, Jack, not since my first month in Korea when my two best buddies got torn to bits with mortar fire on the same goddam bitter cold morning. But… I broke up after this call from Leah. Tears are coming down my face. Al Goldstein was like a brother to me. I walk back to my seat at the bar where Greenberg is sitting. He sees how upset I am. He says, 'Moe, what is it?'

"I tell him, 'Jerry, our great friend Al passed away this afternoon.' I put my face down in my hands. Maybe a minute goes by. Then I feel a tap on my shoulder. I look up at Jerry. He says, 'Uh, Moe? Were there any calls for me'?

"Jack, I thought about hitting him in the nose, but it broke me up laughing even with the tears on my face. I said, 'You son of a bitch.' I didn't say thanks. But I should have."

He drained his glass and stood up. "Sometimes, Jack, you just have to try to laugh your way through. Dance between the rain drops. Know what I mean?"

Chapter Forty

August 6, 2009

This was one of the best times of the day for Marty Higgins. Between six and six-thirty on a clear summer morning. Breathing in the cool air as he stretched his legs on the patio of his River Woods home. He had on shorts, a cut-off gray sweat shirt, a Chicago White Sox ball cap, his New Balance cross-trainers.

Ever since Higgins had taken up jogging a dozen years back, this period of anticipation always made him smile. The next best period was when he finished his daily four-mile run through the Cook County Forest Preserve path that bordered his home. In between, well, it could get a little tough for him around mile three. "Ain't getting any younger," he told himself, "but still moving." Then he'd kick it into another, final mile gear. Marty had turned fifty-five three weeks earlier. When he stepped on the bathroom scale once a week, he weighed one pound less than thirty-eight years ago, when he was a defensive back at Mount Carmel High School, perennial football power of the Chicago Catholic League. Coming out of high school and entering the UW, he knew his football career was over. Too small for the Big Ten. But he took pride years later in his dedication to fitness. The endorphins from these morning runs seemed to propel him through his busy business days.

◇◇◇

Orth had parked his Big Dog cycle off the Forest Preserve tree-lined roadway behind a thick stand of bushes. He'd gotten there just after dawn. Assured by Sanderson that this was "one of Higgins' jogging days," Orth made his preparations, then began waiting patiently in the cool silence. At six-fifteen, a slender young woman trotted past on the bicycle path that ran parallel to the roadway, pulled forward on a long leash by an energetic black Labrador. Not another person came by. Orth knew Higgins never used the bike path, preferring the roadway.

The sound of pounding footsteps alerted him. Orth peered from behind his helmet shield to make sure it was the target. He recognized Higgins from the photos Sanderson had provided. Higgins passed him. Orth looked at his watch. He waited the ninety seconds he calculated Higgins would need to reach the bridge across the Preserve Creek. He pushed his bike out from behind the bushes and drove up the roadway.

Orth had been on the bridge an hour earlier. Working with a small light in the dark, he strung a light gray trip wire two inches off the ground from one side of the bridge's far end to the other. It took him less than a minute.

Throttled down in the quiet morning, Orth moved ahead. Higgins was running in the middle of the roadway, running easily. He heard the cycle begin to accelerate. Irritated at this unusual and unwelcome sound, Higgins muttered, "All of a sudden we've got a biker on my route. Damn."

He started to sidestep off the roadway and onto the bridge walk. His left foot caught in the nearly invisible trip wire. Higgins yelped as he pitched forward onto his chest, face smashed down against the pavement.

Orth did a quick wheely with the front of his "Big Dog" in order avoid the trip wire. His back wheel rolled over it easily. Orth brought the front wheel down on Higgins' prone figure. He had to struggle to retain balance and keep the bike wheels from sliding off Higgins.

Twenty yards down the sidewalk, Orth braked his cycle and turned it around. He drove back slowly. Higgins was inert. Orth saw the trail of blood leading down the curb and the definitive geometric angle of Higgins' broken neck.

Orth raised his helmet and wiped sweat off his forehead. He felt the exhilarating adrenalin rip that always accompanied his kills. No feeling in the world like it for him, not ever.

He pulled the helmet back down again and drove quickly to the east end of the Forest Preserve where he'd parked his small truck and trailer, rented from an outlet more than one-hundred miles south of his Wisconsin cabin. The parking lot was empty except for his vehicles. He loaded the Big Dog into the trailer, jumped into the truck, and took off. He'd have to remember to clean the blood off the Big Dog's tires when he got home.

Chapter Forty-one

August 11, 2009

Doyle walked into Petros' Restaurant, waved at Darla the waitress, and went to his regular booth. Minutes later, Damon Tirabassi hurried through the door and slid into the booth across from Doyle, who said, "Coffee?" Doyle signaled Darla.

"Where's Karen?"

"She's in D.C.," Tirabassi said, "meeting with the director about one of our cases."

"Obviously not the sponger case, since we've gotten nowhere with that."

"Obviously," Tirabassi said.

They sat in silence until Darla brought their coffees and took their breakfast orders. Then Doyle said, "What other case?"

Tirabassi frowned. "You think I could tell you if I wanted to? Forget it. Just keep in mind that various segments of Illinois politics will keep FBI agents busy here for years. The newspaper business may be dying. Not the corruption business." He set his cup down. "That's enough talk about that. What did you want to see me about?"

"Well," Doyle started, "I've been up and down the Heartland Downs backstretch every day in the past few weeks. I've talked to trainers I know, some I didn't, plus grooms and hot walkers and security people. You can add on bartenders, waitresses, mutuel clerks, veterinarians and their assistants and, in one case, Travis

Hawkins, a blacksmith. The entire result of this research has been *nada*. Major *nada*.

"Whoever is doing the sponging must be like a ghost. Never seen, never suspected. It *has* to be somebody good with horses. That," Doyle said, finishing his coffee, "narrows the list of suspects down to about two thousand. Damon, I've got to say it: this assignment you've given me is a no-hoper—unless the sponger makes a major mistake. And I wouldn't bet on that happening."

Tirabassi spun his coffee cup, eyes down, shaking his head. "The Bureau brass in D.C. are laying a lot of pressure on our boss here, Dave Goodman. And he's transferring it to Karen and me. The big boys hate to read about fixed races. Some of them in D.C. go back almost to days of J. Edgar, who was a big horse-racing fan."

"He had reserved boxes at racetracks all around the country is what I've read," Doyle said. "And he was a big bettor."

"And an occasional night-time cross dresser," Tirabassi replied with an embarrassed grin. "You didn't hear me say that, Jack," he added.

"Say what?"

Tirabassi nibbled at his raisin toast as Doyle concentrated on Petros' new special-of-the-house breakfast offering, "A Greek burrito, with gyros and goat cheese and olives and etcetera," as it was described on the menu.

"I don't know how you can eat like that and still move your limbs in the afternoon," Tirabassi said.

"Hey, if I didn't eat like this, I wouldn't be able to," Doyle said.

Darla swept past, dropping the check in the middle of the table, like a hockey ref letting go of the puck at the start of a period. Doyle reacted at once, sliding the piece of paper on to Tirabassi's place mat.

Tirabassi shrugged and picked it up. "The Bureau can expense this out," he said. "Ready to go?"

"No. Let me ask you something. You have any thoughts or theories about all these horse-racing partners, The Significant Seven, dying off so rapidly? "

Tirabassi said, "Sure, I've read about that. Very strange. But there's never been a criminal complaint that I know of. Nothing has come to us. How many have died?"

"Five. In the span of a couple of months. Pretty fucking weird."

Tirabassi waved Darla back. "One more coffee refill, please," he said. She was quick about it.

Tirabassi said, "I've had a few cases where partnerships went very bad. Old friends, new friends, acquaintances, whatever. One of them would wind up killing another of them, or trying to get somebody to do it for him, or burn down the failing business. It always, always, had to do with money. One partner needed cash badly for whatever reason—women, gambling debts, escape from his boring life. He'd try to get it by somehow stealing, or raiding, or getting control of the partnership's assets. In the worst sort of way. There is crap like that going on all the time."

"I can't see that applying to this Significant Seven stuff," Doyle said. "I mean, these guys were friends since college, and on. Years and years. And starting what, six, seven years back, they started making tons of money in horse racing. All divided up equally from what I know."

Tirabassi said, "Maybe."

"Maybe what?"

"Maybe the divisions of the spoils, or profits, is not as much as some of them, or maybe one them, wants. Greed plays a big role in these scenarios." Tirabassi made a weak attempt to slide their breakfast check back to Doyle, but Jack caught his wrist and stopped him. Doyle said, "I'll take care of the tip."

Tirabassi gave Darla his Bureau-issued credit card. He signed the receipt and placed his copy in his well worn wallet before saying to Doyle, "You know what a Tontine is?"

"Say again?"

"Tontine."

Doyle laughed. "My old man used to tell me about the Lone Ranger and his faithful companion Tonto. Is that what you're talking? Are you kidding me?"

Tirabassi's jaw set. "Would you pay some attention to me, Jack? I'm serious about this."

"Sorry. Go ahead."

"Back in the sixteenth or seventeenth century, there was a brilliant banker in Italy. I think Naples. Maybe not. Anway, his name was Leonardo Tontine."

Doyle said, "I thought Italy only had one memorable Leonardo."

"Don't be such a smart-ass. Now that I think of it, I'm sure the man's name wasn't Leonardo, it was Lorenzo. Lorenzo Tontine. You want to hear this or not?"

Doyle said, "Damon, please proceed." He sat back in the booth, arms crossed, a model of receptivity

"Lorenzo Tontine's brilliant idea was for a money fund that a group of people would contribute to over the years. It was kind of like insurance, or a lottery. That kind of idea was pretty rare back then. From what I've read, Lorenzo couldn't get his scheme going in Italy, so he went to France with it, and he found people there who were interested. The idea was that the last surviving member of the group of contributors to the fund would wind up with all the benefits. He was able to get quite a number of people, rich people only, of course, interested and involved in this. Naturally, Tontine took a cut of the action."

Doyle said, "So, people put in money. Monthly? Annually?"

"I think Tontine had different programs for different groups. Listen, this guy was a tremendous hustler and salesman. He made plenty setting this thing up. As I said, he sold it as a form of insurance, an annuity. And it worked. People liked it. Especially the last man standing. Tontine got a whole bunch of these deals going before he died."

"Did he invest in them?"

Tirabassi said, "Not that I know of. But I guarantee you that Lorenzo skimmed his percentage off the gross. Very bright guy."

Doyle sat back in the booth, arms extended over its back, thinking. He said, "What we're talking here with this Tontine set-up is, essentially, one final winner. Right? The so-called last man standing gets all the money in the deal they created?"

"From what you've told me about The Significant Seven's deal, yeah, I guess it is a Tontine situation. Among people who trust each other. They must have thought they were doing the right thing when they set this up. They were very fortunate men who made a lot of unexpected money in horse racing, deciding to give back to the sport, right? I'm sure they never imagined that the Tontine would be so, well, accelerated by all these deaths. Weird," Tirabassi said. He got up out of the booth.

"Beyond weird," Doyle said. "Thanks for breakfast."

Chapter Forty-two

August 14, 2009

The message Doyle found on his home machine was barely understandable, punctuated as it was by muffled coughs and long pauses. After two replays, he figured it out. Arnie Rison was asking to see him. Doyle called Cindy and cancelled their plans to attend that night's White Sox-Red Sox game at the Cell. "There's some urgency to this," he told her. "I've got to do it." She said she understood.

It was almost seven when Doyle drove his Accord up the long circular driveway leading to Rison's Palos Heights home. The red sports car he parked behind was recognizable to him by the vanity license plate that read "Cool Grl."

She opened the front door before he rang the bell. "Thanks for coming, Jack. Come in." Renee wore a yellow sun dress under a light black sweater she had thrown over her shoulders. Following her down the hallway, Doyle felt a blast of air conditioning.

Renee preceded him up the wide stairway of the expansive Tudor home to the second floor. At the end of the corridor, a large bedroom overlooked the back yard and pool. "Hello, Mr. Doyle," said a woman who identified herself as "Audrey Hartman, Mr. Rison's hospice nurse. He was hoping you'd come tonight."

Doyle momentarily stopped in his tracks when he saw Rison. The lanky horse owner was propped up in a hospital bed, as pale as the pillow on which his head lay. He had lost dozens of pounds just in the few weeks since Doyle had seen him at Heartland Downs. Rison carefully removed the oxygen mask from his face and whispered, "Thanks for coming, Jack."

Audrey Hartman said she'd go down to the kitchen and get coffee. "Fine," Renee said. She closed the bedroom door behind the nurse and walked over to stand next to her father's bed. She motioned Doyle toward the large arm chair nearby.

"Go ahead, Jack, sit down. I've been sitting all day."

It took an effort for Arnie Rison to elevate his back and head to address Doyle. "As you can see, Jack, I'm in the home stretch." He smiled briefly. "Of a great life. With a great daughter at my side." Each sentence was followed by a gasp for air.

Doyle leaned forward. "What can I do for you, Arnie?"

Renee helped her father take a few sips of water through a plastic straw.

"I need only one thing from you, Jack. A promise to protect Renee. When I'm gone."

They waited as Arnie applied the oxygen mask for a minute. Doyle found it hard to watch. Renee walked over to the window and looked out, arms crossed. Like Doyle, she didn't want to witness this struggle for waning life.

Arnie removed the oxygen mask and motioned them to listen. "Jack, if something happens to Mike Barnhill, God forbid...And I wind up as the last of our guys, The Significant Seven...My daughter will be in charge of the monies from our partnership once I'm gone...I am afraid for her...Whoever has caused these deaths, and I am positive it's somebody's sick, sick plan...may target my Renee as the last survivor....I want her protected, Jack Doyle. I'll pay you a lot of money to do it...if you would."

"Where is Barnhill now?" Doyle said.

"He and Peggy are in England, Yorkshire...On a walking trip with some group...Mike said he had to get away from here with all this happening."

"Dad, when do the Barnhills get home?"

"Early next week. He's having some kind of exterior security system put in while they're gone...Electrical fence around the sides and back of his property, I think…Peggy and Mike are both damned worried…Why wouldn't they be?"

Doyle said, "This whole scenario is off the charts. Unless…"

"Unless what?" Renee said.

Doyle thought of what Damon Tirabassi had told him. He said, "Do either of you know what a Tontine is?" They said no. Doyle recounted what he'd learned from Tirabassi about this financial arrangement. "Actually," Doyle concluded, "the deal with The Badger Express amounts to a Tontine. Doesn't it? Last man standing is the big winner?"

"No," Rison said, coughing. "The big winner was never going to be one of us. It would be the horse industry, the salvaging of old retired thoroughbreds from slaughter and…shipment to Europe for food. We all just…hated that stuff. How racehorses were sold…at auctions…for cents per pound…Then shipped to slaughter houses…We, all my guys, loved horses…We couldn't imagine discarding them the way so many people do…That was the whole idea of the contract, the foundation."

Renee said, "This is crazy. Each of the five men now dead apparently had no enemies, no reason to pass away at their ages. If this Tontine thing is what you say it is, my Dad and Mike Barnhill are the last members of the partnership alive. And, Dad…" She turned away and broke into tears. Doyle stood up and went to put his arm around her. Out of the corner of his eye, he could see the pained expression on Arnie's face.

Nurse Hartman poked her head in the door. "Do you need me? Can I get something?"

"No," Renee murmured. "We're okay, Audrey. We'll be done soon."

Not soon enough for me, thought Doyle. He said, "Arnie, I'd like to help you. But I am obligated to my work with Ralph Tenuta. I can't drop that and start shadowing Renee, something I probably wouldn't be much good at anyway. When she comes to the backstretch, of course I'll be on my toes.

"I suggest," Doyle continued, but Rison waved him off. "You do what you can...at the track...I'll be satisfied. That's all I'm asking of you. The pay..."

"Forget the pay," Doyle barked. "I'm not charging you for anything."

He sat down in the chair again next to Rison's bed. "Here's a suggestion, Arnie. I'll talk to Moe Kellman. There's a guy he knows, I'm sure between the two of them they could come up with some major league security talent for you and your daughter."

Rison reached out his hand and placed it on Doyle's wrist. His smile was evident even behind his oxygen mask. "You watch out for my Renee at the track," he whispered. "I've get her covered otherwise. I'll talk to Moe. And a guy my son Cal knew in the SEALs has an agency now...does private security work...He contacted me when he read about the deaths of...of the other Significant Seven. Very nice young man...smart...said he knew our Cal over in Iraq."

Rison's head dropped back on the pillow.

Doyle said, "What's this guy's name?"

"I think Dad has talked enough," Renee said. "This is exhausting for him. Audrey," she called out.

Surprised at this abrupt dismissal, Doyle stood. He put a hand on Rison's bony shoulder.

"He'll do a good job," Rison said, "this fellow that my son Cal knew... His name is Sanderson... Scott Sanderson. He works with another ex-SEAL in the private security business..."

Rison paused to summon strength. "The other man...I don't recall his first name...last name is Orth."

Chapter Forty-three

August 15, 2009

"Did Arnie Rison call you?"

Moe said, "Last night. After I guess you talked to him, Jack."

Doyle said, "Can you help him out?"

"No problem. I've lined up a couple of Pete Dunleavy's ex-cop buddies, plus some talent from the other side of the law. You remember Fifi Bonadio's bodyguards? They'll be splitting shifts, too. Should ease Arnie and Renee's minds."

"Arnie said he thought he was okay with some ex-SEAL his son knew."

"He told me," Kellman said, "that he wanted extra protection for him and Renee. So be it."

Doyle stopped pacing his condo living room. He put down his coffee cup. It was just after seven and he had caught Kellman in his car on the way to Fit City. "You got a couple of minutes?" he said.

Kellman laughed. "For you, Jack? Naturally."

"You know about a Tontine? It's something I never heard of. What happens is, as I understand, the contributors' money builds up and last guy standing gets it."

"This is the Italian thing, right? Yeah, I know about that kind of deal. Far as I know, some of those old dagoes on the west side where I grew up are keeping those things going even now. Not many, though. It's an old-time, old-country thing."

Doyle started pacing again. "It's amazing to me sometimes, what I don't know," he said disgustedly. He could hear Kellman ask driver Dunleavy to pull over in front of the Hancock Building, site of the little furrier's business suite.

Moe said, "Jack, knowing a lot is great, though not that many people do. Knowing *how* to know a lot is for the rest of us who are not geniuses, but not *schlubs* either. If you learn how to find what you don't know, kid, it's a trampoline-life moment." There was a pause. Doyle heard Kellman say, "I've got to take a quick call here from a guy I know at City Hall. Hold on."

Not a minute had elapsed before Kellman said to Doyle, "Let me tell you a story."

Doyle stopped pacing and sat down, smiling, knowing that Kellman could usually be relied upon for instructive episodes from his past.

"When I was a kid and got back from Korea, I lived in a cheap apartment—you could do that back then—just off Rush Street. I hung around a bar called The Interlude a lot of that summer. I was going to start college on the GI Bill at Illinois in the fall. I had a little money saved up, and a lot of free time. The Interlude was a lively place, with sports fans, a bookie in residence, good-looking waitresses dropping in from the great jazz places downtown Chicago had then. I'm talking about Mr. Kelly's. The Blue Note, the London House, the Back Room. The Gate of Horn was a block or two over. I heard Odetta sing there. I saw Lennie Bruce arrested by Chicago cops who hauled him off the stage, after laughing at his routine, which was hilarious. But they were under orders from the top.

"The owner of The Interlude was a very funny, hip Irish Catholic guy named George Sheehan, who had been in the bar business all his life. Big, round-faced, bald-headed guy, strong as an ox. George ran tabs for a lot of his customers, many of whom came from the Loyola night law school down the block. George's famous pronouncement was, 'If I'm ever arrested, I'd rather have a Jewish bail bondsman rep me than a Loyola lawyer. What have the Jesuits done to produce so many deadbeats like you?'

"He'd holler this out, usually late on a Saturday night, and the people at the packed bar would howl with laughter, and George'd say, 'The next round's on me, you lousy bums.'

"Funny thing, George made a lot of money when they were putting up the Hancock Building, which is close to the old Interlude. He'd open up at six in the morning for the iron workers going up on the girders at seven. He served hard-boiled eggs and shots of whiskey to these guys, many of them Mohawks from upstate New York. Fearless when it came to heights. That's not an urban legend, that's a fact. Well, that's neither here nor there, although it's some kind of coincidence that my business is located in the tall building built by not drunken Indians, just Indians who drank a couple of ounces of cheap bar whiskey before working their way up a hundred stories.

"Anyway, Jack, what I'm getting at is that there were many arguments in the Interlude, especially late at night, especially between two guys, one named Fischer, the other named Jansen." There was a pause. "Paul Fischer, Jimmy Jansen. I'm sure that's right, although this took place back there in the so-called mists of time.

"These two would argue trivia about politics and sports and movies, so on, so on, and bet each other who was right. Before I got to know them, one would go to the Newberry Library the next day to find the answer to their dispute.

"One night, the subject is how many times did Willy Pepp fight Sandy Saddler. Who won the most of those fights? Fischer said Pepp, Jansen insisted it was Saddler. The argument was on. After observing these two for a week or so, I would listen to them, quietly get off my bar stool, head for the men's washroom down a dark hallway, get on the pay phone there, and call my Uncle Bernie. Bernie Glockner. Brilliant man. He was known as the 'Wizard of Odds' because he set the betting lines for the Vegas casinos run by the Chicago wise guys. He had sports record books at hand, a set of encyclopedias, the almanacs and atlases, plus a memory like a herd of elephants. The man was a human Google.

"There wasn't a time I called Bernie that he didn't immediately give me the right answer. Fischer would bet that he knew the 1946 Kentucky Derby winner, which he did. But Jansen would say 'I bet you a double sawbuck you can't say who rode that horse.' On and on. What was President Garfield's middle name? What was the name of the Indian woman who helped out Lewis and Clark? This was long before they put her on the dollar coin. Etc., etc.

"So, after calling Uncle Bernie, I'd go back to the bar and tell Fischer and Jansen who was right. *If* either one of them was. And actually, most of the time, one of them *was* right. These two should have been on *Jeopardy*. They would have hauled down the green. But I don't think *Jeopardy* was on then. Also, these two were kind of battered-up veteran drinkers, not exactly TV types. At least in those days. Now, who knows? Both divorced, with alimony, child support they struggled to make. Not really what you would call likeable people, but they weren't bad guys. They both worked and they paid their bills. You could probably make a reality TV show about them today.

"At first, Jansen and Fischer would check out my answer the next day before they learned to trust me. Once they did, the winner always bought me a couple of nightcaps when I came back with what they were convinced was the right answer.

"One late night," Kellman continued, "Jansen says, Moe, how do you do it? You listen to us, you go to the bathroom, you come back, and you come up with the right answer. It's amazing for a young fellow like you, even bright as you are.'"

"I played it very cool. I told Fischer and Jansen, 'I can't explain it but, for some reason, pissing seems to jog my memory.'"

Doyle was laughing now. "You rascal, you," he said. "Thanks, Moe."

Chapter Forty-four

August 16, 2009

Teresa Chandler tapped on her friend and employer's office door. As always, she entered without waiting for a reply from Renee. Having been in business together in this boutique Chicago travel agency for almost six years, their routine of familiarity was a given. But when Teresa noticed the expression on Renee's face, she paused. "What's wrong?"

Renee leaned back in her desk chair. "I just had a call from my Dad. Kind of shook me up."

Teresa reached across the desk to pat her friend's hand. "Has he suddenly gotten worse?"

Distracted, Renee did not answer immediately. Then she looked up at Teresa. "Let's have an early lunch. I could use a super double margarita over at Lupita's."

"Sounds good to me," Teresa said.

Renee said, "But I have to make one phone call first. I'll be out in front in a few minutes."

Teresa shut the door behind her. Renee's voice shook slightly as she began her long-distance conversation.

◇◇◇

The disturbing phone call from her father had come thirty minutes earlier. "Renee, I just want to bring you up to date on some syndicate matters."

"What, Dad?"

A coughing spasm preceded Arnie's reply. "My partners' wives, widows I should say about five of the poor women, have been talking to each other about these deaths. Certainly understandable. Peggy Barnhill, I guess she's their appointed spokesperson, called me this morning. She said they wanted to have a meeting to review the original Significant Seven contract agreement. I told her, 'Fine. Let me talk to Frank Cohan. He's the attorney who drew it up. He's got the original in his office. I was the only one of us to take a copy. Remember, Renee, when I showed it to you last year?"

"Yes."

"Turns out Cohan is in Scotland on a golfing vacation. Doesn't get back until next week. I asked Peggy to tell the other women we could have a meeting then. Here at my house, if they'd agree. Because I'm really not up to traveling into downtown Chicago. Peggy said okay, she understood.

"Anyway, I just wanted you to know about this. I want you to be at the meeting. You can host it better than I can," he laughed. Then his coughing resumed.

Renee said, "Dad, what would it take to amend the contract?"

"Why would we want to amend it?"

"Well, why do these widows want to examine it?"

Arnie said, "It's their right. But as I remember the terms, it would take a majority of the partnership to make any change in the agreement." He paused. "There's only two of us now. Isn't that a goddam shame?"

Chapter Forty-five

August 17, 2009

The phone button was blinking when Orth returned to his cabin.

"Bro, we got to talk. Tried your cell. See you at the same place on the big river, two afternoons from today. Any problem with that, get back to me quick." Sanderson hung up.

Orth had been out on the lake, trolling for bass, without his latest cellphone, the most recent in a series of such instruments he bought and used for one week each before discarding. He'd caught and released eight bass, one them about three pounds he thought, a real battler. He kept the one walleye he'd snagged. It wasn't legal size, but big enough for his dinner, fuck the DNR.

He drove to Boulder Junction's Qwik Stop to use its outdoor phone. Called the airline. Called Sanderson to say, "Confirmed." Went back to his cabin and made his dinner, some fingerling potatoes to go with his pan fried walleye. One of his favorite meals. After eating and washing his plate and utensils, he knocked back a couple of Leinies and turned on the radio repeat of his favorite political commentator, a man regarded by many citizens as the most vicious right-wing bloviator in the business. Orth got out his rifle and two pistols and cleaned and oiled them as he did every week, smiling as he listened to the strident radio voice raging about "this once great country's continuing decline."

◇◇◇

Sanderson opened his St. Louis motel room door right after Orth's one tap. They were in a Holiday Inn Express. "Hey, man," the Sanderson said, slapping his hand onto Orth's. "You made good time from the airport. Let me turn the TV up so we can talk. I guess nobody knows you're here?"

"Nobody but that nerd at the front desk who checked me in."

"What name did you use?"

"I went with Eddie Mathews. My old man's favorite Milwaukee Brave. How about you?"

Sanderson said, "I'm here as Don Moore. About as forgettable as I could come up with."

"How about some food?" Orth said. "All they had on the damn plane were five buck junky looking sandwiches in plastic. I need something."

Sanderson swung open the door of the mini-bar. He took out two beers and a can of mixed nuts. "Make do with this for now," he said. "We'll order from room service later. Gotta talk first."

"Shit," Orth said as he twisted the cap off his beer. "This must be serious, you putting business before food. What's up? Anything wrong with our contract?"

"No, no. The deal is still on. The money keeps coming in. I came up here to talk to you about slightly alterering our schedule. Not a major change, but a change. I figured it was best for us to go over this in person."

Orth frowned. "Go on," he said.

"The original number of targets," Sanderson continued, "was six. Now it's seven. The change is that the seventh target is not from the group we've been, well, dealing with. And we've got to move fast in taking out the last one of the original six. That's vital."

"Why?"

Sanderson said, "We don't have to get into the reason for that. The less you know, the better."

Orth, who had been lying on one of the beds, stretched out and relaxed, sprang up and moved over to the window. He reached down to the air conditioner controls and dropped the temp to sixty-five, fan whirring. He said, "Who's the new number seven?"

"Guy named Doyle, Jack Doyle. A little older than us, a former amateur boxer, no military. Worked in advertising or some kind of white-collar shit, then at a little racetrack south of Chicago. I found him on Google. A few years back he was in the newspapers when he helped the feds convict a ring of rich guys killing their horses for insurance money in order to get richer."

Orth said, "Tell me how and where and why this Doyle comes into it? Is he hooked to this Significant Seven bunch?"

"No, no, no. But our client is concerned that if Doyle sniffs around too long trying to figure this all out, he's liable to get lucky. He's close to the situation. He's evidentally a sharp guy. The client thinks Doyle may figure out something the client doesn't want him figuring. Doyle is just a concern that the client doesn't want to deal with, okay?"

Orth kept looking out the window. "I hate changes like this, Scott. You know that. We had a schedule, targets, boom boom, it's fuckin' over."

"Hey, bro, it's no big deal. We had to change course way more than our underwear back in the hell hole of Iraq, right? We did it and survived. Hell, thrived. Doyle works for some horse trainer at a track near Chicago. So he was a fucking AAU boxer, big deal. There's no way he's like us. Just eliminate the man, okay?" Sanderson finished his beer and tossed the can halfway across the room directly into a waste basket.

Orth turned from the window and lay down on the carpet on his back. "I got to do some sets, man. Just like in the old days. Helps me think."

"Go to it," Sanderson said. He sat back in the chair closest to the TV, which was turned to a dance contest program featuring a very aged actress trying to spin and vamp her way back into her past. He had to laugh; she was pretty good.

Sanderson counted silently as Orth did two-hundred crunches, two-hundred pushups, another hundred crunches. This took slightly less than nine minutes. When Orth finished, there was not a hint of perspiration on his tanned, taut face. He sat up on the floor, not even breathing hard.

"You bastard, you're still in unbelievable shape. Not like this married father," Sanderson smiled, patting his belly. He waited.

Orth said, "Okay. I'll go along. What's the schedule?"

Sanderson let out a whoop and jumped up from his chair and gave the still sitting Orth a series of low fives. "My man," he said. "I got some recon to do. I'll let you know real quick. Number six from the original group has to come first and quick. I'm talking this week. Doyle comes after that. Then we're done."

Chapter Forty-six

August 18, 2009

"Would you *look* at that dipshit," Ralph Tenuta shouted, yanking his truck's steering wheel to the right and aiming its wheels off the pavement on the Heartland Downs backstretch road. He slammed to a halt. Ahead of the truck, completely unaware that Tenuta had barely missed crashing accidentally into him and his stable pony, was Frank Lester, the track's leading trainer. Lester was in charge of an upscale seventy-horse local stable. As usual, Lester was wearing his designer sun glasses, embroidered jacket, white hat, saddle-soaped leather chaps, $500 boots. Lester continued to ride slowly across the narrow roadway completely oblivious to the fuming Tenuta.

Doyle said, "I believe Frank Lester is texting on his cell phone. On horseback. As oblivious as one of those little woman drivers who veer into your lane with their big SUVs while yakking on their phones. Frightening sights."

"What do you mean, 'texting'?"

"Ralph, let's not go into that."

Tenuta said, "I'd blow my horn and tell numbnuts Lester there to get his head out of his ass, but I don't want to scare the pony. Remind me to give him a call later."

"Will do," Doyle said, "if you can get through to him." He leaned back in his seat as Tenuta pulled off the grass and back onto the road leading to the entry clerk's office. It was just before eight. The truck's front windows were open, letting in the distinctive aroma of newly cut grass and, between barns, scents from the growing mounds of horse manure. The sun dominated the cloudless blue sky. Doyle tried to Zen himself into enjoying this particularly pleasant part of his working day. It didn't work. He and Tenuta were soon talking about the latest Significant Seven fatality, Marty Higgins. "That's five of the guys in the syndicate gone, Jack. Unbelievable."

"Except it's happened," Doyle said. After thinking about the apparent hit and run accident that had killed Higgins, Doyle phoned Renee Rison at her travel agency. She said she, too, was shocked at Higgins' death. "Promise me," Doyle said, "that whenever you come out to the track you'll let me know." She said, "I will."

"How's the other security working out?"

"Fine, Jack. Dad is still very shook up about Mr. Higgins. Of all the other six, Higgins was the one my father felt closest to. And, naturally, he's worried about Mike Barnhill. And me. But I feel very protected now, and I think Dad does, too. Jack. I've got to go. One of my best customers just walked in."

Doyle looked down at the notebook in his hand. "Ralph, why are we putting Clever Carolynn in to be claimed? She's run pretty decently in her allowance races."

Tenuta shook his head. "Clever Carolynn is losing confidence. That's natural. She's been in over her head. I'm trying to help her out here."

"What if she's claimed?"

"It will be what it will be, Jack. I've had this filly for almost a year. She started out real promising. Then she hit a kind of class wall."

Doyle said, "What's that?"

"Look. You take a horse like Clever Carolynn and run her over her head, she'll try. That time. The second time you do it, she'll try again, but not as hard. Third time, your biggest problem is going to be getting her to the paddock. Because of what's happened in the last two races, she is not going to want to go there and run. These are dumb animals, but they are not stupid.

"So, what I'm doing is I'm dropping Clever Carolynn down in class, into a $50,000 claiming race. I think she's going to sit back there early, and then come running and beat some horses, not like in her last three races. I think she can do it, probably even win. Clever Carolynn's reaction is going to be, 'Hey, okay now. I'm getting good.' That's because she's in the class where she belongs. She'll be a happier, eager horse. Horses know this, Jack."

There was a blare of horns. "Holy fuck, Ralph! What the hell are you doing? You almost threw me onto the damn dashboard." Doyle glared at the trainer, who had wheeled his truck into the parking lot and hit the brakes in a dust-producing thrust. Tenuta said, "You didn't see that I just missed that little Mexican kid on his bike who came around the corner? What else could I do? Take it easy."

"No," Doyle said, "*you* take it easy."

Tenuta glanced sideways at Doyle. "Aw, Jack, I'm sorry. I apologize. I'm just kind of agitated this morning about poor Marty Higgins. Plus, I've got *agita*. Reach in the glove compartment there will you and get those Tums."

"Agitated I can understand," Doyle said, "since you almost ran down Frank Lester and the horse he was texting from. But what's *agita*?"

"It's a kind of super heartburn. It comes from stress, or too much drinking, or spicey food. I don't drink much anymore. Let's say my case comes from stress and bad food."

Cindy Chesney and Doc Jensen drove past in the veterinarian's truck, both waving. Doyle waved back. Tenuta, morose, stared straight ahead, hands on his steering wheel.

"Well," Doyle kidded, "as they say so often today, 'Do you want to talk about it?'"

Tenuta sighed. "What can I say, Jack? I think my wife is trying to kill me."

"C'mon, Ralph. Rosa? That sweet woman. What are you talking about?"

Tenuta said, "Okay, okay, not trying to kill me. Just destroy my desire to live. With her goddam Kentucky cook book. Jack, you wouldn't believe what Rosa's been putting me through. I haven't had a decent meal in weeks. This, from a woman my mother taught to cook!"

Doyle had to turn his head to avoid looking at his doleful employer.

"I know you're laughing, Jack. Don't try to hide it. You think this is some kind of domestic comedy. It isn't," Tenuta said, slamming his hand down on the dash board.

They sat in silence. Doyle said softly, "You want to say anything about last night's dinner?"

"I really don't even want to think about it. But, yeah, I'll tell you. You'll get an idea of what I'm up against here. Hand me those Tums again." Tenuta crunched and swallowed two.

"I come home, I'm starving, thirsty, I make myself a big cold martini, then go to the dinner table and open a bottle of nice red. Minutes later from out of the kitchen Rosa comes with some kind of shrimp cakes under green chili sauce. Something she called an 'Asian stir-fry vegetable salad.' Then there was a tiny piece of meat, a little filet, I had to scrape another terrible smelling sauce off the top of it. There were I think green beans under a yellow sauce with toasted nuts on top, cashews maybe, I don't know. And something Rosa said was Wasabi or something mashed potatoes. They *looked* like mashed potatoes.

"By now I'm starting to ask myself, 'Who the hell in Kentucky eats like this?' Nobody *I* know."

Doyle struggled to restrain his laughter. He said, "Was there dessert?"

"Poached pear and kiwi tart," Tenuta said bitterly. "No biscotti like Rosa used to make. The best. Or the homemade gelato from the machine she has in our kitchen. No."

Chapter Forty-seven

August 21, 2009

Sanderson laid the plans for target number six. Orth listened in disbelief. Standing in the parking lot of the Boulder Junction Qwik Stop, he said, "Are you telling me this guy Barnhill is still going about his regular routine? Business as usual? No precautions, no guards? Hard to believe, man."

Sanderson said, "Hey, the guy's an old football player. Maybe he took too many hits and they've caught up with him. I don't know, and I don't give a fuck. I'm just telling you where you can find him, where you might take him out. I'm leaving it up to you as to how. One thing he has done," Sanderson added, "is electrify the fence that runs around the back and sides of his property. Why he did that and didn't install an alarm system is a mystery to me. Maybe he thinks he's invincible or something."

There was a pause before Sanderson said, "You getting your money all right?" Orth hardly heard him. For him, it was never really about the money. He said, "Oh, yeah. The Bahamas account is booming." He didn't thank Sanderson. Both of them knew Sanderson should be thanking him for the monetary bonanza for which Orth was the primary provider.

"Call me when it's over, bro," Sanderson said before hanging up.

◇◇◇

Orth scouted the Barnhill home for two days. The electrified fence would be no problem. There was an overhanging tree branch easily thick enough to hold the rope he would knot and toss over it before pulling himself up and launching himself into the yard. Nothing to it for a man in his condition. With his night vision glasses, he had been able to stay on the other side of the fence, which bordered a forest preserve, and confirm Sanderson's report on Barnhill's after-work routine.

Mike Barnhill's wife Peggy opened the door leading to their basement and hollered, "Mike, how much longer? Dinner'll be ready in fifteen."

"Give me twenty," came the grunted answer. "I'm almost done here, then I'll take a quick shower. Okay?"

"All right, honey," Peggy said, closing the door.

On the floor directly beneath Peggy's kitchen was her husband's workout room. He had converted an old basement storage space into an area containing a treadmill, weight bench and stand, weights, and mats. He'd finished this project three years earlier. "I can't jog anymore," he'd explained to Peggy, "my old football knees are making it too hard. And I've put on weight, which I don't like. I've got to get back in shape."

"Why don't you join a health club?" Sharon asked.

Mike said, "I've spent more time in locker rooms and athletic facilities with bunches of other guys than I ever want to do again. Now, if somebody directed me to a nearby health club near here with a co-ed locker room, I'd consider it."

"Go ahead and do the basement," Peggy shot back.

They both laughed before Mike said, "Tell you the truth, I like working out alone. No distractions. Just concentrating on what's got to be done. Call me old school."

Barnhill's three nights per week routine was soon launched. He returned home via Metra from his Chicago Loop law office by six o'clock each Monday, Wednesday and Friday, quickly changed into sweats, took a couple of bottles of water out of the kitchen fridge, and told his wife, "I'm going below."

"Up periscope," Peggy would respond, making both of them laugh.

This evening Barnhill toweled himself off after stepping down from the treadmill. His old gray sweatshirt, with its cut-off sleeves, was dark with sweat. Since starting this regimen, Barnhill had dropped twenty of the most droppable pounds he'd accumulated. He slapped at his much diminished belly before walking over to the black-leather covered, rectangular weight bench. A quick look at his watch convinced him to do just three sets of ten reps with the barbell holding one-hundred fifty pounds of plates. He didn't want to have Peggy chide him for delaying dinner. He tugged on his gloves, sat down, and lay back on the bench. On the wall in front of him, ESPN's *Sports Center* was on the television, running highlights of that afternoon's Major League baseball games. He smiled as he reached for the weight bar, saying aloud as he usually did, his own self-motivating mantra: "Not so bad for a fifty-five-year-old one-time jock. Let the bench press begin."

Sports Center producers had for some reason called in basketball Hall of Famer Charles Barkley to offer some of his questionable opinions about baseball. Barnhill reached down beside the bench and hit the mute button on his television remote. He started lifting, slowly at first.

As Barnhill went through his routine, avoiding Sir Charles' fulminations, he chuckled as he recalled the incident a sports writer friend of his, Neil Ruklick, described to him regarding another famous American sports announcer, Howard Cosell.

According to Ruklick's report, a New York Jets cornerback had been overnighting at the Manhattan apartment of the team's star quarterback following a Sunday victory over the Steelers and a long night of carousing. Near noon, the cornerback emerged from his bedroom and saw his famous host and teammate being interviewed by the famous announcer. Bleary-eyed, the cornerback walked up to Cosell to say, "Jeez, I came out here to turn you off. I thought you were on television." He then ruffled the famed announcer's toupee and went back to bed. The memory of that incident always brought a smile to Barnhill's face.

He was still smiling as he began his last set of reps. Engrossed in the exercise, Barnhill barely felt a brief flush of cool air invading the room. Figured it was the air-conditioning kicking on. When he knew it was six o'clock, he reached for the remote and turned the television to PBS and the *Lehrer NewsHour*.

Orth silently slid shut the basement patio slider door he had pried open with his knife. The sound of the television drew him across the carpeted part of the basement to the workout room. He peered around the doorway as Barnhill put the remote down and his hands up on the weight bar. On the television Jim Lehrer said, "Good evening. Here are today's top stories."

Barnhill boosted the barbell well over his head, extending his arms. It was abruptly snatched from him. Startled, he looked up and back of him at the black clad figure now holding the one-hundred fifty pounds. He said, "Wait…" But the intruder did not pause. He flung the barbell directly down on top of Barnhill's throat. Larynx crushed, Barnhill had time only for one last look at the nightmare figure behind him. Then he stopped breathing. Orth felt for and found no pulse. He slipped out the patio door and hauled himself back up on the rope and over the fence.

At six-fifteen, during Judy Woodruff's report from the Obama White House, Peggy Barnhill opened the kitchen door to the basement. "Mike, c'mon, honey. It's getting late for dinner. You've still got to shower. Please."

Getting no response, Peggy stepped down the stairs. When she walked through the door of the workout room, she began screaming.

Chapter Forty-eight

August 23, 2009

"Jack, calm down. You're like a raving maniac. You're talking so loud and fast that I can hardly understand you. What happened to Mr. Cool?"

Damon Tirabassi turned to Karen Engel. She was driving as they headed north on Lake Shore Drive. "It's Doyle," he said. To their right, the unusually gray summer waters of Lake Michigan were ruffled with waves. It was one of those rare August mornings that set boats to rocking in Belmont Harbor, wind surfers calling into work sick. Rain pounded he windshield. Karen turned the wipers to high.

"Bull shit I'm a raving maniac," Doyle said. "Are you listening to me or not, Damon?"

"Of course I'm listening."

Doyle said, "Two evenings ago, a guy named Mike Barnhill died in the basement workout room of his home. Name ring a bell?"

"No."

"I figured as much. Well, for your information, and for the information of what portends to be your vaunted Bureau, Barnhill was the sixth member of his horse-racing syndicate to kick off this summer. Sixth. And there has not been even one official inquiry into these deaths. Even Inspector Clouseau might prick up his ears at these statistics. How about the cream of American law enforcement?"

Karen motioned for Damon to hand her the phone. "You're on the muscle today, aren't you Jack? I could hear you even without the speaker phone." Doyle did not reply.

She switched over to the second lane when she saw a Chicago Police Department car flying up ready to pass her on the left. "Jack," she said, "I'm sure the reason we've not been ordered to investigate is that there hasn't been any evidence of foul play in these deaths. Yes, I'm aware of The Significant Seven. I agree, it's pretty weird, even when just when the first two or three died. But not one of the police jurisdictions involved reported a possible murder. We can't get involved unless we're asked, or told. We haven't been either up to this point. I've got to turn off Hollywood. I'll give you back to Damon."

Doyle said, "Damon, get serious. You're telling me something murderous hasn't gone on with these guys? Their fatality rate—six different deaths, six different kinds of dying—is way off any actuarial able. And you know it."

"Where are you, Jack?"

"I'm at the track. I just hung up with Renee Rison. She's scared shitless her father's going to be next in the death line. Even though the poor guy is doomed."

"What do you mean doomed?" Tirabassi said.

Doyle said, "Arnie Rison has lung cancer. Advanced, untreatable. Renee's concern is that some madman, maybe resentful of the success and luck Arnie and his buddies enjoyed in racing, is carrying out some kind of vendetta against them. Some jealous, resentful, murderous lunatic. Like the guy who killed Lennon. That fucker in the Oklahoma City bombing. The Columbine creeps. Don't think there isn't a legion of them out there, burbling beneath civilization's surface. You think that sounds crazy, Damon?"

"Unfortunately, no."

Karen swerved sharply to just miss hitting a Loyola student pedaling his bike through the Sheridan Road curve around the university. She didn't bother to honk her horn. The young man was riding into her lane, his head down and not seeing what was behind him, ear phones plugged in. Straightened away, she said, "Damon, let me talk to him."

"Jack, we're on our way to Highwood Park to arrest one of their leading citizens for fraudulent stock dealings. A nationwide scam. By the time we get her booked and processed and taken downtown, it's probably going to be late afternoon. We'll get back in touch with you then and talk about the Seven. That's the best we can do today. Okay?"

Doyle had calmed down. He said, "Karen, are we talking here about a north suburban white-collar criminal? Female? This is huge. What a dent in the glass ceiling!"

"Goodbye, Jack."

Chapter Forty-nine

August 25, 2009

Once, sometimes twice a week, on a completely random basis, Doyle would get in his Accord to ostensibly depart Heartland Downs in the evening at the end of his work day. He'd then park the car behind a small grove of trees on the far side of the track kitchen and walk back to Tenuta's barn, keeping off the roadway, trying not to be recognized. Once in the dark office, he positioned a chair so that he could observe the area between the barns without himself being seen. The first couple of times he did this, he used his CD player to listen to some jazz, sound turned down low. That was before he realized that if he were ever to discover the silent, secretive sponger, he'd best have absolutely no aural distractions. So, with the office door slightly ajar, Doyle spent boring nights listening to the snuffling nasal sounds and shuffling feet of nearby equines. Once each hour, he left the office to quietly walk up and down the shed rows of barns he chose at random. The more nights he spent in these attempts to spot the sponger, the more discouraged he became.

A week earlier Editorialist, the meanest horse in America, had been scheduled to run the next afternoon in a minor stakes race. Editorialist would be an odds-on favorite, everyone knew that. The morning before Editorialist's race Doyle said to Tenuta, "Ralph, who's on security tonight?"

"Tony LaVine. Used to groom for my dad, then for me. Retired now. But he's bored and needs something to do. So, I hire him once in awhile when one of my regular guards needs to be off. Nice old guy, Tony."

Doyle said, "Are you talking about that skinny old guy who shuffles around here some mornings, looking to read your copy of *Racing Daily*?"

"Yeah, that's Tony."

"You can't be serious! That old man can hardly locate the front page of the paper. You're relying on *him?* With Editorialist running tomorrow?"

"Jack, ease up. Tony's done this work for me before. He'll be fine."

"You hope."

Tenuta said, "I've got to go into Chicago to talk to some potential new owners. I'm not worried about Editorialist, or old Tony. You shouldn't be, either. C'mon, walk with me to the car. I want to go over tomorrow's work schedule."

In the parking lot, Tenuta handed Doyle the clipboard with the schedule. He was smiling as he leaned back against the car, saying, "I've known Tony LaVine, like I said, for a long, long time. But I hadn't seen him in years until the start of this meeting. I'm walking out of the track one day and there he was. I was shocked. He looked terrible. Skinny, in a raggedy old sport coat, crusty looking pants, it was pitiful.

"We talked for a couple of minutes. Tony told me he could use a little work. I said, 'Come to see me next week. I'll see what we can do for you. By the way, Tony, would you like a cigar?' I had some great Cubans with me from my good owner Sam Murray. I'd planned to enjoy one on the way home. Rosa doesn't like me smoking around the house. But Tony says, 'Naw, Ralph, thanks, but I don't smoke anymore.'

"I said, 'Tony, how about we go across the street to the Paddock Lounge? I'll buy you a beer.' Tony says, 'Thanks, Ralph, but no thanks. I don't drink anymore.' By this time I'm taking an even closer look at Tony. Besides his miserable wardrobe, he's wearing these ancient shoes, and his shirt collar is so frayed it could lift off in the next slight breeze. I said, 'Tony, how about I loan you a few bucks to bet tomorrow?' I said this because, in the old days, Tony LaVine was a regular at the mutuel windows. Tony used to say, 'You've got to make at least one bet every day. Otherwise, you could be walking around lucky, and never know it.' Anyway, this day Tony says, 'Ralph, thanks for the offer, but I don't bet anymore.'"

One of the Heartland Downs security patrols slowly drove past. Tenuta waved at them before turning back to Doyle. "So I said, 'Tony, how about coming to my house for dinner tonight?' Well, the old guy's face lit up. 'Sure, Ralph, thanks.'"

Doyle said, "That was nice of you."

"It was, but I had, what do you call it, a superior motive."

"Ulterior?"

"Yeah, Jack, that's right. Tony rides with me to my house. Rosa opens the door for us. She takes a long look at Tony, who she's never seen before. I said, 'Rosa, this is Tony LaVine. An old friend of mine and of my dad's. He's here for dinner.'

"Rosa slowly looks Tony up and down again, which is when I take my shot. 'This, Rosa,' I said, 'is what happens to a man who doesn't smoke, drink, or bet.'"

Doyle laughed along with Tenuta.

"Rosa didn't think it was all that funny. But we gave Tony a good meal—this was before the Kentucky cook book disasters—and I worked it out so Tony could get a few hours of work a week as a stable guard for me. He was happy as hell about that. And that's how I've kept the old guy going."

The next afternoon, after Tony LaVine's night of apparent vigilance, Editorialist won "like a thief in the night," as the jubilant Tenuta put it.

Two mornings later, the chief state veterinarian reported that, in the race prior to Editorialist's, the heavily favored filly Mady and CeeCee, trained by Frank Lester, had been sponged. She finished eighth and last, her first loss of the year. The resultant exacta and trifecta payoffs were huge.

◇◇◇

Doyle leaned back in the chair, his feet on one of the window sills in Tenuta's office, looking out at the moistly developing evening. He'd just checked down the shed row. Tony LaVine was seated there in a camp chair under the roof, looking alert. The lingering drizzle suddenly accelerated into a hard rain. A hard rain falling. Doyle started to hum Bob Dylan's song on that subject, remembering most of the words for a change. That led him into "Oxford Town" and "Corrina, Corrina." Doyle loved the early Dylan music that his parents had played when he was a kid.

The rain stopped as if a faucet had been turned off. The evening was still gray and gloomy, but Doyle saw movement across the stable yard and heard voices. Two people, decibels rising as they argued. He could hear them clearly. Doyle jumped out of his chair and went to the doorway, recognizing one of the two voices, the woman's. He opened the door all the way and saw the woman give the short man a shove that forced him back a couple of feet. She pivoted and started to quickly move away. Then she slipped in the mud, and dropped her exercise rider's helmet, and went down on one knee as a white envelope slipped out of her other hand, disgorging dozens of bills of currency.

"Aw, Christ," Doyle said. He dashed out the door and splashed across the muddy yard. She heard him coming. She'd quickly snatched up most of the $20 bills she'd dropped. Startled, she looked up at Doyle, mouth open, money in each muddied hand. She looked down and plucked the last sodden bills out of a puddle and stuffed the now refilled envelope into the back pocket of her jeans. She lowered her face again. Her shoulders started shaking as she sobbed, "Oh, Jack."

Doyle reached down and jerked her to her feet. "Have you got all the money, Cindy?" he growled. He marched her into Tenuta's office. Junior Garza, there a minute ago arguing with Cindy, had slipped away into the advancing night.

Slamming the office door closed, Doyle yanked down the window blinds before turning on the desk light.

"Why? Why in *hell?...* " He pounded the desk top with his left hand. "Answer me, woman."

Cindy wiped her face and tried to compose herself. She took a deep breath and sat back in the chair. Tear-tracked and mud-streaked, her face was so heart-striking to Doyle that he felt even more angry, disappointed, betrayed.

She started to get up but Doyle put a hand on her shoulder and forced her back down into the chair, hating the desperate look on her tanned and earnest face.

"Let me talk, Jack. Let me talk."

"Go."

Cindy said, "I am truly, truly sorry. Not just that you caught me out, but that I had to start doing the sponging in the first place."

"It was all for Tyler, wasn't it?"

"You have to *ask?*" she said bitterly. "Everything I do is for Tyler."

Doyle said, "That motive isn't enough for me. It doesn't justify your sneaky, cheating, horse-hurting actions. Don't pretend it wasn't for the damn money."

Cindy slapped his hand off her shoulder and jumped up. "Yes yes yes, it was about the money, Jack. Of course it was. I've got this beautiful, damaged, challenged, different kid. And I want the best for him. And the only way for me to manage, or try to, was to bring in more money than I ever could through my regular work—no matter *how* hard I worked, *how* many hours." She dropped her head downs into her hands.

"I exercise horses early in the morning. I help Doc Jensen most days. I spend three nights a week behind a cash register, selling beer and cigarettes to punks who try to pick me up. And when I finish, I'm so tired I can hardly stand up. Next day, I start over."

She rubbed her hand over her tear-streaked face and slowly looked up at Doyle. "When that creep Garza first came to me with his sponging plan, I turned him down cold. I told him he was nuts. But he kept pressing me. He had a pretty good idea of my financial situation. And he figured out that because of where and how I worked, I could get the sponging done if I was smart. I asked the little bastard right off, 'Why don't you do it?' Garza said, 'Oh, no, *chica*, horses don't like me the way they get along with you.'"

Doyle walked around the desk and sat in Tenuta's chair. Cindy said, "I have to use the washroom, Jack. No, no, don't worry, it's just down at the end of the shed row. I'm not going to run off."

"Like I can trust you," Doyle muttered. He waited in the doorway until she returned, when he said, "Tell me this. Why didn't you ask me for money. I would have helped you."

"You came along too late. I wouldn't have asked you anyway. I was too ashamed. I *hated* doing that to those horses. But I had no choice. Garza paid me $5,000 for each horse I got to. All of them were favorites, all of them lost. I've saved all that money for Tyler's special schooling. I may be trailer trash, but I've never begged for money, or taken a handout, or a dollar of welfare money. Neither has my Mom."

"You want a medal for that?" Doyle shot back. "What you did to those horses, helpless animals, damn it, I don't care what your motive was. Not to mention cheating bettors all over the country by fixing races. If this story ever got out, it'd be a huge black eye for racing." He took a deep breath. "You're a menace to the sport that gives you a living," he said.

Cindy didn't answer. She stood up, back to him, arms crossed across her chest. Doyle fought down an urge to put his hand on her shoulder in an attempt to comfort her. Without turning around, she said, "What are we going to do, Jack?"

"I have a question. Who else is involved in this besides you and Junior Garza? He doesn't strike me as a mastermind of betting strategies."

"I have no idea," Cindy said. "I know he calls somebody when I've done the sponging. Who it is, I have no idea. I never wanted to know."

Doyle said, "You tell Junior Garza that if there's ever another horse that gets sponged at any track he's at, I will turn him and you over to the FBI in a minute. Understand?"

"Yes."

Doyle sat down in the chair behind the desk. He held his head in his hands before saying softly, "I'm letting you off the hook, Cindy."

Cindy whispered, "Thank you." At the doorway she stopped and looked back. "And…what about us, Jack? Could you ever forgive me for what I did? For what I had to do?"

Doyle slowly shook his head. "I'm quits of you, Cindy Chesney."

The next morning, when Junior Garza's employer Marty Alpert arrived at the barn, he was informed by his head groom that "Junior quit, boss. We don't know where he's going. He didn't say nothing. He just got all his stuff and left last night."

Chapter Fifty

August 28, 2009

Orth heard Sanderson say, "He works late on Fridays. The track starts the races later that day and they finish later. He's the last one to leave that barn that he's in, except for the security guards. There's an interval between when he's there alone, waiting for the nighttime guard. That's the window of opportunity, bro. It should work for you."

"That's the deal with him every Friday?"

"Yeah. You're not going to trick this guy into meeting you anywhere. The way he lives his life, he'd be hard to sneak up on. You got to jump him and take him. Take his wallet, make it look like a robbery. Surprise the bastard."

Orth said, "It's always by surprise, ain't it bro?" He replaced the receiver, got into his Jeep Cherokee, and pulled it up next to one of the Qwik Stop pumps. As usual, he walked inside and told Dwayne the cashier "sixty bucks worth" and paid in cash. They talked for several minutes about the currently good walleye fishing on the area's lakes.

Three of the Ralph Tenuta-trained horses had competed on that Friday's program. The best finish they managed was a third. The mood around the barn was dispirited. Ralph tried to revive the flagging spirits by shouting down the shed row, "Remember, we've got the Big E going tomorrow." Editorialist was scheduled to run in the featured stakes race the next afternoon. He was usually a money earner for all concerned, including Tenuta's stable employees because the horse's owners, The Significant Seven, most often represented by Arnie Rison, always "staked" them with bonus payments. Doyle wondered if the ailing Rison would instruct Tenuta to carry out this practice if Editorialist won. Or Renee. Doyle considered these pretty meager stipends. But to people making $350 a week, they were much appreciated gifts.

Orth exited his rental car at the far end of the Heartland Downs parking lot just before eight o'clock. The last of the ten Friday races was under way. He heard track announcer Jason Dooley calling out, "And it's Round Man in front by a length, Twags Two in second by two lengths, followed by…."

Orth wore old blue jeans, a gray cut-off sweat shirt, Chicago Cub ball cap, Western boots into one of which he'd tucked his sheathed combat knife. "*Hola,*" he said to the woman running the tamale stand on the roadway two barns down from Tenuta's as he strode past. She smiled back at him. "*Buenas tardes, Señor.*"

Doyle was locking Tenuta's office door when he heard a deep voice say, "Hey, Doyle." He turned around.

"Yeah?"

"Has Tenuta got any job openings here?" Doyle watched the easy, confident stride of the tall, fit-looking man as he approached.

"Sorry, buddy. There's hardly ever a vacancy in his work force. Tenuta's too good a boss for that. Do you groom? I could give you a couple of the names of trainers who might be looking to hire help. Why don't you come around tomorrow morning after I ask around."

Doyle put the door key in his pants pocket, then stopped. "How do you know my name? And what's yours?"

The man shook his head as he closed in on Doyle. "I'm not waiting till tomorrow morning, Doyle. My business is with you, right here, right now." He yanked his knife out of the boot in a movement so swift Doyle hardly tracked it. Doyle stepped back. Thinking, I don't believe I can outrun this mean-looking son of a bitch, whatever his name is. Doyle's usually effective left hook would not match up against the weapon in this man's right hand.

Doyle kept retreating, slowly, hands up in front of him. He said, "What is this?

"You want money, take my wallet." He reached behind him, not for his wallet pocket. He doubted it was robbery that had sent this man here. Doyle's left hand landed on a stall door handle. He pulled it. The door swung open and Doyle ducked into the stall, reaching back to slam shut the door.

The intruder braced one large, strong hand against the swinging door, stopped it, and pushed it back against Doyle. With his two hands on the door, Doyle could hold the man out. But only by staying within the range of the knife. Doyle jumped back toward the rear of the dark stall, brushing against the legs of a large, irritated thoroughbred.

Doyle kept his eyes on the man. Doyle's right shoulder brushed against the agitated horse's left side. The horse shifted his big butt and lashed out with a powerfully driven left hind foot that narrowly missed Doyle's right shoulder, resounding when it thumped against the stall wall. Doyle dropped down in the straw and scuttled to the stall's darkest rear corner. *Christ,* Doyle thought, *it's Editorialist. I'm in that crazy bastard's stall. He's liable to kick the shit out of me before whoever the hell is over there with the knife gets his chance to slice.*

Orth removed a small flashlight out of his pocket and aimed it first at Editorialist, then at Doyle. The horse threw his head up and away from the light. Doyle put his hand over his eyes. "Turn that thing off," he said.

"Then come out of there. I just want to talk to you."

"You always launch your conversations waving a knife around? Fuck you, pal." He paused. "And what would we talk about?" Doyle thought if he could prolong this discouraging-looking encounter, the night security guard might arrive for duty and see what was happening. Then he remembered that the night's assigned watchman was Tony LaVine. *Oh, Christ.*

Orth, no trace of irony in his matter-of-fact voice, said, "What will we talk about? We'll talk about death. Yours." He slid sideways through the stall door.

Editorialist lashed out again with a back foot. Orth, startled, aimed his light upward. Editorialist's eyes rolled in his upraised head. *This horse is either terrified or pissed,* Doyle thought. *God help me, whichever it is.*

The increasingly loud sounds emanating from Editorialist brought a wave of response from his nearby stablemates. Snorts, loud whinnies, feet scraping nervously on stall floors. None of this racket attracted any help for Doyle, who felt in his jacket pocket for his cell phone. The stranger quickly leaned forward delivered a karate kick that knocked the phone out of Doyle's hand. He spotted it on the stall floor and kicked it out the way.

The man now in the stall said, "I wouldn't want to slash this horse's jugular, Doyle. But if you don't come out of there, I sure as hell will."

"What is this bullshit? You with PETA? Spare the horse and carve up Doyle? Go to hell."

Orth slowly moved farther into the stall. Doyle ducked to the other rear corner of the twelve by eighteen foot box, putting Editorialist between him and his attacker. When the flashlight came on again and found Editorialist's eyes, the horse freaked. He reared up so violently Doyle thought his head might hit the stall ceiling. Editorialist made a screaming noise and brought his front legs down, his left front hoof crashing onto Orth's right shoulder with a *cracking* sound. Orth grunted loudly. Dropped his knife. Grabbed for his damaged shoulder with his left hand. He sank into a pile of straw near the stall door, on his back, writhing. Doyle heard him mutter, "Oh....man."

Doyle thought about making a grab for the knife. Editorialist changed Doyle's mind. He unleashed another vicious backward kick that scraped the air over Doyle's lowered head. Then Editorialist was back up on his hind legs, frightened and furious.

His front hooves pawed high up in the evening air. When they came down and landed again, they produced a sound Doyle would never forget. Orth's face was smashed apart by the aluminum shoes of the enraged animal. He would never answer Doyle's question of *Who the hell sent you after me, mister?*

Doyle crept to the front of the stall and got to his feet, keeping a wary eye on Editorialist. He picked up Orth by his ankles, swiveled the body, and dragged it out of the stall onto the dirt pathway, followed by the smell of blood and horse sweat and fear. The killer horse turned around and moved to the rear of his stall, facing out the screened back window. Editorialist's nostrils flared as he shuffled his back feet, sending up little clods of straw.

Doyle, drained, leaned back against the stable wall and reached into his jacket for his cell phone to call track Security. His shirt was wet with sweat. Then he remembered he'd dropped his phone in the stall. He crept back in and found it in a near corner.

Back outside, Doyle glanced at the corpse's hideously destroyed face and splintered shoulder before quickly looking away. He heard a cell phone ring. Not his. Trying to ignore the man's gory features, Doyle bent down and patted his pockets. He found the cell phone in the left back pocket of the man's jeans.

Flipping open the phone, Doyle saw the caller's name. Stunned, he took a breath before hitting "Talk" and saying, softly, "Yes? What is it?"

There was a brief intake of breath on the other end of the line before the connection was abruptly ended.

Chapter Fifty-one

August 28, 2009

Doyle secured the lock on the stall door of the still excited Editorialist, then leaned back against the barn wall. He was breathing hard. There was a trail of blood where he had pulled the corpse out of the stall. Doyle looked away, trying not to retch. The man's face had been pounded so hard by the horse's hooves as to be unrecognizable as anything once even remotely human.

He spotted the knife that had fallen from the attacker's hand. Doyle used his handkerchief to pick up the weapon by the handle and place it on the ground next to the body. It was a weapon obviously designed to rip through tissue and organs and bones. "You got what you deserved, you bastard," Doyle snarled.

Track security people arrived within minutes after Doyle called them. An ambulance soon followed, then township police. Doyle answered questions for nearly three hours before he was allowed to phone the incredulous Tenuta to inform him about what had taken place at his barn.

"Who was the guy Editorialist killed?" Tenuta said. "What was he doing there?"

"I can't answer the first question, Ralph, but I think I know the answer to the second one. I'll tell you later. I can't talk about all that right now. Whoever he is, this guy will be identified pretty quick I would think. DNA, fingerprints, they'll find out who he is. Was."

Finally excused by the lead detective, Doyle got into his Accord and drove out of the racetrack. On Willow Road heading east, he used the speed dial on his cell phone to reach the sleepy but soon instantly alert Damon Tirabassi—instantly alert after he'd heard what Doyle had to say.

Engel and Tirabassi were waiting for him when Doyle reached his condo building. The three of them rode the elevator in silence after Doyle said, "Wait until we get upstairs. I've got to change my clothes." There were blood spatters on the cuffs of his khakis. "Karen," he said, "would you please make some coffee? I'll be out in a few minutes."

Showered and dressed in clean clothes, Doyle picked up a cup of the coffee from the living room table. "Thanks, Karen." He opened a sideboard and took out a bottle of Bushmills. "I'm having a taste. You two? No, of course not, you're on duty."

Tirabassi said, "Jack, let's get to it. It's after midnight. We know what happened out there at Heartland Downs. I called the track security chief right after I talked to you. So you were approached by a man, carrying a knife, and he somehow got killed by a horse. Who do you think this guy was?"

"Like I told the cops at the track, I'm sure when they run this guy's prints they'll find him. He's either ex-military, or ex-con. Probably the former. He had that look about him. He told me he came there to kill me. He was very cool, scary cool. Like he'd done this before. What saved me, thank God, was that he didn't know anything about horses. Or, at least, a horse like Editorialist."

"Why would this man want to kill you?" Karen said. "Is this connected to the spongings?"

Doyle muttered, "I wish it were."

"What?" Tirabassi barked.

Doyle sat back in his chair. He felt drained. "First, the good news, folks. The sponging at Heartland Downs is over. Kaput. Finito."

"What do you mean, Jack?"

"Just what I said, Karen. I've taken care of that matter. The person, the people involved in the spongings are out of business."

Tirabassi put his head in his hands before asking, "Did you kill anybody, Jack? That you won't tell us about?" He got up from the couch and walked over to a window. "What next?" he said.

"What *next?* What kind of crack is that, Damon? I haven't killed anybody. At least not since that meth freak at Monee Park, which was done in self-defense. But I almost got killed earlier tonight when I was again aiding *you* people. Almost like what happened in Kentucky, when I was helping you out down there to nail the insurance thief. That, of course, was involuntary. This sponging business is completely voluntary. And you're looking at me like maybe I screwed up?"

He replenished his Irish coffee, took a deep breath, sat back. "Hey, haven't I always been straight with you? Rhetorical question," he smiled, and Karen smiled back. "Damn right I have. So, you can take it to the bank, the sponger is *done.*"

Tirabassi said, "Jack, come on. Who is the sponger? We need an arrest. We need a name."

"You're not getting one from me. And that is fucking that."

Karen, not smiling now, face flushed, said, "You're setting yourself up as the presiding officer, judge, in this case? You've made a unilateral decision to shield somebody you know is guilty of a federal crime? This isn't going to fly, Jack."

"Try to shoot it down, then." He was as angry as she was. "You two have a water-boarding kit down there in that crappy car you drive? Bring it on up!"

Karen slammed her notebook and pen down on the table.

"Jack, I've heard about loose horses, but you are way out of any herd I could imagine. Why won't you identify the sponger? Why didn't you call us right away from the track when your attacker died? For all we've done for you…" She got to her feet. "I'm going to the washroom," she said, "before I do something rash."

Karen started down the hallway, then came back. "Have you thought about the $50,000 reward for the sponger, Jack? It could be yours."

Doyle shrugged. "What's fifty grand to a man of my unlimited potential?"

Karen glared at Doyle and slammed her hand against the wall before stalking off. Even usually dour Damon smiled at that crack of Doyle's.

Doyle and Tirabassi avoided looking at each other while they waited for her. When Karen was again seated, Doyle said, "Hear this. If you two will go along with me on the sponger, I'll give you the chance to crack six murder cases. Six of The Significant Seven horse owners. Can you wrap your heads around that?

"Two days ago, I went to see Mike Barnhill's widow Peggy. I called ahead and said I was a good guy. Helping the FBI on a racetrack project. I told her she could call either of you because I knew you would vouch for me."

Karen said, "She never called me." Damon also shook his head. "But," Karen said, "I'll bet you talked yourself in anyway. Why didn't you tell us what you were planning? The way we've worked together, Jack, there's no need for you to be so secretive."

"Hah! Me, secretive? Compared to you? You Bureau people being secretive is like, what is the old saying, 'bringing coals to Newcastle?'" Doyle paused before adding "foals to Newmarket… Jazz to Newport…Bigots to a Klan Klonklave."

"Cut it out, Jack," Tirabassi said. "That's enough of that. The Irish coffee must be getting to you. Get serious, damn it. Tell us what happened with Mrs. Barnhill."

"She said for me to come out to her home the next afternoon. I did. When I got there, she looked like she was still under the influence of those numbing drugs their physicians make available to spouses of the recently deceased. I've seen a few new widows at their husbands' wakes, and they all look half-stoned. So what, if it helps them?

"Mrs. Barnhill went on and on about how gracious the other widows of The Significant Seven had been. Bringing food to her house, flowers to the funeral home, comfort on the phone. Mrs. Barnhill was also very impressed with Renee Rison's solicitude, although Renee is not a widow."

Karen said, "Jack, you're rambling. Get to it, please."

"Peggy Barnhill still can't quite come to grips with what she refers to as 'Mike's accident.' I didn't want to disabuse her of that notion. I didn't want to tell her, at this time, that I think Mike was murdered. That I think the other members of The Significant Seven now in the ground were also murder victims. I couldn't bring myself to mention that possibility. But Peggy brought it up herself. 'These six hearty, healthy, happy men all dying over the course of one summer? How can that be?" she asked me. "Was somebody killing them?"

"I told Peggy Barnhill I thought that was a good question. That's when I asked to see The Significant Seven's ownership contract. She said she'd only recently gotten a copy. A Chicago attorney named Frank Cohan had written it. It was signed by all seven men and notarized."

Doyle poured another half cup of coffee, leaving out the Bushmills. "When I got to the final paragraph of the contract, I understood what was going on. I don't know if lawyer Cohan was in a hurry when he he wrote it, or what. And I guess the trusting partners didn't question his work. But there was, I'm assuming unintentionally, a loophole you could drive a Brink's truck through. And somebody spotted that. And acted to exploit it."

Tirabassi leaned forward. "In what way, Jack?"

"I'm going to have to look at my notes for this. Wait." He took his notebook out of his jacket pocket.

"The contract states that the heir or heirs or heiresses of the last surviving member of The Significant Seven shall 'Devote proceeds from the stallion career of The Badger Express and other profits from the racing stable, if any, to the creation, financing, and administration of a retirement farm for racehorses.'"

The agents looked at each other, puzzled. "So?" Tirabassi said.

"So," Doyle replied, "it says proceeds. Not *all* proceeds. Frank Cohan, or his typist, left out the *all*. Big mistake. And none of

The Significant Seven caught that omission. But somebody else did. Actually, that may have been the reason for Judge Toomey being the first to die. The fear that maybe Toomey, an attorney, might some day review, amend, and correct the language by adding the *all*. I think that's what led to Toomey dying first. And what led to the rest of the six deaths.

"The trustee," Doyle continued, "under the terms of this contract, would be free to use *some*, not all, of the proceeds to fund the horse retirement plan. That trustee, of course, will be Renee Rison, little Miss Bereavement. Once her father dies, which could be any hour now, she's going to be in complete control of a revenue stream measuring in the millions. Even if The Badger Express were to keel over tomorrow, he's insured for $20 million. With the trust as the beneficiary of that policy, and her soon to be in control of the trust, devious little Renee could easily set aside a million bucks or so for the care and keeping of several dozen old racetrack warriors, just to make it look good, and use the considerable rest for herself.

"I do not believe that that is what The Significant Seven had in mind," Doyle said.

There was a brief silence before Karen said, "Are you saying Renee Rison killed all those men?"

"No. But Renee Rison is cunning enough to find people to do that kind of work for her. Then she winds up with all the money. I asked her some questions about the partnership deal when we were at Ravinia. She brushed me off. Talked just about her Dad's impending demise. She must have gotten worried about what I might suspect or discover. She decided that I was a threat to her plan. I'm sure she sent the man with the knife to the barn to kill me."

Tirabassi said, "How can you tie Renee and the dead man together?"

"By cell phone. When the dead man's cell phone rang, I picked it up. The caller ID said Renee Rison. She must have realized I was not the man she was calling. She hung up without saying anything."

Karen said, "If the motive was money, why? She had her own business. She was due to inherit her father's businesses."

"Her Dad's car dealerships were in trouble, like most of them around the country. I think you'll find her travel business was on the slide, too. She probably used what savings she had, or went into her equity line—I know she owns the building her travel agency is in—to finance this operation. I don't imagine professional killers come cheap, even in a bad economy like this one. Let's say she had to spend hundreds of thousands on the killer or killers. So what? At the end of the day, little Renee planned to be sitting on many millions."

"I don't know, Jack," Tirabassi said, shaking his head. "Even if your theory is right, what can we do about it? Unless the guy who tried to kill you left some kind of trail to her, we don't have anything to go on."

"Maybe the unknown man knew her late brother in the service," Doyle said. "You can check that out once he's been identified," Doyle said.

Tirabassi remained doubtful. "That could be pure coincidence. We'd need more than that to go on."

Doyle downed the last of his coffee. "Well, Damon," he smiled, "you've always got me to fall back on. Here's my idea."

The next morning, the story about the unidentified man who had been stomped to death by a horse at Heartland Downs was all over the national news. Scott Sanderson spotted it on the Internet as he sat in front of his home computer in Dallas, sipping his morning coffee. He quickly turned on the television to a morning newscast. A photo appeared showing a body covered by a blanket, only the feet uncovered. A horse's head could be seen in the near background, the animal peering out of his stall at all the activity. When the camera zeroed in, Sanderson sat up in his seat. "God damn it to hell," he said, "I know whose Western boots those are."

"What?" called Sanderson's wife from the nearby kitchen.

There was no answer. When she looked around the corner, her husband was hunched over, his head in his hands. She knew better than to ask him what was wrong. In his world, nothing was ever wrong. She kept quiet.

Finally, he got out his chair, his face drawn, jaw clenched.

"I got to take a trip," he said. "Right away. Today."

Chapter Fifty-two

August 30, 2009

Doyle scored a parking place across the street from Renee Rison's travel agency. He pumped the only eight quarters he had on him into one of the recently privatized and newly rapacious Chicago parking meters, buying part of an hour. He walked through the door with his iPhone at his mouth, a new one provided him earlier that day by Damon Tirabassi. Doyle nodded to Renee's assistant, Teresa Chandler. She was headed out the door. She waved at Jack. "We're closing up a little early on this rainy evening," she whispered to Doyle. "Renee's in her office at the back."

The office door was partially open. He tapped on it lightly. Renee, startled, put down her phone. Doyle pretended to be concluding a conversation on his phone. "Right," he said. "I'll see you later.

"Jack, I'm surprised to see you here." *I'll bet you* are, he thought.

Renee rose from her chair behind the cluttered desk. She gave Doyle her best welcoming look. She wore a short-sleeved red dress that fit her perfectly. Her hand was warm as she shook his. "Please sit," she said. "Were you planning to surprise me by asking me out to dinner?"

"I don't think I'm going to surprise you at all, Renee. I think you know why I'm here." He took one of the chairs in front of her desk, placing his iPhone down on the empty chair next to him.

She walked around the desk to the small refrigerator in the corner of the office. "Water? Soda? Something stronger?" she said, smiling back over her shoulder as she bent down and looked into the fridge.

"I'm here to ask you about the man you called on his cell phone yesterday evening."

She hesitated before reaching into the fridge for a small bottle of Veuve Clicquot, opened it, and returned to her chair before saying, "What are you talking about?" She took a plastic cup out of a lower desk drawer and filled it. Doyle saw her hand shaking as she drank.

"Yesterday evening," Doyle said, "a man came to Heartland Downs intent on killing me. Didn't happen. Instead, he got stomped to death by Editorialist."

"*What?* Why would someone want to kill you? And what do think this has to do with me?"

"The dead man's phone rang as he lay there in the straw in Editorialist's stall. His face nearly obliterated. I heard a cell phone. I found it in his jeans pocket. The caller's name and number were on it. Yours."

She returned to her chair. "You don't even know who this man is and you're saying I know him?" she said dismissively.

"Oh, they'll find out who he is. Either fingerprints or DNA. He was in his thirties, hard-looking guy, so I'll bet he turns out to be ex-military, or ex-con. They'll find out."

She said, "What if they do identify him? What does that mean to me?"

"I think they'll eventually find a link between you two, maybe with other parties involved. People you employed."

Renee laughed. "For what purpose?"

"To gain control of the money accumulated by The Significant Seven."

She sat back in her chair. Her hand shook again as she refilled her champagne cup.

"When you knew your father had only months to live, you came up with your murderous plan. If the six other members of the partnership preceded your Dad in death, you would be in charge of the financial jackpot produced by The Badger Express once your father died. The Badger Express. The stallion who keeps on giving.

"You had to act quickly. Your father only had months to live. Somehow you were able to employ a very professional assassin, who I presume was the guy that came after me at the barn. He took care of the first six of The Significant Seven. Leaving you all alone in the catbird seat."

He stood up. "That's the way I see it, Renee. And that's the theory I'm going to tell two FBI agents I know when I see them tomorrow. Let them start to look into this. You screwed up, babe. You should have hired a killer who knew about horses. This dead man is eventually going to lead to you."

"Oh, Doyle, you cocky bastard," she spat out, "why should I plan to spend millions of dollars on the upkeep of damaged old horses? I don't even like the damn animals. You think I was going to stand by and watch all that money being blown on nags? No way." For a moment her angered face was almost the color of her dress as she glared at Doyle.

"What would your father think of your plan, Renee?"

She drank from the champagne cup. "He'll never know about it. And neither will anyone else. Daddy's car dealerships started going into the dumper about a year and a half ago. When the economy crashed. He was embarrassed, tried to keep them going and not lay off his workers, but he couldn't pull it off. I'm sure the stress from all that accelerated his cancer. Some of the biggest car companies in this country, which he'd made tons of money for over the years, just shut him off. He was devastated. He closed three of the four dealerships, sold the other at a bottom price. He made clear to me that my inheritance was going to be very, well, disappointing. My own business had almost collapsed. I had to take steps to remedy my situation," she smiled. "I'll have to take another step now. Too bad you told me what you'd figured out, Jack. I couldn't allow allegations such as those to get around, could I?"

Doyle said, "You are one cocky bitch, Renee."

She reached into the middle drawer of her desk. "You're just smart enough to be dangerous, Doyle." When she came around the desk, she was holding the .22 pistol.

"You're a smart guy, Jack, and a smart ass. I never could stand guys like you."

"What the hell do you think you're doing, Renee?"

Renee smiled. "What am I doing, Jack? Why, I'm 'protecting myself from an attacker.' And I'm getting rid of you."

She reached behind her for her champagne cup and threw its remaining contents onto Doyle's chest. Dropping the cup, she ripped open the top buttons of her dress to reveal one of her braless breasts. With the same hand, she tousled her hair into disarray.

"Doyle, you animal," she smiled. "I'm lucky I have this weapon for protection. Three years ago, Teresa and I were held up here in the store on a Friday night. The guy took all our cash and made fun of us. I swore then I wouldn't let that happen again. I got a permit and the pistol.

"'Oh, officer, this man Doyle, I dated him once, we went to a concert at Ravinia. I didn't wish to see him again. He was too forward for me. He's been calling me repeatedly since then, and I never answer. Then, tonight, he charged into my office and tried to force himself on me. It was horrible. He pulled down my dress top. He said terrible things. "I know what you like. You'll like it from me." He was like an animal. I've always had a fear of rape. I was terrified.'

"'Thank *God* I had that pistol in my desk and was able to defend myself. I'm sorry I had to shoot him, but I had no choice.'" She gave Doyle another mocking smile.

Doyle flashed a left uppercut into Renee's gun arm. She screamed. The little .22 flew up out of her hand and hit the ceiling before bouncing down on top of the refrigerator and then onto the carpet. Renee, face pale, clutched her wrist. "You've broken my wrist!"

She bent down trying to pick up the pistol. Doyle kicked it under the desk out of her reach. He shoved her down into her chair and retrieved his iPhone, hitting the recording button. Renee heard herself say, "Thank *God* I had the pistol in my desk and was able to defend myself. I'm sorry I had to shoot him. But I had no choice."

"You bastard, Doyle."

"Uh, uh, Renee. I'm no bastard, and I've got the birth certificate to prove it."

He put the phone down on the desk. "The FBI will find that very useful, my dear."

"No, Doyle, they won't." She stood up, still clutching her injured wrist. "Scott," she screamed. "Get in here."

The side door to the office banged open. In walked a tall, tanned man with a military buzz cut. He wore dark sunglasses, a black tee-shirt and jeans. In his left hand, he carried a black Glock .19 with sound suppressor attached. For a moment he looked straight at Doyle. He raised the pistol. Pivoting slightly, he turned to Renee and shot her in the forehead.

Doyle jumped toward the door. But the man quickly turned to aim the weapon at him. "Stop right there, Doyle. I want to take a look at the man that got my buddy killed at the racetrack."

Doyle turned around slowly. "I didn't get him killed, you jerk. He got himself killed by the horse." Nodding toward Renee's body, "What was that for? I thought you worked for her." Pieces of her skull were plastered against the back of her chair.

"We both did. Me and Orth. Then she started to get shaky on us. When I found out Orth was gone, I was afraid she might come completely apart. Threaten me with exposure. Renee was calling me every half-hour, driving me nuts. She said I had to come up here and get rid of a pain in the ass named Doyle. I flew in this morning to get the rest of the money she owed me and Orth. She paid me today. Told me to stay close, that Doyle might show up looking for her. If not, I'd go looking for him." Sanderson smiled. "Hello, Jack."

"Why kill her?" Doyle said. He was sweating now. Thinking where the fuck are the Feebs. He said, "She could have been a meal ticket for a guy like you. She'd be sitting on millions. You could have squeezed her." He shifted his feet slightly, but Sanderson kept the Glock aimed directly at Doyle's chest.

"Stop fucking moving," Sanderson ordered. He glanced at the dead little woman in the red dress. Shook his head. Said, "She'd paid us most of the money she owed. She was getting wacky. The chick had to go, man. She was a loose end. Just like you."

Doyle snatched his iPhone off the desk. He threw it as hard as he could toward Sanderson's face. Instinctively, Sanderson reached up to deflect the phone, his Glock now pointed at the ceiling. Doyle jumped forward and unleashed a crushing left hook into Sanderson's throat. Sanderson dropped the pistol. He fell forward onto the floor, gasping. Doyle kicked the Glock under the desk next to Renee's .22.

He picked up the iPhone. "Damon. Karen! Where the hell are you?"

Chapter Fifty-three

September 10, 2009

Ralph Tenuta passed the large white bowl of mostaccioli down the dining room table. "Have some more, Jack."

"I will, Ralph." Doyle turned to Rosa Tenuta before helping himself. "What a great dinner, Rosa. I might have another piece of that chicken Vesuvio, too." Rosa beamed as she forked a breast from the platter onto Doyle's plate. Ralph was smiling at the other end of the table at whose middle Doyle was seated. The meal had been long, lavish, and delicious. Even Doyle's notable capacity for food was being tested. *Early to the gym tomorrow,* he vowed to himself.

This dinner at the Tenuta home was to mark Doyle's final day as Ralph's stable agent. The mood was festive. Two of Tenuta's trainees had won their races at Heartland Downs that afternoon, Editorialist as the favorite, Clever Carolynn at 13-1. Doyle parlayed the pair, starting with a $100 win bet on Editorialist. He was flush. Thus far in the evening the talk had all been about horses, flavored by Doyle's effusive praise of the meal, delivered to the delight of Ralph. But Rosa's curiosity came to the fore with the main course.

"Jack, we read all about Renee Rison's death. And the arrest of the man who shot her. That must have been terrible for you, being involved in the death of a young woman."

Doyle almost choked on his pasta. "Involved? Rosa, I was just there. As a witness. That woman maybe didn't deserve to die that way, shot to death by a man she'd hired. But she was sure as hell set to kill me. She was an evil little person."

He sighed and looked around the dining room. Reached for his glass of chianti. "Watching people die has never been fun for me," he said.

"So you'll be testifying against Sanderson?" Ralph said.

"Yes. He's expected to come to trial in about two months. They'll have my testimony as well as the iPhone recording of what went on there in Renee's office."

Rosa said, "The papers reported that the FBI people were late going in to help you."

"Almost too late," Doyle said. "Damon Tirabassi set up the iPhone connection. Mine worked fine. It was recording and the voices also were being carried to where the agents were out in front of Renee's building. One problem. Their phone was malfunctioning. They were only getting snatches of the conversation. Government-issued equipment, Jesus. Anyway, Damon finally got his phone to work properly. And they charged in. I hit Sanderson pretty good. Damaged his larynx. When he was writhing on the floor, I couldn't resist. I put my phone next to his ear and started playing back what he'd done and said. It was great."

Rosa said, "I still don't quite understand what Renee was up to. Wasn't she going to inherit a load of money from her father?"

"Not as big a load as she had in mind. So she used her savings, and borrowed against the equity in the travel agency building she owned, to finance the crimes. If she could get sole control of The Badger Express, she'd be sitting on the mother lode. That's what the greedy little bitch set out to do. She nearly managed it."

Rosa said, "But wouldn't you think Renee would be vulnerable to these men she hired after it was carried out? Wouldn't they have a hold over her?"

"I don't know what she figured," Doyle said. "Maybe she was counting on their loyalty to her late brother, the dead SEAL. Who knows what she had in mind? She hired these two men,

Sanderson and Orth, who had been in the service with her brother. Guys who had later done dirty duty as private security workers in Iraq. Before they went too far and got sent back. Sanderson did the recon, Orth the killing. The bastards wiped out six innocent men. Just for money. Or maybe, in Orth's case, because he liked it. I don't know, Rosa. I don't understand people like that."

"How do you figure this stuff, Jack?" Ralph said. "Arnie Rison was as nice and honest a man as I ever had as a client. How could he be the father of a woman like Renee? It's beyond me."

"And a lot of others, too, Ralph," Doyle said.

Rosa said, "What happens to The Significant Seven's money, Jack?"

Doyle drained his wine glass before saying, "Arnie Rison was understandably shattered by his daughter's confession. To his credit he called in Frank Cohan, the attorney who had prepared the original Significant Seven contract. Cohan, as he should have done in the first place, inserted the word 'all' in regards to distribution of the syndicate's proceeds. The amended contract was notarized and copies distributed to the widows of the other men the next day. That next night, poor Arnie Rison gave up the ghost.

"To *their* great credit, the widows of the six dead men have agreed to an arrangement whereby *all* future proceeds from The Badger Express are to be used exactly as their late husbands originally intended. For the benefit of retired race horses. They've appointed a trustee to administer the funds. These good women have put this money where their husbands' hearts were."

Rosa offered Doyle another piece of chicken, which he declined. Her husband said, "Jack, I've kind of stayed away about asking you something else. You and Cindy Chesney? I noticed you didn't even speak to her when she came to the barn with Doc Jensen yesterday."

Doyle hesitated before answering, "To put it bluntly, Ralph, Cindy and I are over with."

There was an uncomfortable silence. Rosa said, "Are we ready for dessert and coffee? I've made the cannolis that Ralph loves."

Doyle smiled at this most accommodating of hostesses. "I am, Rosa. Thank you."

Rosa went into the kitchen. Ralph sat back in his chair, arms crossed on his chest, pouting. He said, "You don't want to tell me anything more about you and Cindy, that's up to you."

Doyle's face tightened. He thought about Tyler and Wilma. He knew he could never tell Ralph, or anyone else, about him and Cindy Chesney without potentially screwing up her already terribly difficult life. He hated the sponging of horses she had done, but he could not bring himself to hate her or to hurt her.

Ralph sat back in his chair, patting his belly, a look of satisfaction on his face. "What a meal, hey, Jack?"

"Outstanding."

"Rosa's her old self again. We're back where we should be," Tenuta said.

"Some of us are," Doyle said softly to himself. "Some of us."

To receive a free catalog of Poisoned Pen Press titles, please contact us in one of the following ways:

Phone: 1-800-421-3976
Facsimile: 1-480-949-1707
Email: info@poisonedpenpress.com
Website: www.poisonedpenpress.com

Poisoned Pen Press
6962 E. First Ave. Ste. 103
Scottsdale, AZ 85251